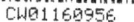

ANDY McD

X by ANDY MᶜD
www.andymcd.com.au

First published in Australia by McDermott House 2022
P.O. Box 395 Coolangatta
Queensland 4225 Australia
info@andymcd.com.au

Copyright © ANDY MᶜD 2022
All Rights Reserved

 A catalogue record for this book is available from the National Library of Australia

ISBN: 978-0-6453709-0-4 (pbk)
ISBN: 978-0-6453709-1-1 (ebk)

Cover design by ANDY MᶜD © 2022
Cover background image: © DAE Photo (Shutterstock)

Typesetting and design by McDermott House © 2022

All characters and events in this publication are fictitious, any resemblance to real persons, living or dead, or any events past or present are purely coincidental.

No part of this book may be reproduced in any form, by photocopying or by any electronic or mechanical means, including information storage or retrieval systems, without permission in writing from both the copyright owner and the publisher of this book.

For Kirra

**Other titles by
ANDY MᶜD**

Flirting with The Moon (2022)
The Tiger Chase (2022)

Quest of the New Templars series:
Book 1 – Resurrection (2022)

Children's books:
The Last Tiger (2022)

AUTHOR'S NOTE

Kirra is a small beachside suburb at the southern end of the Gold Coast in Queensland, Australia. Until recent years Kirra was basically a place you drove through on the way to the more popular Coolangatta or the Queensland, NSW border. The area has seen some great times and some not so great times. In the 50s, 60s and early 70s, Kirra Point was arguably one of the best surf breaks in Australia, and a popular holiday destination. A surf culture grew in the town that many of the locals still look back at with great fondness.

Recently, Kirra has enjoyed a massive resurgence, which has pushed up the median house and apartment prices to an all time high, as well as cementing it as Australia's premier holiday resort.

Since the writing of this book, the area has entered a new phase of development. In the chapters where I mention The Kirra Hotel, I am referring to the since demolished pub that stood on the corner of Marine Parade and Miles Street. Although the place will be sorely missed by the locals – and the new development holds great promise – I've attempted to keep the essence of the old establishment intact and how I remember it.

Scotty Stephens is a bloke I know. I've worked with him, we've shared many a yarn over a beer at The Kirra Hotel. He introduced me to the footy, the schooner, the Sunday arvo session, the barby, and the age-old saying, 'She'll be right, mate!'

Scotty is not one person, he's a product of all the Aussie blokes I've met and worked with over the thirty plus years I've lived in Australia. He's a good mate – reliable, funny and smart. The kind of person I am proud to call a friend.

Good onya, Scotty!

1

3 September
Unable to look at the victim, the ruddy-faced security guard watched me with industrious eyes as if awaiting instructions.

'Who found her?' I asked.

He nodded towards a group of students huddled close by.

'You know her?'

He shook his head. 'Seen her around the campus, that's about all ...' The mints he'd recently consumed did little to mask the smell of cigarettes on his breath.

'Do any of you know her?' I called back to the group.

'Yes,' a tall, skinny guy with a beard said. 'Her name is Lisa ... Lisa Wei.'

'Okay, I'm gonna get you guys to move back.' Pointing towards the edge of the building. 'Over there, please.'

Surveying the area where the killing had taken place. It was outside the entrance to Varsity Towers – privately owned student accommodation at the outer edge of the Bond University campus.

'And I'll get you to make sure no one comes out the exit,' I instructed the security guard.

He nodded, willingly taking up post in front of the glass doors, his back to the scene.

This would be the seventh murder in only three weeks. I'd only seen pictures of the previous crime scenes. The killings had been identical—all young women, their throats slashed in an X, jugular veins skilfully severed on either side, causing the victims to bleed out in a matter of minutes. On each occasion, the victim had been laid out with a large pool of blood at their feet.

Although I was the first on the scene, the wailing sirens in the distance meant I wouldn't be alone for long, so there wouldn't be much time to look around.

The victim was about twenty years old. Asian, possibly Chinese. Her body and clothing were saturated in blood from the gaping wounds on her neck, but her face was as white as chalk. Looking straight ahead as if startled, eyes that only moments before would have sparkled with the inquisitive energy of a carefree student, now dull and void of life.

Kneeling beside the blood, I could clearly see where she'd fallen to her knees, supported herself with one hand while probably clutching at her throat with the other. But there was no sign of her collapsing forwards. The killer must have grabbed her hair from behind, yanking her head backwards, increasing the dwindling blood flow. Then, once she'd lost consciousness, he'd laid her out.

With so much blood, there had to be footprints—or at least some sign of a struggle. Squatting, I followed the edges of what was two pools of blood combined as one, but I found nothing. All the marks appeared to be from the victim.

Suddenly, the whole area lit up as the first of a zillion squad cars came to a squealing halt.

'Step away please, sir,' a uniformed constable yelled as two of them jumped from the first of the cars.

I held up my detective's badge as more units arrived.

Detective Inspector Dion Gardner, the first detective to arrive, immediately took charge.

'What the hell are *you* doing here?' he asked, noticing me.

'Doing what a detective does, mate.' I had a problem with calling him 'sir.'

'Detective? Ha! I'll get you to step away.'

X

Reluctantly, I rose to my feet and moved to one side. Ignoring Gardner, I continued to scan the scene as if he wasn't there.

The ground floor of the building was a car park. Entry to the apartments was accessible via a double glass door leading to a small foyer and lifts. Looking up at the security camera, I realised that from the angle at which it was set the murder scene was out of shot–but only just. The killer had positioned the spot perfectly.

I imagined him waiting out of sight, and Lisa, possibly late from a class, marching back towards the dorm with her head down. The blood spray facing away from the door indicated he must have approached her from behind, making her turn. A tap on the shoulder perhaps?

'You still here, fuck face?' Gardner said loudly enough for all the uniforms present to hear. 'Why don't you go get us all a cup of coffee, eh?' he continued, clumsily stepping in the edge of the blood. 'Shit.'

I was about to reply when the detective in charge arrived– Detective Inspector Des Williams. By this time, the uniforms had cordoned off the area. Forensics personnel continued to arrive, and a white tent was erected over the scene.

'Who found her?' Des threw the question into the air, aiming it at everyone present.

Gardner shrugged, wiping his shoe on the ground.

'Over there,' I pointed to the group of students. A crowd was now forming on the other side of the police barrier.

'Scott? What are you doing here?'

'I was on my way home, sir. Picked up the call.'

'You the first here?'

'Yes, sir. I was heading along Bermuda Street.'

'Okay, come with me.'

Des was my boss. He was a good bloke. Already at the top of his game and having been so for some years, he had nothing to prove.

'Which one of you guys found her?' he asked the group.

A small Indian girl raised her hand. She was being comforted by the tall bearded guy.

'Did you see anybody else in the area? Anyone at all?'

'No.'

'Is there anything you can tell us?'

'No, I was just coming back to the dorm and … and she was lying there.' She turned into the tall guy's chest, sobbing.

'Do you all know the victim?'

The group nodded in unison.

'Okay. Detective Constable Stephens here is going to ask you some questions, but we'll need you to come down to Surfers Paradise Police Headquarters to make official statements.' He marched back towards the crime scene.

I pulled out my notebook.

X

It was after midnight when I finally returned to Surfers Paradise. Des had called the team together for a briefing. When I say 'team,' I mean the group of detectives and selected uniforms who had been brought together to form the catalyst of the investigation. All were privy to the more delicate details of the case. But in reality, every police officer on the coast was part of a much bigger team, canvassing the surrounding neighbourhoods and taking statements. There was also a 24/7 presence on the streets and in the air, ensuring a visible vigilance was maintained. Two floors of Police Headquarters had also been allocated to over a hundred officers and staff manning the phones and sifting through possible leads.

As usual, I sat at the back of the room. Jenny Radford, our newest detective, joined me.

'Hey.' She was friendly, a bit younger than me perhaps, but a fellow surfer. 'I hear you were first on the scene.'

'Yep.'

X

I was surprised to see Superintendent Andrew Ripley enter the room. He took his place by Des's side.

Des stepped towards a large whiteboard that displayed photographs of the previous victims. 'Okay, you all know why we're here.' He added another photograph to the board. 'Victim number seven. Twenty-year-old Lisa Wei, a Bond University student, was killed at approximately nine o'clock this evening.'

Without being prompted, Dion Gardner stood. 'As usual, there was no evidence at the scene—no prints, nothing, but I …'

'Take a seat, detective.' Des cut him short, preventing him from showing off in front of Ripley.

Gardner slunk back into his chair like an ostracised schoolboy.

'We know very little about the victim at this time,' Des continued. 'Scott, perhaps you'd like to fill us in?'

I was listening but not comprehending. Was he talking to me?

'Scott?'

Shit, he was! I rose to my feet. 'Uhm …' I'd never spoken in front of the team before.

'Tell us what you learned about the victim.'

I pulled out my notebook. The only information I had to add was that Lisa Wei was an overseas student from Hong Kong. She'd been studying social sciences at Bond University for two years. Her parents—the father, an eye specialist; and the mother, a clinical psychologist—had been notified. She had a small group of friends, whom she usually met on a Tuesday evening at Varsity Lakes Tavern for trivia night.

'Is that all you got?' Gardner sneered.

'You were first at the scene,' Des said, ignoring Gardner, 'notice anything out of the ordinary?'

'I did get the chance to have a bit of a look around before anyone else got there.'

Superintendent Ripley raised an eyebrow.

'This was a very cleverly planned operation. The attack took place literally millimetres out of shot of the entrance's security camera, and at the time of night when most students were either in their dorms studying or over at the tavern for the trivia.'

'So, you think the killer is carefully picking the locations?' Des questioned.

'Yes.'

'And the victims too?' Ripley threw in.

'It's obvious the victims have been preselected and watched in the days leading up to the killings,' Gardner said.

I was surprised when Des and Ripley looked to me for confirmation.

'I don't agree. I think the location is the important factor. A spider will build a web in a high-traffic location.'

'Right, so the victims are like flies. That makes sense,' Ripley said, glaring at Des as if to say, *Why the hell hadn't you thought of that?*

'Each crime scene has been in an area where young women come and go,' I continued. 'Look at tonight–student accommodation. Perfect!'

'Did you notice anything else about the scene before it was … contaminated?' Des asked, shooting an irritated glance at Gardner.

'I would have expected to see some tracks, but once again, this killer knows exactly what he's doing.'

I'd always liked Des. He was an honest cop who treated people with respect.

'What are your thoughts, detective?'

It felt good to be spoken to as an equal. 'With the amount of blood at the scene and the rate at which it would have sprayed from the victim, some had to have landed on the killer.'

'You think he was covered up?'

'Yes. Perhaps a coat of some kind, or an overall, but something he could arrive at the scene wearing without being too conspicuous, then remove and get away without being noticed.'

X

'Have all the bins in the area been checked?' Des asked Senior Detective Constable Dale Mason, who was seated at the front.

'Being done as we speak, sir.'

'Like on the previous occasions, I don't think you'll find anything,' I added. 'My guess is it would be something he could stuff into a backpack and take away with him.'

'Good work, detective,' Des said.

'Yes, good work indeed!' Ripley agreed, his gaze lingering in my direction.

'Wow. Look at you,' Jenny said in a hushed voice when I returned to my seat. 'You actually sounded like a detective!'

'Perhaps I *am* a detective.'

2

4 September
Although I didn't get home until 3.30 am, I still woke up early, thanks to the old surf clock in my head. Des had given me the morning off. Normally I'd relish the chance for some extra time in the surf, but thanks to an ongoing offshore, Kirra Point was as flat as Lake Eyre.

The crescendo of beer bottles cascading into a wheelie bin was a familiar morning sound on Ruby Street. Taking out the empties was one of those things you couldn't do quietly, so you did it as quickly as possible. As the last bottle was bouncing around in its acoustically enhanced tomb, I'd already ducked back into the house with my shoulders up to my ears.

Even though I hadn't had a drink the night before, I didn't mind cleaning up after the boys. I had a lot to think about and this mindless chore offered a cogitative solitude. Not as good as a surf perhaps, but it was a reasonable substitute. Thankfully, it was a house rule that we kept the partying to the man shed, so the house was always – bachelor pad grade at least – tidy.

Elvis is the king, or so he tells us *every single day*. Tetley is just a tea bag who makes tea, or so we've been telling him for the last twenty odd years. The former is my long-time housemate. The latter lives around the corner but spends most of his time at our place.

According to Elvis, he doesn't snore. I beg to differ – he's a window rattler! I could hear him in his room as I padded through the

X

house and out to the bindy-infested back yard. A second-generation Greek from my hometown of Essendon, Victoria, Elvis (real name Nicholadas Papageorgiou) has been my best mate since preschool. At ten years old – when everyone else sported mullets – Elvis paraded a black quiff as sharp as the Sydney Opera House. We played footy for the same team, and apart from a five-year gap when I moved to Queensland, we'd spent most of our days together.

When he left school, Elvis's parents funded his move to the Gold Coast to attend the Southern Cross Uni in Tweed Heads. At that time, I was working as a security guard at Coolangatta Airport prior to enrolling at the Police Academy. We ended up sharing a house together in Kirra Beach. Twenty-four years later, and we're still in the same house.

Thankfully I haven't lost my hair or put on much weight, but the Elvis quiff has long gone, replaced with a close-cropped head. So too has the AFL physique in favour of a much-nurtured beer belly. Elvis is an accountant by day and, like me, a lifelong Essendon supporter.

The man shed, like the house, is made of fibro, and I suspect the only things holding it up are the fences on either side. Stretching across the full width of the garden, it's big enough to house a small bar, the all-important beer fridge, a pool table, an old lounge, and a flat screen TV. This all sounds a bit flash but in reality, everything was either scavenged or purchased on special.

Tetley was still asleep on the lounge and didn't stir when I snapped off a bin bag from the roll and began to fill it with Doritos bags and discarded dips. I knew what he was doing – he'd pretend to be asleep until he was sure all the tidying was finished, then he'd wake up and ask what was for breakfast.

We'd been fourteen when we both started at Palm Beach Currumbin High School on the same day. He'd recently immigrated to Australia from the UK with his parents and sister. I'd moved up from Victoria with my dad and my brother and we've been mates ever since. His real name is Sean Webster. The nickname, Tetley, came from an English tea bags ad in the 90s.

I know it sounds like we're living the bachelor dream – steady jobs, surfing, drinking, following the footy – and we probably are. Truth is though, I've been growing tired of the lifestyle for quite some time. Now in my forties, my health, my future and my career have been on my mind a lot lately.

3

The Gold Coast had never been hit so hard. The COVID-19 outbreak had been disastrous for the tourism industry. Businesses struggled and life changed, but like the rest of the world, we got through it. However, this serial killer wasn't just murdering innocent victims, he was killing the city. After the third attack, and the worldwide media coverage, the tourists stopped coming. Schoolies Week was cancelled again, and local businesses were taking another hammering. Only this time, we weren't part of a worldwide pandemic and there was no government assistance. This new virus was confined between Burleigh Heads in the south, and Sanctuary Cove to the north. The news had spread quicker than any germ could – the Gold Coast was a no-go area.

That afternoon, I'd been summoned to be present at a press conference outside the police headquarters in Surfers Paradise. I looked over at Des Williams. He was tough, but he was going to cop another hiding from the press. We all knew it. He knew it too. I could see him shaking. After thirty-five years on the force, he didn't deserve this. Rumour was, he was going to be removed from the case.

Mayor Julian Monroe was coming up for re-election. '*Smug bastard*' seemed to be the general opinion of him. Around the same age as me, he was tall, blond, insincere, and arrogant. He'd only won the vote of mayor because of a lack of credible opposition, but the media seemed to love him. An ex-AFL player, ecotourism magnate and high-profile property developer, he'd also dabbled in mining, but got out at the right time and made a fortune – in the billions they reckon.

I listened to him banging on about what he was doing to catch this menace to society, and that it would only be a matter of time before the killer was brought to justice. As usual, he went on and on. The questions rolled off him like waves over Snapper Rocks. I'll give him one thing, he could handle the media. He answered only the questions he wanted to, while cleverly deflecting those he didn't.

Finally, he handed over to Queensland Police Commissioner, Edward Singleton. Approaching retirement, Edward had been flying under the radar since COVID-19 had hit. A recent *Gold Coast Bulletin* article suggested he followed Monroe around like a little puppy.

I'm not sure if the look that invaded Des's face was one of shock or relief. But it certainly was a surprise to everyone present when Singleton suddenly dismissed him from the press conference before he even had a chance to speak. I felt glad for Des, but sad at the same time. Glad because he'd been spared the humiliation of trying to explain himself in front of the press for the umpteenth time, but sad because I knew this could be the end of an illustrious career. He'd been dealt an impossible hand. I doubt anyone could have handled this case any differently.

Then my world suddenly changed forever!

I was hardly listening to Singleton. He was going on about Des and how he wasn't being dismissed, merely redistributed, when he looked right at me and said, 'I'd like to introduce you to the new detective in charge, Scott Stephens!'

'What?' There was a tiny splatter of applause from somewhere in the back of the room, then the press surged forward, redirecting microphones and mobile phones in my direction.

'What can *you* do that hasn't already been done?'

'What makes *you* a better detective than DI Williams?'

X

'Do you feel *bad* that Detective Williams has been discarded for you?'

'Will you catch "X"?'

Singleton raised his arms and spoke into the microphone.

'Detective Inspector Stephens hasn't been briefed yet. In fact, he's only just found out about his appointment.'

You're not kidding! And detective inspector? Last I knew I was just a detective constable.

'That will be all for now. We'll schedule another conference as soon as possible once DI Stephens has been brought up to speed.'

What the hell? Why didn't anyone tell me? I wanted to yell. These were the first questions I asked when the last of the journos had been shepherded from the room.

'We couldn't bloody find you, that's why,' Singleton growled. 'Where the hell have you been all morning?'

'It was my morning off, sir.'

'No such thing from here on. You've only one thing to concentrate on now.'

'You're seriously putting me in charge of the "X" case?'

'Yes. I suggest you liaise with DI Williams and exchange data, but first, you'll need a full briefing. I hope you haven't got anything planned for tonight.'

'But why me?'

'You're next in line for promotion. We feel you're the right man for the job.'

'But Gardner, surely?'

Monroe stepped forward. I wondered if the politician smile was surgically enhanced. He wouldn't remember me. Both from Victoria, we went to different schools and moved in vastly different circles – him the public schoolboy from Hawthorn, me the state school scrapper from Essendon. I knew him from the footy. We'd played against each other regularly in the same position – full forward – but he was in a different league. He went on to be a professional player, later a star, and winner of the prestigious Brownlow Medal. 'Detective, after a recommendation by Superintendent Ripley, you've been hand-picked by Commissioner Singleton and me.' He'd moved in close, had taken my hand and was shaking it slowly and forcefully. 'We haven't made this decision lightly. We need results, and we're willing to bank everything on you.'

Apart from on the TV news – just about every bloody night – the last time I'd seen him there'd been an altercation between us. We were fourteen years of age and playing the quarter finals of the AFL Youth Championships. He'd probably remember if I prompted him. But perhaps now wasn't the time.

'But why me?'

'Because you're young.'

I'm the same age as you, and you're not looking that great up close, mate, I almost said.

'We feel you're going to bring the energy to this investigation that it needs.'

'But old Des is the best detective on the force!'

Monroe threw his head back, his smile turning to a sickly laugh. 'He may have been once, but not anymore.'

'There's no negotiation, Scotty,' Singleton pipped in.

Scotty? Like he knew me.

'You start immediately.'

4

It was a typical late spring Gold Coast evening – warm and sticky. I strolled into Surfers from Police Headquarters on Ferny Avenue. It was Sunday, so it was quiet. Just a few tourists and families heading back to their hotels after a day on the beach or at the theme parks.

I hadn't smoked for almost six years, but I tell you, if someone had offered me a cigarette at that moment, I would have taken it.

I'd spent the rest of the afternoon being briefed on the investigation, which was a complete waste of time. Although I certainly hadn't been one of the big players, I'd been working on it since the beginning, albeit in more of an admin role.

It was 6.15 pm. A meeting with the mayor, the commissioner and Superintendent Ripley was scheduled for 7.30 pm, so I'd decided to duck out and get something to eat. Turning into Cavil Avenue, I was approached by a young woman.

'What are you going to do?'

'Excuse me?'

'You're out of your league and you know it.' She was short with dark hair and fierce green eyes.

I suddenly felt hands on my shoulders from behind.

'Don't say a word, Scotty.'

I turned to see Des Williams. He took me by the arm and led me away.

'You won't be able to hide from me, Detective *Constable* Stephens. I'll be watching you!'

'Who was that?' I asked Des as we headed along Cavil Avenue.

'*Gold Coast Bulletin*. Trouble that one, mate. Come on.'

Des led me to Kitty O'Shea's, the Irish bar.

I turned down the offer of a beer but put in an order for food.

Des shook his head apologetically. 'You're right, sorry. You need to keep a clear head.'

'What's happening, Des?' I asked after we'd taken our seats outside.

Des sipped his pint of Guinness, leaving a white moustache that he quickly wiped away with the back of his hand.

'They've thrown me under the bus.'

I wasn't going to pretend I didn't know what he was talking about. 'Why have they picked me?'

'Because you're a nobody.'

'Thanks.'

'I don't mean that as disrespectful. I mean you'll be easy for them to manipulate. And if, when, there are no results, you'll be thrown on the scrap heap, just like me. "Scotty who?" they'll be saying a year from now.'

'You don't think I'm up to it?' The "when there are no results" comment rubbed me up the wrong way.

'You tell me.'

'I *am* a detective, Des.'

He took another swig of his drink, longer this time, savouring the malty taste. I noticed the blooming around his nose and cheeks and guessed he also enjoyed something stronger than Guinness. 'Like I said, mate, I'm not disrespecting you. But there are a few things you need to know. This case isn't all it appears to be.'

'Fuck me dead!' I suddenly yelled, a lot louder than I would have liked. Above the bar was a TV. An evening news bulletin was showing the press conference from earlier. Julian Monroe appeared as his usual immaculate self, but it wasn't him that had caught

X

my eye. It was the scrawny looking bloke standing next to him, looking like a frightened parolee wearing a cheap suit … me! 'I'm on the telly!' I blurted out.

A young female reporter appeared on the screen standing outside the police headquarters. The voice of the anchor from the studio asked, 'What do we know of Detective Inspector Stephens? Is he really the man for the job?'

'We know very little at this time, Alex,' the reporter replied. 'We've only just learned of his appointment, but we know he's not a detective inspector at all, only a detective constable. He's never even been in charge of a case before. It's almost as if he's been plucked from the lowest ranks.'

'Do we know anything else?'

The reporter shook her head. 'No, but I'm sure the Queensland police commissioner and the Gold Coast mayor had good reasons for picking him. One thing for certain though, working on a high-profile case like this there won't be any secrets. I'm sure we're going to learn all about Detective Scott Stephens over the next few days.'

Des looked at me, his eyes full of sorrow. 'You're fucked, Scotty!'

'What do you mean?'

The waitress interrupted with my order of burger and chips. I tucked in, while gesturing for Des to continue.

'We haven't got time to go into it now, and this isn't the place.' He took another drink, this time half finishing it. 'You're going to be flat out busy from tomorrow morning. Your life is about to change forever. Let's agree to meet up as soon as possible.'

'Sounds a bit dramatic, mate.'

'You've got no idea. I've got to go.' He finished his drink, then handed me his card.

'Ring me when you get the chance, preferably tomorrow. I need to fill you in on the facts, not the bullshit they're feeding you.' He rose from the table and offered his hand, 'Good luck,

Scotty. You're going to need it. And remember, if there's anything you need at all, give me a call.'

'Thanks, mate. Listen, before you go, I'm really sorry about all this.'

'Don't be. I'm fine. In fact, I'm better than fine. These last three weeks have been hell. I'm looking forward to a break. Relax a bit.'

'Good on you.'

We shook hands and he rushed off into the twilight.

5

It only took a few minutes to stroll back through Surfers, but in that time my mind was swirling. That morning I'd been cleaning up after Elvis and Tetley. Now I was in charge of one of Australia's biggest murder investigations. It couldn't be right.

From the moment I walked into the station, I could feel things had changed. The way the staff sergeant on duty looked at me before quickly averting his eyes. The way WPC Mandy Hobbs, who I'd been trying to tap for a couple of months, nodded to me respectfully like she would a superintendent or someone of high stature.

'If you'd like to take a seat, sir. The commissioner will see you shortly,' the staff sergeant said.

Sir? Since when did anyone call me sir? 'No worries. I'll go up to the office.'

'He specifically said you were to wait here in the foyer, sir.'

I shrugged and took a seat in one of the plastic chairs.

Uniforms came and went–all looking my way. It was as if I was the new bloke on show for the first time. Another WPC entered with her partner–a strapping lad I didn't know. I noticed slight smirks on their faces as they passed. *Or was I just imagining it?* I nodded at them, but like everyone else, they quickly looked away.

I waited for an hour before a young woman appeared and introduced herself as Lucy, Commissioner Singleton's assistant. I followed her up to the main boardroom. The door was open. Inside was Singleton and Monroe sitting at the oval table, along with Superintendent Ripley. There were other people there too – suits. Only one vacant chair was left at the table.

'Ah, here he is,' Monroe said, rising to his feet as I was shown into the room, 'the man of the moment.'

Everyone turned to look at me while Lucy showed me to my seat.

'How are you holding up, Scotty?' Ripley asked.

'I'm not quite sure, sir.'

'Everyone, I'd like you to meet the new detective in charge of the X investigation. Detective Inspector Scott Stephens.'

Had I really been promoted without knowing it? He introduced me to the people in the room. Most were Gold Coast personalities in some form or another, including a couple of local politicians, businesspeople, and two high-ranking uniforms. As introductions took place, Monroe didn't take his eyes off me. With his unnerving grin, he seemed to be analysing my every move. Commissioner Singleton was doing the same.

Ripley remained on his feet. 'So, Scott, firstly I'd like to apologise for the speed at which things have taken place. As you know, these are unprecedented times.' He looked around the room, making eye contact with everyone present as if trying to justify his/their decision to appoint me. 'We've called this meeting to firstly congratulate you, and to welcome you to your new role as the lead DI in the X investigation.'

There was a moment of awkward applause. I just sat there blushing.

Ripley continued, 'I want you to know you'll have the full support of the Queensland police, and indeed the community as a whole.' Everyone nodded their heads enthusiastically. 'Now, before we bring you up to speed, do you have any questions?'

My mind had wandered a bit. It does that. All eyes were on me.

'Scotty? Any questions?'

'Yes ... why me?'

Among the laughter, I also noticed a few nervous sideways glances. Monroe and Singleton however, kept their eyes firmly on me.

X

'You're very modest, detective, and that's one of the reasons we were drawn to you.'

'I am?'

'We've studied your career. You are an exceptional detective. I'm just amazed you've been overlooked for promotion so many times. There'll be an inquiry into that. But before we go any further, I think it important that you get to know everyone present.'

One of the high-ranking uniforms stood. He was a middle-aged man, stocky, balding. I didn't know him, so suspected he was a fed. He introduced himself as Detective Sergeant Keith Roper from Sydney and his partner as Detective Sergeant Todd Bannister. My suspicions were correct, they had been drafted from the federal police to assist us with the investigation.

Janet Carson, Member for Surfers Paradise, stood next. She covered the disastrous impact the killings would have on the Gold Coast economy if the perpetrator wasn't brought to justice before he killed again.

Next up was Jack Mento, a well-known Gold Coast identity, successful businessman and philanthropist. I remembered him from his TV ads for mobile phones in the nineties. Now one of the biggest property developers in Queensland, he spoke about the impact the case was having on the community. Of course, it was really a thinly veiled concern about the real estate market.

I was fighting to stay awake when the final person at the table introduced themself then sat down.

'We can do this,' Monroe began, rising to his feet once more, 'we can fight this disease in the same way we did COVID-19, and we will win. I want you all to understand we are doing everything in our power to stop these deaths and bring this killer to justice. And we have a new weapon in our armoury.' He held out his hand in my direction, 'I just want to personally welcome you to the team, DI Stephens ... Scott ... Scotty, if I may?'

I shrugged.

'We have every faith in you, my friend. We *know* you will deliver. Ladies and gentlemen, Detective Inspector Scott Stephens.'

More applause followed and everyone at the table stood, except me. Instead, I sat there blushing and wishing I'd had that beer.

When the applause finally died down, everyone took their seats once more, but I noticed they were all gawking at me expectantly. *Oh god, no!* They expected me to speak! I hadn't spoken in public like this since ... since I was best man at Johnno's wedding. I slowly rose from the table.

'Uhm ... firstly, I'd just like to thank everybody for coming ...' Shit! I was delivering the best man speech.

There was a sudden knock at the door. A uniformed constable, not waiting for a reply, stepped into the room and addressed Singleton.

'My apologies for the interruption, sir, but there's been another one!'

6

Superintendent Andrew Ripley and I were ushered into a waiting car and whisked away, south, towards Carrara Stadium. The streets of the Gold Coast were eerily empty. Even though not quite in season yet, there would usually be more tourists than this, milling around, eating in the restaurants, patronising the bars. Those establishments that hadn't already closed early were empty and still.

'We need you to smarten yourself up, Stephens,' Ripley said suddenly as we crossed the bridge onto Chevron Island.

'I'm sorry, sir?'

'There'll be someone to help you tomorrow, and you'll need to lose the mullet.'

Mullet? I consciously ran a hand over my head. Granted, my hair was due for a cut, and because it was thinning slightly at the front, it may have looked a bit bogan.

'Your life is going to change, detective, and you need to be ready.'

In the gloom of the back seat, I was beginning to sound like a parrot.

'But why me?'

'And you need to stop that, too.'

'What?'

'This lack of self-belief. It's tiring. If you don't harden the fuck up, the press will crucify you!'

'But I don't get it. Yesterday, I was just a detective const—'

'You've been flying under the radar for far too long. It's time to step up.'

'But Gardner or Mason ... they're more qualified, surely?'

The car turned left onto Bundall Road.

'Put all that out of your mind. We've got great expectations of you, Master Pip.'

I didn't have a clue what that meant, but he seemed hellbent on avoiding my questions. I leaned forward and tapped the driver on the shoulder. 'Stop the car, mate.'

'What are you doing?' Ripley frowned.

'I'm getting out. If you're going to ignore my concerns, you can get fucked!'

Ripley obviously wasn't used to being spoken to in that way. Until then, his expression had been authoritarian, smug even. Now he sat open-mouthed, eyes agape. 'How dare you speak to me like this.' he demanded as the driver pulled over at the entrance to the HOTA complex.

'Because although I may just be a detective constable, I'm not a bloody idiot. I want to know what the hell's going on.'

Ripley sat silently, staring at me through narrowed, calculating eyes for what seemed like ten minutes, but was probably thirty seconds. Then his face suddenly broke into that smile he usually reserved for his peers. 'That's the spirit!' He slapped me on the back.

I desperately wanted to get out of the car. I wasn't thinking of my career. The only thing going through my mind was that this wasn't right.

'This is exactly the kind of energy we need.' He'd changed his tone, it was now soft and friendly, almost like he was talking to an injured child. 'Look, you're right, we could have chosen anyone. Yes, there are detectives who may seem more suitable, more capable perhaps, but we didn't want them. We didn't make our decision lightly. I honestly believe you're the right man for the job, Scotty. Trust me. Great things are going to come your way. Drive on, Alan.'

As the car pulled away, I realised I was wasting my time. Ripley would have made a good politician with his smile and the make-you-feel-good answers that weren't answers at all.

X

The Metricon Stadium complex, home of the Gold Coast Suns – south-east Queensland's second premier AFL team – was situated in Carrara, a suburb west of Broadbeach.

I made my way to the forensic tent that had already been set up over the crime scene, close to the turnstiles at the northern side of the stadium. Forensics in medical garb and face masks were busily hovering. A series of bright flashes illuminated the interior as a police photographer took pictures of the body from all angles. I noticed a man wearing a surgical mask standing at the entrance, looking inside. Before he even turned, I realised it was Gardner.

'You know DI Gardner, of course,' Ripley said.

My nonchalant shrug was an attempt at hiding the disdain.

'Dion was in the area and got the call.'

Gardner had one of those practised stares that made you feel as if you needed to justify yourself. It probably worked well when questioning suspects, but I was having none of it. I pushed past him and entered the tent.

I'd been a detective for six years, and in uniform for fifteen years prior to that, so as you can imagine, I'd seen some sights. It wasn't the blood and the horrific scene that lay before me that captured my attention, like the last time, it was the expression on the poor girl's face. It was a mixture of shock, horror and surprise, like all three emotions had been captured and solidified at the very first moment of the attack.

The signature X cuts on her throat were prominent and her clothes were saturated, making them appear dark red. And, just like before, the enormous pool of blood was below her feet.

I moved in for a closer look.

'Excuse me, sir,' said a young woman in full forensic gear. 'If you don't mind, you're … in the way.'

I glanced at Ripley, who quickly averted his eyes. Gardner, however, continued to watch me, and even though his mouth was covered by a surgical mask, I could tell he was grinning.

'There's not a lot we can do here,' Ripley said, trying to mentally shepherd me out of the tent. 'We'll meet up in the morning. I'll introduce you to your new team, then we'll be able to get to work.'

'What do you mean?' I was confused. 'There's work to be done here, right now.'

'That's okay, you don't have to worry about that. Gardner will finish up.' Placing a hand on my shoulder, he continued, 'You've had a massive day. Be good to get some rest. Tomorrow will be even bigger.'

Was I leading this case or not? 'I'm not going anywhere.' I returned Gardner's stare, 'As for you mate, you can fuck off!'

'Now then, Scott, there's no need for that,' Ripley interjected, 'DI Gardner has been assigned as your number two.'

'What?'

I imagined Gardner's grin widening. I wanted to rip that mask off and stuff it down his throat. 'And when were you going to tell me about this?'

'Tomorrow, at the meeting.'

Whether it was pride, or just a product of my mother's Irish roots, I dug my heels in. I was out of my depth; I'd known that from the moment Singleton dropped the bombshell at the press conference that morning. I knew just as well as anyone else that you didn't pull out the roadie to sing at a U2 concert, but I wasn't

X

about to go along with their charade. If they were putting me in charge of this case, that's exactly what I'd do – take charge.

'Still here, Gardner?' I continued, before Ripley could protest. 'Listen up everybody.' My voice was raised so everyone in and outside the tent could hear. Then I waited while the stunned personnel stopped what they were doing and turned to look at me. 'I'm Detective cons ... Detective *Inspector* Scott Stephens, and I'm in charge of this investigation.' I paused, scanning their reactions. 'This means you *all* answer to me. I'm happy to wait while you finish up whatever it is you're doing, but then I'll be expecting the reports of your initial findings, as well as full access to this site before anything else is touched or removed. Do you all understand?'

At first there was hesitance in the response, but everyone present finally nodded. I turned to Ripley and Gardner. Ripley looked away and headed back to the car. Gardner was no longer smirking. I could tell because his mask was kind of puckered, and his eyes had lost their fire.

'And yet *you're* still here,' I said, squaring up to him.

'You haven't got a clue what's going on, have you?'

'That's where you're wrong, mate. I know exactly what's going on.'

Pulling the mask down onto his chin. 'Like I said, you haven't got a clue.' He strutted off into the night.

7

5 September

Like the day before, I didn't get home until the early hours. As tired as I was, I hadn't been able to sleep. The victims' expressions were haunting me. It was if they were asking the same question as everyone else, *What the hell are you doing here?*

According to the early morning radio report, the waves were back, so it was unusual for me not to go for an early morning surf. Instead, I was showered and eating a bowl of Weetbix while only half listening to the news. The main story, of course, was last night's killing.

Answering a knock at the front door, and wearing only a pair of board shorts, I was shocked to be confronted by a small crowd of jostling faces – it was the media.

'DI Stephens, what's the latest news on the *X* killings?'

'Are you any closer to finding the killer?'

I closed the door on them as my phone rang.

'Scott, it's Superintendent Ripley. I'm sending a car for you.'

'What?'

'Should be there in half an hour.'

I've got a car. Then I realised my old Volkswagen Beetle, aka "the Dub," probably wouldn't fit the image of a high-profile detective. Nothing I owned did. I went into the bedroom and picked up my suit jacket from where I'd thrown it the night before. It was grimy, old, cheap and worn. Another trip to the dry cleaners wouldn't do a lot for it.

X

My second suit was hanging in the wardrobe, and although clean, was no better than the first. As I put it on, a strange feeling of self-consciousness suddenly overcame me. I guess it had something to do with being in the limelight, something I hadn't experienced since my schoolboy footy days.

A text message dinged on my mobile. It was an unknown number, but the message was clear. 'I'm at the front door.'

When I opened it, two uniformed cops were holding back the media pack.

A well-groomed young man stood on my doorstep with something slung over his shoulder. He was also carrying a large sports bag. 'Hi, I'm Bradley.' Marching in like he was leading the gay Mardi Gras, he turned, offered a wet-lettuce-handshake, and looked me up and down. 'Oh, thank goodness. Looks like I got here just in time.' He quickly scanned his surroundings. 'Where's the bedroom?'

'What?'

'The bedroom?'

He swung a vinyl bag from over his shoulder and I realised it was a suit bag. 'Here you go. Put on one of these.'

It was heavy–there must have been two or three suits in there. Opening it, I found seven–one for every day of the week. 'Bloody hell!'

'I know ...' Bradley had followed me into my room. 'Aren't you the big superstar now?'

I laid the suits out side-by-side on my bed. Not that I'd really know, but I could tell they weren't cheap. The styles were the same, but they differed in colour from brown to blue to black, except for one which was a leery tan.

'These are all for me?'

Bradley skipped over to the bed and picked up the tan-coloured suit. 'Yes they are. Here, put this one on.'

'Not bloody likely.'

'But it's ... sexy.' He fluttered his eyelids.

I picked up the grey one. 'This'll do.'

Bradley gave a patient sigh.

'Well, thanks for dropping these off,' I attempted to shepherd him from the room.

'No, no, no, no.' He held up the palms of his hands in front of his chest and squeezed in his shoulders like a showgirl. 'You don't understand. I'm all yours!'

'Excuse me?'

With great theatrics, he lifted his right hand to his brow and held it there like a damsel in distress. 'To do with whatever you will.'

'What the hell are you going on about?'

'I'm your new assistant.'

'You're kidding.'

'Or your new partner, perhaps?'

'I've got an assistant?'

'Or ... partner.'

I tried again to usher him out of the room but noticed the sports bag was on the floor.

'Wait. There's more.' He picked up the bag, plonked it on the bedside chair, unzipped it, and pulled out a stack of new shirts, ties, socks, underwear, handkerchiefs, and a couple of shoe boxes.

'I'll make coffee while you get changed.' He swanned from the room. Everything he did had a sense of drama.

Along with a pair of new dacks, a shirt and socks, I put on the grey suit. It fitted perfectly, and I have to say it felt good. In one of the shoeboxes was a nice pair of deep brown brogues. In the other was a black pair. I put on the black ones. Once again, they fitted just right.

When I walked into the kitchen, Bradley wolf whistled and clapped his hands like a hummingbird. 'Whoo-hoo. You look amazing!'

'Uh, thanks.'

'But wait, there's still more.'

On the table was a mug of coffee, but next to it were two more boxes. The simple logo on the bigger of the two told me it was a brand-new iPhone. The other was a Wallace Bishop jewellery box.

Bradley was watching me closely.

'Go on, open it.'

Inside was a Tag Heuer Aquaracer Quartz watch. I put it on. It fitted as if it had already been sized to my wrist.

'Perfect! Look at you.'

It may have all looked perfect, but it didn't feel real. None of it. How could it have? Every item of clothing I was wearing, right down to the pair of Calvin Klein dacks, was brand new and significantly more expensive than anything I could have bought myself. The only Tag Heuer watch I'd ever owned was a knock off Elvis brought me back from Bali.

'Okay, drink your coffee. We have to go.' Bradley snatched up the iPhone box and opened it. 'Give us the old thing.'

'Me phone?'

'Yes, just need to switch the sim card.'

Reluctantly handing him my phone, then drinking my coffee – which was particularly good – I watched as he skilfully transferred the sim.

'There you go, all done. Now come on, drink up. We've got one more stop before we go to the station.' He was like a mother rushing to get his child ready for preschool.

'Where are we going?'

'To the hairdressers. Time to lose the mullet, I'm afraid.'

'It's *not* a mullet.'

'It *so* is.'

I checked my new watch. Wow, this would take some getting used to. 'I don't know if Chilly'll be open yet.'

'Chilly?'

'Me barber.'

'No, I've got you an appointment at Bernaard's in Broadbeach.'

'You've what?'

'8.30. Come on or we'll be late.'

'I'm not bloody going to no place called "Bernaard's."'

'Why not?'

'Well, it's for bloody p—' I thought twice on what I was about to say and cleared my throat, 'women.'

'No, it's not, they do men as well,' Bradley replied in that mother-knows-better tone.

'Not gonna happen, mate. Chilly's my bloke.'

Bradley sighed once more with exasperation. 'Where?'

'Just down the road.'

'Coolangatta?'

'No, here in Kirra.'

The damsel in distress returned. After some patting of his brow and cheeks, he reluctantly gave in. 'Okay, but I'll be giving this "Chilly" instructions.'

'No need. Number three all over as per usual. Five-minute job.'

I thought he was going to faint.

Chilly's Barber Shop was only a two-minute walk from my place, but seeing as the media were still out front, Bradley and the two uniforms ushered me through the crowd and into a Range Rover.

Following my directions, Bradley drove to Chilly's shop and parked around the corner.

'Seriously?' he said as we climbed from the car.

'Yep, come on.'

Thankfully, there were no other customers waiting. It looked as if Chilly had just opened. He was busying himself around the till. His hair was damp, so I guessed he'd been for a surf.

'Chilly.'

'*Fuckin' hell!*' His eyes almost popped out of his head when he saw me.

I stood tall and grasped the lapels of my suit jacket. 'Not bad, eh?'

'Where'd you get that?'

X

'All part of the new look.'

'Saw you on the telly. Big shot now, mate.'

'I wouldn't say that.'

'How'd you do it?'

'Do what?'

'Get the job? I thought you were just a traffic cop.'

He was kidding. I'd been coming to Chilly's for the last five years and had had the odd drink with him at Kirra Hotel. A surfer, like me, he had a dry sense of humour, which a lot of people didn't get. I did, fortunately.

'Detective Inspector Scott Stephens to you, if you don't mind.'

He made his way to the empty chair. 'Okay, who was first?'

I noticed Bradley's body immediately stiffen as if he'd just been asked to strip naked.

I climbed into the seat. 'Just me. This is Bradley.'

'Ahh, a new friend, Scotty?' Chilly smirked as he looked Bradley up and down.

'He's my ... assistant.'

'Partner,' Bradley corrected.

'Ohhh, partner ...' Chilly said, parenthesising the word partner with his fingers.

'Assistant. You can wait in the car, sport. Won't be long.'

'I bloody will not wait in the car.'

Chilly placed a gown around my neck and was about to grab the clippers when Bradley gently led him by the arm to one side. After a bit of whispering, Bradley produced what looked like a magazine clipping from his pocket.

I heard Chilly say, 'That's what you want?' I couldn't see the picture he was looking at, but the mischievous grin was unmistakable.

'Number three, as usual, Chill,' I said.

Bradley stepped forward and stood behind the chair, looking at me through the mirror. 'You need to trust me, Scott.'

'Why, what do you think you're gonna do?'

'We're going for the new look, *remember?*'

'No. I don't *remember* anything of the kind.'

'Trust me, Scott.'

Chilly was unusually quiet as he went to work. I'd never had anyone give me a shave before, especially a tattooed surfer. When he'd finished, he lifted the electric hair clippers and changed the blade cover.

'Number three?' I asked.

'Of course,' he said, side-glancing Bradley. He turned on the clippers and drove them up the back of my head. 'Oh shit, Scotty.'

'What?'

'Fuck me, I'm sorry, mate.'

'What?'

'I've used a number one by mistake.'

'You what?' I lifted a hand from under the gown and ran it across the back of my head. There was a three-inch track of stubble from my neck to just below the crown. 'You're kidding me, aren't you?'

Chilly was desperately trying not to laugh.

'It's okay, it's okay. Don't panic,' Bradley said, taking charge, 'we can fix this.'

'I know what you bastards have done.'

Chilly stood back, tongue-in-cheek.

Reluctantly, I had to let them continue. Twenty minutes later I had a number one crop to the back and sides, with a close trim on the top.

Chilly didn't make eye contact as I stood from the chair, but I could tell from his smirk he was enjoying himself.

Bradley was the opposite, jumping like an excited schoolboy. 'Wow, look at you. From the Tiger King to James Bond in minutes. You're one good looking chap, DI Stephens.'

Before we left, I noticed the magazine cutting lying face down on the bench seats along the back wall. I picked it up to see a picture of Daniel Craig.

Chilly couldn't hold it in any longer. 'I'm good, mate, but I'm not that bloody good!'

8

Before he could climb into the driver's seat, I nudged Bradley to one side and grabbed the car key from his hand. 'I'll drive.'

'But—'

I was already in, ignoring his protests.

With heavy traffic, it took us just over thirty minutes to reach Surfers and park in the basement below the station on Ferny Avenue. I checked my reflection in the rear mirror. What I saw would take a bit of getting used to. Not just the short crop, everything, the new look, clothes, the car. Would they be telling me how I should act and speak next? I was guessing that was to come. I didn't have to wait long.

As we strolled across the basement from the car, Bradley began to do a kind of slow strut. 'Like this, look. Chin up, look straight ahead, lose the hunch ...'

Totally ignoring him, I continued with the old PBC High shuffle. Maybe it should have been me teaching *him* a few new tricks. He stopped me just before we got to the lift.

'Scott, this is important. You walk like a Melbournian stevedore.'

'I walk like me.'

'I know this is all new, but everything I'm doing is to protect you.'

'Protect me from whom?'

'Everyone. The press, your peers, superiors, the public. You're going to be one of the most scrutinised men in Australia over the next few days, maybe weeks–months even. If you're not ready, they're going to crucify you.'

Pressing the 'up' button at the side of the lift doors, I tried to sound casual. 'I think I'll be right, mate.'

'You won't be, trust me. That's why I'm here.'

'She'll be right,' I insisted as the elevator arrived.

We reached the top floor, and just before the doors opened, Bradley turned to me. 'This is it. The new order in the life of Detective Inspector Scott Stephens begins as soon as these doors open. I hope you're ready.'

'I am.'

Who was I kidding?

The first noticeable difference was the way everyone seemed to stop what they were doing when we stepped from the lift into the busy heart of the station. The expressions, the body language, it was like when you know someone's talking about you and they suddenly shut up when they see you approaching. All eyes were watching as I walked over to my desk to find it bare. 'What's going on?'

Dale Mason, a mate, took me by the arm. 'You're no longer in here with the minions, Scotty.'

Bradley had also appeared by my side.

'Where's me things?' I instinctively straightened my back and lifted my chin.

'My things ... you mean, *my* things,' Bradley corrected. 'Follow me.'

As I followed him out the door and into the corridor, the chin stayed up. It felt strangely right, seeing as everyone was watching. Perhaps Bradley had a point after all?

'You're kidding me, aren't you?' I said as he opened the door to Des's old office.

'No. This is your new office.'

'But it belongs to Des.'

'Not anymore.'

I noticed a slight smell of disinfectant mixed with the aroma of fresh roses as I entered the office. The room was nothing flash. It

X

housed a desk, a chair, a computer, and a filing cabinet, but it was much more than that. In the world of offices, it was like owning the penthouse suite. A dozen red roses in a vase adorned the top of the filing cabinet.

Bradley checked his watch, announcing, 'Okay, we have a team meeting in two minutes.'

He was about to rush off again when I grabbed him by the arm, pulled him into the office and closed the door. 'Now just slow down a bit Brad—'

'Bradley.'

'I'm feeling a little bit like a sheep being led to slaughter here.'

'Good analogy.'

'How do *you* know what's going on and I don't?'

'This is my job. It'll be up to me to make sure you're where you're supposed to be and when, and to ensure you're prepared.'

'Mate, I don't need you telling me when or how to wipe me own arse.'

'*My* arse, my—'

'I'm going to get awfully tired of that, too.'

'Scott, I know my ways may seem totally alien to you, but believe me, you're going to be on the TVs of just about everyone in this country *every day* until you've solved this case. This is much more than just being a good detective. You're going to have to learn diplomacy and tact. You'll need to be in charge, and you'll need to stay in control of the media while keeping them on side. Please just trust me. I'm here to help you.'

'Do you know what's pissing me off the most?'

'No, what's that?'

'Nobody even asked me if I wanted this job. It's just been thrust upon me. I was actually happy doing what I was doing.'

'Really?' This seemed to confuse him.

'Really.'

'But surely, this is the kind of case you've always dreamed of?'

'Nope.'

'Every detective would sell their soul to be in your situation right now.'

'Not me. I don't even want it.'

The damsel in distress returned. He appeared to be genuinely shocked. 'But you've been chosen above all those hard-working detectives out there.'

'And why is that? Can you tell me? Because I don't bloody know.'

'You're the right man for the job, Scott!'

'Am I, though?'

X

Superintendent Andrew Ripley made a grand entrance once everyone was present. I must admit, I didn't have a clue what I was doing, and I was glad when Bradley guided me to a chair at the front of the incident room. Five detectives, two uniforms and Jacob Tyler, the young profiler, were present. I was glad to see Dale Mason and Jenny Radford. However, I wasn't so happy to see Dion Gardner sitting there with his ever-present sneer. The two other detectives were Roper and Bannister from Sydney, who were now both in plain clothes. Constables Wayne McDonald and Dee Forester were the uniforms, both good cops.

Ripley stood at the front of the room and cleared his throat, 'Good morning, everybody.'

'Good morning, sir,' said the group in unison, sounding like primary school children.

'This meeting was originally scheduled as a vehicle for us to get to know one another, and of course, to introduce you all to the new DI in charge, Detective Inspector Scott Stephens,' he gestured towards me with an open hand.

With a few nods, I acknowledged everyone present.

'But, as I'm sure you're all aware by now, there was another killing last night.' He paused momentarily. 'I'm sure I don't need to

X

tell you about the importance of us bringing this killer to justice as soon as possible. We've already seen a drop in tourism by sixty per cent. If this continues, it will have devastating repercussions. We'll need to keep this meeting short because there is much work to do. So, without further ado, I'd like to hand you over to DI Stephens.'

All heads swivelled in my direction.

I'd been biting my tongue long enough while listening to Ripley banging on about the effect the killings were having on the coast. 'But let's not forget why we're really here, eh?' I said, rising to my feet and turning to face the team. 'This killer has murdered eight innocent young women! Stuff the bloody economy.'

From the corner of my eye, I caught sight of Bradley's hand rising to his brow.

9

Although somewhat reluctantly, I'd always been a team player, never a team leader. Standing at the head of the packed incident room, I began to wish I'd paid more attention over the years instead of just taking instructions. The core team had been joined by the rest of the personnel working on the case–over a hundred detectives and uniforms. Was I supposed to give a pep talk, or should I get straight down to business? It was great to have a team to ease the burden, but what was I supposed to do with them all?

'Uhm ... for those of you who don't know me, I'm Detective Inspector Scott Stephens – Scotty. I'll be leading the investigation from now on. I want us to ... uhm ... work as a team, and I think if we all pull together ... we should be able to stop this bastard from killing again.'

'Prodigious words of wisdom, *sir*,' Gardner said, 'thank you so much!'

He was bigger than me, but I'd have a go. I matched his stare for a moment, but he wasn't going to back down. All eyes were on me. I guess everyone was interested to see how I'd handle this.

'Thank you, DI Gardner.'

Although everyone present was familiar with the case, I asked Constable Dee Forester to bring us up to speed.

'The first killing took place on the former Iluka Resort development site at the corner of Hanlan Street and the Esplanade, Surfers Paradise on August 13th. The body of twenty-two-year-old,

X

Brazilian born Maria Santos, a waitress who worked at the Guzman y Gomez Mexican restaurant on Cavil Avenue, was discovered by a man and his wife while out walking their dog. They found her after they noticed the gate to the site was open. The victim had died from fatal wounds to her neck in the shape of an *X*.'

'At about what time did the killing take place?' Everyone present already knew the answer, but I felt the need to engage.

'Around 9.00 – 9.30 pm.'

I watched while the team, apart from Gardner, scribbled down the information. I nodded to Forester to continue.

'The second killing took place three nights later, Aug 16th, on Burleigh Headland. The victim was Angela Dale, a nineteen-year-old student from Sydney, up here visiting her father. The MO was exactly the same. The victim had bled out from the same wounds to the neck.'

'Time of death?'

'About the same, 9.00 to 9.30 pm.'

This time she carried on without my prompting. Over the next thirty minutes, she listed the remaining six victims. August 19th, Nadia Cowen, a twenty-one-year-old usher was found beneath the overpass walkway between the Gold Coast Convention Centre and The Star Casino. August 20th, Michelle Morgan, a twenty-three-year-old real estate agent, was killed leaving her office at Sanctuary Cove. August 25th, Liz Staniforth, a twenty-two-year-old waitress, was killed in the grounds of the Home of The Arts (HOTA). August 29th, the body of Stella Simpson, a twenty-four-year-old tennis coach, was found behind the Pizzey Park Sporting Complex in Miami. September 3rd, Lisa Wei, a twenty-one-year-old student, was killed outside the Varsity Lakes Towers student accommodation, and on September 4th, twenty-three-year-old Denise Shaw, an employee at Metricon Stadium, was added to the killer's resumé.

Dee returned to her seat.

Jacob Tyler, the young profiler, put up his hand.

'Yes?'

'I'm sure you're all familiar with my profile report. But I've been tweaking it in the hope we can establish if there has been a pattern in the killer's movements, and whether or not this will determine the likelihood that we can predict his next move.' Jacob rose from his seat. 'May I, sir?'

'Of course.'

He plugged a memory stick into the laptop, and the projector screen went from a default Microsoft wallpaper with icons scattered around the peripheral, to a PowerPoint presentation. Using the handheld remote, he manually began the slide show with a horrific photograph of the first victim.

'Maria Santos was attacked after leaving work early and heading home to her shared apartment.' The next slide showed a map of the Gold Coast. Red crosses appeared at each of the locations a body was found. 'As discussed previously, all killings took place between 9.00 and 9.30 pm between Burleigh Heads and Sanctuary Cove. The victims were female and of a similar age. The execution was the same on each occasion.' He paused, looking around the room as if he'd just revealed an amazing revelation. 'The killer has not left one single piece of evidence. He seems to have cleverly avoided the hundreds of CCTVs placed around the coast.'

Unaware at first that my mouth was agape, I was hoping he had more to share and wasn't just trying to justify his presence, because this was all old news.

A close-up picture of Santo's throat displaying the *X* cuts appeared on the screen. 'The two initial, and only cuts, forming the *X*, were fatal and identical in each case. The element of surprise was a key factor. The same implement was used on each victim.'

A picture of a small, hooked knife appeared. The handle was curved, with a hole at the base of the blade for the index finger.

X

'This is a gut hook skinning knife. Used for hunting, they can be purchased from any outdoor or fishing store. Not expensive.'

'This shows a level of skill with the blade,' Dale Mason offered.

'Yes,' Jacob replied, once again looking around the room like a magician about to perform his next trick. 'And it could easily be concealed within the hand.'

I still wasn't hearing anything new.

'This brings me to the profile.' A basic photo-fit appeared on the screen of a young, slim man. 'We have absolutely no information about the killer, so we need to rely on the science.'

I noticed Dion Gardner roll his eyes and check his watch.

'*X*, as the press have unfortunately christened him, is between thirty and forty-five years old. He is single and lives alone. There may be a history of depression, anxiety or even bipolar. It's likely he is on medication for this. The precise staging of each scene would suggest a form of OCD, possibly autism.'

This caused a scurry of pens across paper.

'He's a Gold Coaster, introverted, but fiercely proud of his city. It's likely that he even follows one of the football codes at a local level. NRL would be my guess. This might be his only form of social interaction. He works in one of the following occupations: a hospital porter or some kind of technician, the morgue perhaps. A butcher. A vet. He's a loner, so he's the guy at work who keeps himself to himself. He appears to be shy, the strong silent type. He's heterosexual, but not very attractive to the opposite sex, either due to his awkward shyness or maybe a physical abnormality, a speech impediment perhaps. He's a bit of a computer geek—'

'You've just described yourself,' Gardner said.

Ignoring the chuckles, Jacob blushed and continued, 'Something happened during his childhood, some event that embedded a misogynistic gene in his being. An incident with a girl, a teacher, his mother perhaps. Whatever it was, it has left him with an inferiority complex towards women, so much so that he has the need to exhibit his control over them. This isn't something that comes easy to him, and it's not something he could ever do in his daily life. For this he's created a kind of alter ego if you like. A persona. There's a chance he actually sees himself as a superhero.'

I was scanning the room as Jacob continued. Dion Gardner kept catching my eye, and each time he did, his chin would rise into the air like he was challenging me to a face off. I looked away and instead concentrated on the rest of the team. *My* team. I began to realise how much I'd need them.

Jacob finished his presentation to a splatter of applause. Call me cynical, but I was unable to establish any of the tweaking he had mentioned. It seemed to be the same as the last half a dozen times I'd heard it.

For an awkward moment, I sat waiting for the next item on the agenda to be announced. Then I remembered I was in charge. All eyes were on me once more.

'Okay. Thank you, Jacob. That was very … enlightening,' I said, rising from my seat. 'Do we have any questions?'

Gardner put up his hand. 'Yes. You still haven't told us how the fuck you got put in charge of this case?'

10

'Press conference?'

'In twelve minutes,' Ripley replied. He'd ushered me into his office after the meeting.

'With all due respect, sir, why are you doing this to me?'

'Doing what?'

'Throwing me to the wolves like this.'

He circled his desk, sat down, picked up his pen, opened a folder, and spoke to me without making eye contact. 'Nobody's throwing you anywhere, Scott. This is normal practice for a high-profile detective.'

'But I need to be out there investigating.'

He flicked through the pages of the folder. 'That's what your team is for. You're the general. They're your foot soldiers.'

'So, what am I supposed to do?'

He checked his watch. 'Address a press conference in nine minutes. And all of the important stuff.' He looked up at me, closed the folder and rose to his feet. After circling back around his desk, he placed a parental hand on my shoulder. 'You'll need to get used to it. This is going to be your life from now on.'

'But I've never facilitated a press conference before. What am I supposed to say?'

He squeezed my shoulder before checking his watch again. 'You'll be fine. We best get out there. Come on.'

X

A bank of microphones had been set up outside the entrance to the police headquarters. There were more reporters than I'd expected. One of the traffic lanes on Ferny Avenue had been blocked off to accommodate a row of news trucks from Channels 7, 9, 10, SBS, ABC, and Sky News, and the crowd of reporters blocked the whole pavement. Soundmen carrying long booms stood either side of the entrance, dangling microphones overhead.

I was still following when Ripley and I exited the building. But instead of approaching the podium, Ripley made his way to the side of the microphones and stood with his hands clasped and his head down, like he'd just entered church. I followed suit. In the awkward silence, I heard whispers in the crowd. Someone chuckled.

Ripley looked up and gestured with his eyes. 'Go on, detective. The world is waiting.'

The new suit suddenly felt like it was made of cardboard. The shoes were loose on my feet. The shirt collar was constricting and sweaty around my neck, while the expensive watch seemed to be sliding off my wrist. It was as if I was shrinking, melting perhaps, and that's exactly how I felt as I stepped forward.

When I lowered my head too close to the microphones, a loud whistle of feedback invited a group snigger and more whispers. 'What the hell?' I heard someone say.

I straightened my back and tried to slow my breathing, but my breaths were coming short and sharp. 'Uhm ... good morning ... I'm Detect ... Detective Inspector Scott Stephens.' I was suddenly startled by a flurry to my left. I flinched, instinctively lifting my fists in defence. The chuckles were upgraded to laughter. A man, who had followed me to the podium without my noticing, had thrown his arms up and began making gestures and movements. It took a moment before I realised he wasn't about to attack me– he was signing for the deaf. Now he was standing motionless and quiet, waiting for me to speak.

The late morning was bright and hot. I was squinting into the

X

eastern sunshine, while the reporters looked up at me like they were waiting to hear the first words of a novice comedian at the local comedy club. 'Uhm ... I'd ... I'd just like to thank you all for coming.' *Fuck, the wedding speech.* I glanced around at Ripley. He still stood with his head down, praying, no doubt, that I didn't stuff this up. *Why the hell wasn't he helping me?*

'DI Stephens, do you feel bad that Des Williams has been relieved?' Still squinting, I recognised the voice of the girl from *The Bulletin*. 'I do, actually. Des is a fine detective.'

'So, why are you on the case and not him?' a middle-aged man asked.

Good question. The one I'd been trying to get an answer to for the last twenty-four hours.

'Is it true you threw him under the bus?' another male voice called from somewhere in the group.

I was drowning. My heart was pounding. As Tetley would say, I was shitting bricks. Thankfully, Ripley finally stepped in.

'Can we concentrate on the investigation please, and the job at hand?'

'Sir, why have you appointed an inexperienced detective to lead one of the biggest murder investigations in Australian history?' It was that girl from *The Bully* again.

'We haven't. DI Stephens is one of our finest and most experienced detectives.'

The group surged forward.

'But he isn't even a detective, inspector.'

I needed to take charge. I may be a man of few words, and I might come across as a bit thick, but I actually am a good detective. I was beginning to feel like it was me who'd been thrown under the bus, not old Des. But I wasn't prepared, how could I have been? The limelight I'd been thrust into was the one from the roof of the big top, following every stumbling move of the clown in the centre ring. Then the face of Lisa Wei appeared in my mind's eye.

I took a deep breath through my nose. The uncertainty of the last twenty-four hours, the anger of the situation, the fear of a man who knew he was a thousand fathoms out of his depth, must have been gradually growing inside me, swirling towards the surface. It was inevitable that it would overflow sooner or later. It always did. Usually for me it would be in the pub over a few beers after a shit day, or in the man shed with Elvis, Tetley and the boys. But who would have thought it would ever happen on live television?

The same questions were being hurled at me over and over, louder and louder, until ...

'ALL OF YOU JUST SHUT THE FUCK UP!'

Ripley ducked his head as if an air raid siren had just gone off. The group instantly fell silent. The sign interpreter stood motionless, his mouth agape.

As I squinted into the crowd, I could still see Lisa Wei staring back at me.

'You all seem to have forgotten that there is a murder investigation taking place. I am Detective Inspector Scott Stephens of the Queensland Police Service.' My shoulders swelled into the jacket of my suit as my wrists expanded until the watch was tight. My feet suddenly felt lighter, and a cool shiver relaxed my neck. 'I am in charge of this investigation, and I will bring this vicious killer to justice!'

The crowd surged forward again as I backed away from the podium and headed towards the station entrance. Their questions followed me, drifting into the air like helium balloons.

11

I'd purposely ignored a request from Ripley to go and see him. I wanted to get out there with my team, but they pretty much had everything covered. I'd paired them off–Gardner and Simpson, Dale Mason and Roper, Jenny was working with Jacob Tyler, the profiler, and Constables Forester and McDonald would be out canvassing together. Each pair had a single task–find new evidence.

We'd arranged another meeting for 5.00 pm to discuss their findings. So, what was there left for me to do? Something Des Williams had said the evening before had been playing on my mind. 'There's more to this case than meets the eye.' I decided to pay him a visit.

'But I'm your driver as well as your partner,' Bradley complained when I told him I was going alone.

'I don't need a driver, I can drive meself—'

'Myself.'

'And you're not *my* partner.'

'But we're a team.'

'Right, so what I need you to do is go through that stack of files on my desk. It's the case history from the beginning to the present.' His top lip started to quiver. 'Write down anything you think may be of use. Look for anything at all that we may have missed.' This was basically all I could think of giving him to do. To my surprise, he began to sob in the hallway where everyone could see us. Embarrassed, I looked around to see if anyone was looking. They were. Pretty much everyone. I took Bradley by the arm and led him into my office. 'Are you serious, mate?'

'I need to keep active.' A tear rolled down his cheek. 'I want to be a DI, like you.'

'You're gonna have to man the fuck up if you're gonna get anywhere in this game.'

'I know, I know.' He wiped his eyes with the palms of his hands, then straightened the bottom of his jacket as if it were a petticoat. 'I'll take the files home with me tonight. I'll study them. I'll find something if it's there.'

It wasn't that I wasn't used to working with other people. It wasn't unusual for us to be paired off and given tasks to fulfil, just as I had done with my new team. And I liked the lad, I really did, but I wondered what the hell a nice boy like him was doing in the police force.

He looked back at me through moist, red eyes.

'Alright, I'll let you tag along. But you're not driving. I don't need a chauffeur. I don't really need an assistant either, but—'

'Partner,' he said softly as he reached into his pocket, retrieved a handkerchief and blew his nose.

The smile he brought to my face was a welcomed distraction. The muscles in my cheeks felt odd, under used, like the way your lower back feels when you haven't been for a surf in a long time.

As if reading my mind, Bradley said, 'You should smile more often. It suits you.'

X

Des Williams lived in Pacific Pines, a western suburban sprawl stretching from the Pacific Highway at Gaven, to Maudsland and the hinterland beyond that. Des lived on the north-west of the estate, bordering Oxenford. I'd only seen his house once

X

before from the outside, after last year's Christmas party. Des had drunkenly insisted on sharing a taxi with me, even though the ride took me miles out of my way.

Bradley said very little during the fifteen-minute drive from Surfers to Pac Pines. I didn't mind. I considered making him wait in the car as I pulled up outside Des's house. Once again, he seemed to read my mind.

'Can I come in with you, please?'

I turned off the engine, returned my hands to the steering wheel and sat for a moment, looking out at the lowset, brick and tile house that was typical of this earlier stage of the Stockland estate. The only really noticeable thing about Des's house was the magenta bougainvillea that obviously hadn't been trimmed back for a few seasons, and had grown up the side of the house and over the roof of the double garage. I wondered how many times it tore at Des's arms when he put out the bins.

'Okay, you can come in, but you don't say a word, and you don't take notes or anything like that. This is strictly off the record. Do you dig?'

'Yes.' His sad expression disappeared and was replaced with his usual smile.

'Are you there, Des?' I called out as I knocked on the front door, suddenly realising I should have rung first to make sure he was home. 'Des?'

'Listen ...' Bradley said, looking towards the garage.

I cocked my head to one side and listened. Only just audible from the opposite side of the house was the sound of a car engine idling.

'It's coming from the garage,' Bradley said.

We rushed to the double pull-up door and tried lifting it, but it was locked. The side gate wasn't. Negotiating our way past the bougainvillea without being grabbed, I noticed a back door to the garage. Bradley was in front of me. Discovering the doorknob was locked, he instinctively pushed his shoulder up hard against the door. I was surprised at the show of strength.

The door burst open, and a cloud of toxic exhaust fumes bellowed out like steam from a laundry. I lifted the lapel of my jacket and covered my mouth, then rushed blindly into the dark garage. Bradley followed. After almost running into the back of Des's car, I felt my way around to the driver's door. Bradley, bless him, had the forethought to open the pull-up door. As soon as he did, the rest of the fumes rushed out of the building and sunlight flooded in.

Des looked like he was asleep, not slumped over or anything, just sitting behind the steering wheel with his head against the headrest, eyes closed as if listening to classical music on the stereo.

'Des,' I was whispering for some reason, 'Des, can you hear me?'

I gently slapped his face and shook him by the shoulder. His head slumped to one side. He wasn't stone cold, but he wasn't warm either. Turning off the ignition, I pulled my head from the car to instruct Bradley to call 000, but he was already on his mobile doing just that.

There was obviously no trauma to the body, so I knew I was okay to move him. Grabbing him around the shoulders, I pulled as hard as I could. His torso slumped towards me. Although he was a heavy bugger, I managed to turn him and get a better hold beneath his armpits. When I had him halfway out of the vehicle, Bradley joined me, grabbed the opposite arm and pulled. When Des's legs flopped onto the garage floor, Bradley lifted them and we stretchered him out the backdoor and into the garden.

CPR and first aid were something we had to be proficient in, and although I hated giving mouth to mouth, especially after once receiving a mouthful of garlic-tasting puke and hot beer from a bloke who'd choked during a big night watching the

X

footy, my instinct took over and I went to work trying to revive Des. Checking his pulse and any vital signs, there were none, so I began administering CPR. Bradley assisted and took over the chest compressions while I administered mouth-to-mouth. We continued for fifteen minutes without success until the ambulance finally arrived and the paramedics took over.

Ten minutes later we were back in the Range Rover, following the ambulance at speed as it roared out of Pac Pines, siren blaring, towards the university hospital.

12

I know everybody says they hate hospitals. My dislike of them wasn't due to fear or because of the antiseptic smell, mine was from memory. I hadn't been near one since I was fourteen years old. As I stood in the Emergency Department waiting room at Gold Coast University Hospital, memories of the awful day that had plagued my sleep all these years seeped into my consciousness and invaded my insides like a virus. My legs were heavy, and my breathing was short. The beginnings of a dull migraine headache expanded over my left eye, and the world around me seemed to be slowing down, becoming fuzzy around the edges.

'You look terrible, Scott. Why don't you sit down? Can I get you a coffee or something?' Bradley offered.

I didn't want coffee, and I certainly wasn't going to sit. Sitting down in a hospital waiting room would have completed the memory. Suddenly, my legs jittered and my knees almost gave way. Bradley took me by the arm and before I could stop him, he planted me down in one of the hard chairs.

That was it, the memories that had been lapping on the beach of my subconscious for all those years finally broke the seaway levy and flooded in.

X

X

At fourteen, I was enjoying my teenage years. School was okay. I'd never be an academic, but the footy ensured I was popular and well liked. I had a great group of mates and life was good. Trouble is, popularity can breed arrogance if it's not earned for the right reasons. My status was purely due to the fact that I was captain of the Year 9 Aussie Rules school team, as well as the Under 15s Essendon junior squad. I played the show pony position of full forward. I was tall for my age, with the typical Aussie attributes of blond hair, tanned skin and blue eyes. It was a given that I'd move up the ranks of the Essendon age groups over the next few years, become professional after leaving school, and slot into the forward position when it became vacant.

Most teenagers can be arrogant at times, selfish and downright thoughtless, especially the popular ones with talent. I was no exception. In fact, I was a shit from the age of twelve to fourteen. I attracted the cool kids and hung around with them – other footy players, musos, rich kids. To say I was becoming self-obsessed would have been an understatement.

The fact that I would become a professional footballer playing for the Essendon Bombers one day meant I didn't really need school. Footy was the only important thing in my life, except that is, for my mum. Apart from Elvis and Coach Joe – the under 15s coach at Essendon – my mum was the person who kept my feet on the ground. She was the one who made sure I did do my best at school, and who flat out told me, on many occasions, that I was an arrogant little shit. But she also offered me the love and reassurance that only a mother could. The popular kids I hung around with, well, they were friends. Mum was a mate.

Dad was away with work a lot. A sales rep for a mining equipment company. He often had to fly around Australia to remote mining towns in Victoria, Queensland and Western Australia. And when he was home, he seemed to want to spend all his time with my older brother, Todd.

Four years older than me, Todd had just left school and won a scholarship to play rugby league for the Melbourne Storm. He was also smart. Not that I was jealous of him or anything like that, but we just had very little in common.

A devoted follower of the National Rugby League, the Melbourne Storm was Dad's team. Apart from work and fishing, rugby was his life. 'Real football,' he'd say, 'not like that bloody Gay FL!' He hated the AFL. 'Bunch of pansies running around the field. I'd rather watch women's soccer.' He hated soccer, and he was a misogynistic bastard, so this was a fully loaded insult.

Every chance they got, Dad and Todd went fishing. Often during the off season, Dad would hire a campervan and they'd go off together for the weekend. At the time, I didn't think it bothered me. I didn't want to spend time with them anyway.

Mum was the only person in our family who took an interest in anything I did. She always came to the games, but not the night games unless she could get a lift, because she was afraid of driving in the dark. Kate Donovan married Don Stephens at an early age. From the family photos she displayed proudly around the house, she'd been a good-looking girl. Still was when I was fourteen–way too good for my dad. I rarely saw her laughing with my father, or even enjoying his presence. In fact, she always seemed at her happiest when he was away. She somehow changed when he was at home, seemed more servient, not herself. Todd was changing too. It was like he was slowly turning into Dad, and Mum didn't like it. I always felt lucky, because I was the only one she opened up to and shared her wicked sense of humour with. We had a strong bond. That's why what happened on that terrible evening had such a devastating effect on my life – something I've never been able to come to terms with. And something that, after all this time, still kept me awake at night.

X

X

We had a Friday night game, the Essendon under 15s versus Hawthorn. We played at the Hawthorn ground, about an hour from where I lived, and we won. I scored twenty points. Elvis was also on the team. He played half forward flank, and he was bloody good, which in turn made me look good because he was the one supplying the great marks.

'So, you gonna tap it?' Elvis asked as we were drying off in the changing rooms after the game.

'Who?'

'Fuck off! The cheerleader. Like you didn't notice her.'

All teams had their own cheerleaders at their home games. When we'd first run out onto the pitch, I was in the middle of the pack. Blocking my path was the most beautiful girl I'd ever seen – tall, blonde and as sexy as all hell. She winked at me, then playfully shimmied her pom poms down the length of my body. I had to reluctantly run around her to get to the other end of the pitch.

As we ran off at half time, the girls were heading back onto the pitch, and she seemed to make a beeline for me. Once again, she made me run around her. The same thing happened on my return, and at the end of the game.

'If you don't, I will,' Elvis said, flicking me with his wet towel.

It always felt good to win an away game. Home wins in front of the home crowd were special, but an away win always held a greater sense of achievement. I was feeling good as I strutted from the changing rooms with the rest of the team that night. This turned to euphoria when I noticed a couple of girls were waiting outside. One of them was 'Blondie.' She immediately caught my eye, then looked away in a shy, schoolgirl way. Her friend giggled and left her standing there.

Elvis slapped a hand on my shoulder. 'There you go, mate. Told you.'

There was no argument. She was making a play.

'Make sure you're on the bus in ten, though. Coach won't wait, remember?' Elvis said, tapping his watch.

I wasn't hearing him. The fluttering eyelashes, blossoming cheeks and the sensuous flick of the head had rendered me captive. As if in a trance, I wandered towards her.

'Good game tonight,' she said, making quick eye contact. Her voice, western suburbs slang, didn't match her appearance. For some reason, I'd expected something more refined.

'Thanks.'

There was an awkward pause. 'Fancy a drink?' she finally said.

'I can't ... I've got to get on the bus.'

'Just a quickie.' She grinned.

She was obviously older than me. I was tall for my age, but didn't she realise I was only fourteen? I *was* playing for the under fifteens.

'Come on, won't take long, I'm sure,' she ran a finger seductively down my arm.

I checked my watch. The bus would be leaving in five minutes.

'Come on. Just a quickie.'

It was the eyes. The flutter of long, perfect eyelashes. 'Alright, but it'll have to be super quick.'

She grabbed my hand and led me back through the club entrance. There was a bar and gaming room. But before we entered the bar, she grabbed my arm tighter and led me into the ladies' toilets.

As we kissed passionately in one of the cubicles, all thoughts of catching the bus and getting home vacated my mind with the redispersing blood flow.

When I think back now, I emphasise the word 'quickie.' Yes, it was bloody quick. Although I was popular with the girls at school, I hadn't actually done *it* before. I lost my virginity in a piss-stinking stall of the Hawthorn Football Club ladies' toilets. She was disappointed, I could tell. I was embarrassed and was just

X

wondering how to get out of the situation with as little further embarrassment as possible, when I remembered the bus.

'Shit!' I yelled, glaring at my watch. My traumatic little quickie hadn't been quick enough. Coach wouldn't wait–this was the kind of thing he drummed into us often. I pulled up my dacks, apologised to – *shit, I didn't even know her name* – and rushed out of the toilets, through the club foyer and out of the building.

The bus had gone.

13

'Are you alright, Scotty?' Bradley had a hand on my shoulder. 'You're looking a bit pale.'

'I'm fine.'

'I don't think you are.' His tone was both concerned and soothing. He touched my cheek with the back of his hand, like a mother checking her child.

'What the hell are you doing?' I knocked his hand away.

'Sorry. I understand. You're afraid of hospitals.'

'I am *not* afraid of hospitals,' I growled. 'Go and find out what's happening.'

He sauntered off towards the reception.

Of course, I wasn't fine at all. The only thing on my mind at that moment was my mum. Being in the hospital was bringing back the memories I'd crammed into the top of a high cerebral cupboard. Now it was like I'd opened the door and they were falling on me from the top shelf.

X

There were no mobile phones back in the early nineties. My only option was to use the public payphone in the club foyer. I was a schoolboy and didn't have any cash, so I had to reverse the charges. This wasn't a problem though, back then most teenagers were proficient in that little exercise.

X

Mum picked up after the first ring and accepted the charges, 'Hello, Scotty?'

'Hey, Mum. Good news, we won.'

'Yay! That's great, but why are you calling reverse charge? Shouldn't you be on the bus by now?'

'Yeah, that's why I'm ringing – the bus went without me.'

'You missed the bus?'

'Yep, sorry, and I haven't got any cash.' Dad rarely gave me an allowance. It was Friday night, and he'd left early that morning to go on a fishing weekend with Todd.

'But surely the coach wouldn't just leave you?' Her voice was beginning to shake, and I wasn't sure if it was from concern for me or the thought of the likely scenario that was about to play out.

'Can you come and get me?' I tried to play it cool like this was just a normal request, one most parents of teenage kids were used to. There was a long pause. I imagined her standing in the kitchen, her face drained of colour except for a bloom on either cheek. Her eyes searching, she'd be shaking and on the verge of a panic attack.

'But you know I can't ...'

'It's only a forty-minute drive, sixty tops.' I knew this wouldn't help one bit, but I threw it in anyway. My selfish tone made it sound like this was no big deal.

'You know I don't like to—'

'I know, you don't like to drive at night.' The clever deliverance of this line screamed, "Not that old chestnut."'

'Not don't ... can't ...' she said, her voice dropping off to a whisper.

'But I'm stranded here in Hawthorn. What am I going to do?'

'Call a cab. I'll pay the driver when he gets you home.'

Thankfully, through the advancement of time and wisdom, most of us forget those teenage tantrums we threw whenever we couldn't get our own way. We forget them because they're unimportant and embarrassing. That is, however, unless one of those little episodes becomes the pivotal moment that changes your life forever.

'What kind of mother are you that you can't even pick up your stranded son?'

I could hear her breathing down the phone like a slow shiver.

'Don't ask me to do this, Scotty, please.' She was crying now.

I'd already run through the scenario in my mind before making the call. Mum had had a fear of driving at night since she got her licence at the age of nineteen. It wasn't just a fear, it was a real illness – Vehophobia – and I knew that. I fucking knew that!

'Alright ... don't worry about it, eh? I'll just roam the streets. You go to bed. *I'll be fine.*' Normally you'd hang up the phone for effect after an outburst like that, but that wouldn't have gotten me what I wanted.

'Scotty, please.'

'I'll find a shop doorway or somewhere out of the cold. You never know, I might get used to it. Then I can move out of home and not be a burden anymore.' Yes, I was well-practised in the art of the teenage victim.

'Okay ... okay. Stay there at the club. I'll come and get you.' Her tone was a mixture of reluctance, fear and determination.

'No, that's okay.' The final bullet ... guilt.

'Scott, I'm coming to get you.'

'But you don't have to. I'm sure everyone will understand.'

'I'll probably be a bit longer than usual. Stay in the club. I'll be there as quickly as I can.' She would be longer. She wouldn't use the highway.

'Okay, thanks Mum.'

'Love you.' She hung up.

X

'You played a cracking game tonight, son. We could use a player like you at the Hawks.'

The friendly face of a stout elderly man, wearing a Hawthorn

X

blazer and tie, was looking down at me. His face was familiar, I'd seen him at games in the past. I was sitting on the ground against the front wall of the club, having moved outside when the place began to close. From there, I had a good view of the entrance to the carpark.

'What are you doing hanging around here?'

'Waiting for me mum.'

He pulled back his head, stretched out his arm in front of his face and squinted at his watch through long-sighted eyes. 'It's a bit late. How long have you been waiting?'

Checking my own watch was just an automatic response. I already knew I'd been waiting for over an hour. 'She should've been here by now.'

'Is there anyone I can call for you?'

'No, Dad's away fishing.'

I never met my grandparents. Dad's mum lived in an old people's home in Germany, and his dad had died years ago. They never visited Australia and we'd never been to Europe, so the last time he saw them was before he migrated to Australia when he was twenty-one. Mum's parents had both died in a car crash when she was only fourteen. Mum was at a school camp when she learned of the tragedy. They'd been traveling at night along the Monash Freeway when a truck jumped the central reservation and hit them head on, hence her lifelong fear of driving at night.

'Hmm,' he rubbed his chin, 'so she'll be coming from Essendon?'

I nodded.

'The M1, no doubt?'

'No, she won't drive on the highway. She'll take the Dandenong route.'

'Oh well, that's easy then. I live at Ascot Vale. You can come with me. We can drive slowly so you can keep an eye out and flag her down when we see her.'

Deliberation wasn't something my teenage brain had developed at that time. 'Okay, sounds good.'

'I'm Tom Badger.' He offered his hand as we walked across the carpark.

'Tom Badger?'

He chuckled, nodding slowly.

'*The* Tom Badger?'

'The one and only!'

Tom Badger was a Hawthorn legend. He'd played the same position as me back in the 1960s, and played in six premierships, with one of the highest scoring records.

'Hi, it's great to meet you. I'm Scott—'

'Oh, I know who you are.'

'You do?'

We reached a pastel green Holden Kingswood. Tom climbed wearily into the driver's side. I jumped into the passenger seat. Inside were the familiar aromas of vinyl, Mountain Dew air freshener, and a hint of petrol.

The slow speed at which Tom drove was normal, I guessed, which was good because it meant I had a clear view of oncoming traffic. Although, the headlights made it impossible to clearly make out the vehicles until they were alongside us. This meant that when Mum did pass, we'd have to do a U-turn, follow her and flash her down. This might have been a bit of a problem considering how long it may have taken Tom to turn the car around, but at least Mum would have been driving super slowly too. Once again, my underdeveloped teenage brain, lacking both foresight and logic, took none of this into account as we headed along Flemington Road.

When we turned off a gloomily lit side road onto a wide dual carriageway, I instinctively lifted my hands to shield my eyes as the car filled with flashing lights, blue, red and orange. The road was blocked by a fire engine, a tow truck and a half dozen or so police

X

cars. As my eyes adjusted to the change in light, I could also see a stationary semi-trailer resting on the centre reservation.

'Oh crikey,' Tom said, slowing down behind a line of traffic.

My first reaction was relief. This explained why Mum was late. She'd been stuck in the traffic. The thought of turning around and taking another route wouldn't have occurred to her, or it may have, but she would have been too frightened to take it. Instead, she'd be sitting in Dad's Ford Falcon in the line of traffic coming from the opposite direction. She had no way of contacting me to let me know she'd be late. She'd be worried sick and panicking. I explained all this to Tom as I climbed from his car.

'Okay, but I'll come with you, just in case,' Tom said, turning off the ignition.

I was in a hurry but was forced to slow down so Tom could keep up. We passed the queuing cars in front of us, and as we approached the jackknifed truck, a large policeman stepped in front of us.

'I'm sorry. I can't let you past.'

From our position, we had full view of the horrific scene. The truck had crossed the central reservation and ploughed into the oncoming traffic on the other side of the road. It had braked but jackknifed. A car travelling in the opposite direction had either smashed into the front of the cab, or had been unable to get out of the way of the approaching truck. The firies had cut away the roof and the passenger side car door to get the victim out. There was blood and carnage on the mangled vehicle and on the road, but it was none of that which made me faint. It was the make and colour of the car – a silver 1989 Ford Falcon.

14

To be honest, I didn't hear most of what the doctor said. Just those first few words, 'I'm afraid we couldn't save him.' It wasn't until Bradley placed a hand on my shoulder that I realised she'd stopped speaking.

'Oh ... right. Can we see him?'

'Sure. Follow me.'

The last thing I wanted to do was to go deeper into the bowels of the hospital, but apart from it being my duty, Des was also a mate. We followed the doctor through the double doors into a smaller corridor, then through more doors and into what appeared to be a small ward. There were two or three empty gurneys along each of the walls. At the far end was a drawn curtain, like you see pulled around a hospital bed.

The doctor turned to us and gave a look that said *brace yourselves*. Then she opened the curtain slightly and passed through it like she was stepping into the shower. I warily followed, with Bradley right behind me.

Des lay on a gurney. He wore a standard hospital gown, with no sheet to cover him. His skin was a light grey, except for a splay of burst blood vessels around the side of his face and neck.

'I'll leave you alone for a moment,' the doctor said.

'No, that's okay.' I wasn't planning on staying. Not as a sign of disrespect for Des, I just needed to get out of there, and back into the fresh air with the sun on my face.

X

I hadn't seen Todd cry since he was nine years old when Didge, the family dog, died. I'd have been five. He was crying now as we stood around Mum's bed in ICU. Dad's eyes were also heavy with tears. As he stared down at Mum, lying still, her head heavily bandaged, hooked up to a ventilator, with the sound of artificial breathing and the constant beep of the heart monitor, I saw fear in his eyes. He didn't look at me once.

The doctor addressed Dad, but as he explained that Mum was in a coma, his words broke off, drifting upwards into inaudible bubbles. I was slowly slipping under water. The *beep, beep, beeps* of the heart monitor began to echo, and the respirator pump grew louder and louder.

I couldn't look at her. The initial glance when I'd first arrived was enough. I had caused this. Not her stupid fear of driving. Not Dad and Todd being away for the weekend. Me! *Selfish, arrogant, all-important me!*

Mum's sister, Aunty Eddie (Edwina), showed up with her husband, Terry. 'What happened? Oh my god!' She threw herself at Mum. 'How could this happen? How?' she yelled, glaring at each of us, one at a time.

Terry placed his hands on her shoulders and gently pulled her away.

Aunty Eddie was my second favourite member of our family, after my mum. She was cool and funny, unlike Terry, who was a bit serious and dull. They never had kids, so Eddie used to dote on us boys. I had fond memories of when Todd and I would stay at their house when we were young. Eddie used to make me laugh, and she'd always let us do naughty things, like eat ice cream before bed or have a sip of Terry's beer. But on that day, I saw bitter anger in her eyes, the sort I would never have thought possible from her. At that point it wasn't just directed at me. Like Dad, she couldn't know the facts yet, could she? How would she feel when she found out this was all my fault?

Terry took Todd and I to their home, leaving Dad and Aunty Eddie with Mum. Todd didn't want to go, but I couldn't wait to get out of there. I wanted to run away and get as far away from that hospital as possible. If I hid, perhaps everything would be okay. In reality, I knew things would never be okay again.

The next day was Saturday. After a breakfast of scrambled eggs that Terry made but neither Todd nor I ate, we went back to the hospital. Terry had gotten up early and fetched a few things from our house while Todd and I slept. Of course, I wasn't sleeping. I heard him go, and return about half an hour later.

On the drive to the hospital, Terry said, 'Just so you know, Scott. Your mum tried to ring us last night.'

'She did?'

'Yes. We were out at the club. She left a message on our answer machine.'

I shuffled uncomfortably in the back seat of the car. 'What did she say?'

'That you were stranded out at Hawthorn, and that you needed someone to fetch you.'

'WHAT?' Todd swung around in the front seat to face me.

'She couldn't get hold of us, so she must have driven herself,' Terry continued.

Todd reached over and grabbed me by the scruff of the neck, 'You didn't tell us this.'

'I was … I was going to—'

'You fucking lied to us!'

'Now then, Todd,' Terry intervened, 'I'm sure Scott would never lie, especially in these circumstances. Isn't that right, Scott?' He was looking at me through the rear-view mirror.

Should I have continued with the lie, and risk making the situation worse? I didn't know what to do. I looked away and out of the window.

Todd took the cue. 'You bastard! This is all *your* fault!'

X

He grabbed me harder and began to shake me backwards and forwards. If it wasn't for the confines of the car, he would have punched me no doubt, and so he should have. I would have done the same. I deserved everything that was coming my way. He must have weighed up the possibility and decided against it, realising how ineffective it would have been. Releasing his grip on my shirt, he slapped me hard across the jaw with the back of his hand.

'Now that's enough you boys, please?' Terry pleaded as the car swerved slightly. 'We don't want another accident.'

Todd turned back to the front, slumped in his seat, and began to sob. Terry placed a reassuring hand on his shoulder. I watched from the back seat–a spectator of my own terrible deeds.

To his credit, Todd didn't say anything to Dad when we arrived back at the hospital, but I could tell he already knew. Aunty Eddie must have told him about the call. From the moment I stepped back into the intensive care unit, his stabbing, bitter scowl–directed solely at me–hurt more than a back-handed slap ever could. Aunty Eddie's usual warm features also displayed the same sharp bite, but only when looking at me.

Mum never came home. She never cooked chocolate chip cookies again on a Saturday morning, never danced to Bruce Springsteen, never giggled again, and never laughed at my jokes. She never regained consciousness. We were told on the Sunday that her brain was nonresponsive. The only thing keeping her alive was the respirator. Dad had to give his permission for them to turn it off.

15

'Why are they calling you and not me?' I demanded as Bradley and I left the hospital.

'Because I'm your—'

'Assistant.'

'Partner.'

We climbed into the Range Rover. 'Well, I'm not going to just drop everything and come running every time they call.'

'With all due respect, it's the Queensland Police commissioner and the Gold Coast mayor.'

'I don't care. Besides, we've got a meeting with the team in just over an hour. It's a quarter to four now, that'll give us time to get back to Surfers and grab something to eat.'

'Let me tell them six o'clock then,' Bradley said.

I reluctantly agreed. I suppose I was going to have to get used to liaising with Monroe. I wondered if he remembered me. Apart from the recent meetings, the last time we'd come into contact was on 'that night' and he wasn't too happy. It was the last night I ever played footy, the night everything changed.

After a silent fifteen-minute drive, we pulled up in the basement of Police Headquarters.

'Shall I go get sandwiches, or did you want to go somewhere?' Bradley asked as we climbed from the car.

'Get me a pie.'

X

'A pie?' His tone said, 'Haven't I taught you anything, Eliza Doolittle?'

'Tradie pie, ketchup and a coke.'

Bradley sighed inwardly, kneading fingers rising to his forehead. 'What type of meat?'

'Don't care, as long as it's dead.'

'And would you like a donut, chief?' His attempt at a Brooklyn accent would have been funny if it wasn't laced with bitchy sarcasm.

'Just get me a pie and a bloody coke, yeah?'

'Yes, sir.'

As he marched away like a dismissed schoolgirl, I called after him, 'And a chocolate donut with sprinkles!'

X

We ate in my office. Bradley had a healthy salad sandwich and a drink that looked like liquid grass cuttings.

'You're not one of them bloody vegans as well, are ya?'

'As well as what?' His chin shot up defiantly.

I was giving him a hard time, but I wasn't sure why. He obviously wasn't used to banter. I wasn't a homophobic or a meat-munching hater of vegetarians or anything like that. Believe it or not, I'm quite liberal-minded. Years of mate-to-mate banter with Elvis and Tetley had hardened me, but Bradley had obviously had none of that. I needed to test his metal. Was he a sensitive cry baby or a tough copper?

'Well ... you know ... a poofter?'

At first his expression was one of disbelief – mouth agape, eyes wide open. Silence hung in the air as we stared at each other. Finally, I grinned my cheekiest larrikin grin. This seemed to take him by surprise.

'Oh my god ...' the corners of his mouth twitched slightly, 'did you just call me a poofter?'

'No ...'

'You did!'

'No, I didn't. I was just asking—'

'A vegan poofter.' His brow lowered into a scowl, and he puckered his lips. He stared at me as if measuring me up, then burst into laughter. 'I can't believe you!'

'What?'

'You can't go around asking people questions like that.'

'Like what?'

He looked up at the ceiling and exhaled loudly, as if searching for divine guidance. 'Okay,' lowering his gaze back to me, he shuffled in his seat, 'I'm gay and I'm a vegetarian.'

'See, that's all I wanted to know.'

'Do you not realise how offensive that is?'

I'd overstepped the mark, and I knew it. Maybe it was just a release from the extraordinary situation I'd found myself in.

'So, what about you, how come you've never married?' He took a nimble bite of his sandwich.

'Never found the right girl.'

'Oh my god, if you say you're married to the job, I swear, I'll bitch slap you so hard.'

'Nah, stuff the job. Like I said, just haven't found the right girl.'

'Or boy.'

This caused me to inadvertently straighten my back. Now it was my chin that rose.

Bradley giggled, and I realised he wasn't averse to a bit of banter after all.

X

The only person not present at the team meeting was Dion Gardner. I couldn't have cared less.

Before we started, I lowered my voice, 'I just want to let you all know that Des Williams passed away this morning.'

X

Gasps and shocked expressions filled the room.

'Des?' Dale Mason said. 'How?'

'Suspected suicide.'

'Bullshit!' Dale growled, 'Des would never do that. Not with the pay-off. He was glad to be out of it.'

'Pay-off?' I queried.

Everyone looked at me as if to say, 'What? You didn't know?'

'He wasn't sacked,' Dale continued, 'he was given the golden handshake.'

'He must have been depressed,' Jenny Radford offered.

'No,' Dale raised his voice. 'I only saw him last night. He was fine. Planning a trip down to Batemans Bay to see his daughter, even thinking of moving down there.'

I remembered the last time I saw Des on that same evening, and I agreed with Dale, he was happier than I'd seen him in a long time, like he was ready for a new chapter in his life.

X

It was no surprise that there were no new findings. Once again, Jacob Tyler, the profiler, seemed to feel the need to justify his presence by going over the same ground. We were still waiting on the full report from forensics, but regardless, it was obviously apparent that little had been achieved on our first day.

As the team dispersed, Jenny Radford approached me. 'Sir, would it—'

'Forget the "sir" bullshit. It's Scott, remember? The same bloke you had a surf with last week off Burleigh Heads.'

'Sorry, Scott. Would it be okay if I ducked off early?'

I sensed anxiety in her worried tone. 'Sure. What's up?'

'Oh, nothing to worry about. It's just my mum, she's a bit under the weather. Getting on a bit, you know?'

'No worries. I'll see you in the morning.'

'Thanks, Scott.'

16

I stood alone in the incident room, studying the victims' photographs on the whiteboard. That same shocked expression on each of their faces was beginning to haunt me. Usually, at this point in an investigation there would be pictures of suspects also, but there were none. We had nothing but the dodgy photofit picture, created by Tyler. The assignments I'd given the team for tomorrow were pretty much just to fill in time. All we could do was keep going over the facts, like patient archaeologists sifting through the dirt, brushing off every rock, looking for new clues or something that was overlooked.

One thing was for sure, though, I had nothing to report to Singleton and the mayor at our impending meeting. Anxiety was constricting my chest like an expanding block of ice. The only option I could see was for me to tell them I was out of my depth, step down and go back to my safe little life.

Strolling back to the boardroom, it was if the Red Sea was parting before me. No longer that scruffy, scrappy detective no one took any notice of, I was now the guy people craned their necks to get a look at. I was the centre of attention, and I didn't like it.

Superintendent Ripley and Queensland Police Commissioner Singleton were already present when I entered the boardroom. Ripley rose from his seat, 'Scott, good to see you. Come in, take a seat.'

Singleton offered a noncommittal nod in my direction.

X

'The mayor is running a little late, but he'll be here at any moment,' Ripley said.

Singleton and Ripley sat on the farthest side at one end of the table. The seat at the end was reserved, I guessed for Monroe. I took a seat facing my superiors.

'So, how's it going?' Ripley asked. His tone, although friendly, was tinged with despair.

'Uhm ... good, I suppose.'

'Any new leads?'

'No.'

'That's alright, early days yet.' As Ripley said this, the door swung open and in marched Monroe.

Ripley and I rose to our feet. Singleton remained seated.

Monroe headed straight for me, offering his hand while displaying his most dazzling smile. 'Scotty, it's great to see you again.' His breath was a mixture of extra strong mints and whisky. Even his eyes appeared to be smiling as he grasped my hand hard and squeezed it.

Once again, I wondered if he remembered me. Would it be too embarrassing for him to admit it if he did? I was good at reading expressions, especially eyes. The tight skin around his brow, the fixed, impossibly white smile and blond highlighted hair that didn't move were all accessories, products of wealth and vanity. But the eyes, they were the same, piercing Nordic blue, slightly bloodshot. The warmth from his plastic smile seemed to stop at his eyes.

He headed for the seat at the end of the table, apologising for his tardiness. 'Okay, fill me in,' he said, taking off his pastel pink sports jacket and throwing it over his chair.

Ripley and I sat down.

'Stephens?' Singleton said, redirecting his gaze at me.

Ripley jumped back up, 'Before DI Stephens reads his report—'

Report?

Ripley spoke of Des Williams's suicide. Briefly, Monroe seemed genuinely shocked. Singleton obviously already knew. His eyes remained fixed on me.

Way too quickly for my liking, Monroe changed the subject back to the investigation.

Ripley gestured for me to stand. 'If you'd like to share your report with us now, detective.'

My thoughts were momentarily back in Hawthorn. My gut feeling was telling me that Monroe did remember. How could he forget someone who did what I did to him?

There was a hurried knock at the door and Dion Gardner burst into the room.

'What is it?' Ripley demanded.

'Sorry to interrupt, sir, but we have a lead.'

'A lead?' Monroe said.

'Yes, sir. I think we've got the bastard!'

17

I'd been living with a searing guilt for that long I could hardly remember life without it. Prior to that night at Hawthorn, I didn't know what guilt was. I certainly didn't feel guilty after I'd replaced the receiver of the payphone, or even paid a second thought to my mum.

There was some time to kill. I was too young to drink, and apart from the odd stubby with Elvis that we nicked from his dad, I hadn't acquired the taste for beer yet. I needed to use the toilet. Remembering where the ladies' toilets were – how could I ever forget? – I figured the gents' toilets would be next to it. A glance in that direction confirmed this.

Picking up my kit bag, I headed across the foyer. From the corner of my eye, I noticed Julian Monroe and two of his entourage watching me. Nodding smugly in his direction as I passed, my body language said, *in your face, dickhead.* Monroe was a good player, probably no better than me, but like me, he was the full clichéd package–tall, blond and handsome. Unlike me, though, he was from a wealthy family. It was well known that his father owned most of Hawthorn. A dodgy character, according to Elvis, something to do with real estate, booze and the sex industry.

Julian was probably pissed off at me because I'd literally run rings around him during the game. My tally that night made me the leading goal scorer in the under 15s division, and I'd given as good as I took in our scuffles, jeering, pushing, and punching when the referee wasn't looking. All those things a good forward took in his stride, but with Monroe it was different. It was as if he were trying to put you in your place, keep you down where you belonged.

I guess the fact that we thrashed the Hawks on their home turf didn't help either. Even so, I was surprised when he followed me into the toilets, his two burly mates behind him.

'Hey, Stephens,' he said, before I reached the urinal.

I turned to face him. All three of them marched right up to me.

Monroe stood toe-to-toe, fists clenched. 'If I see you looking at her again, I'll fucking kill you!'

'Who?'

He was obviously talking about 'Blondie.' I guessed he had no idea what had happened between us in the ladies' toilets.

'You know exactly who I mean.'

I'd like to say his breath stunk of cigarettes and booze when he moved in even closer, as if positioning himself for a headbutt, but it didn't. Instead, he smelled pleasantly of mint gum and expensive body spray.

'You stay away from her,' he growled.

'And you go fuck yourself, dickhead.' To me it was just a continuum of the intimidation game, the jostling, the name calling that was a part of Aussie Rules footy. I was wrong. Monroe's mates lurched forward and grabbed my arms.

'About time someone taught you a lesson.'

Monroe stepped back, his expression angry and determined. His right fist was clenched. Slowly twisting at the waist, he obviously wasn't going to rush this. If he'd produced a tape measure I wouldn't have been surprised. He was measuring up the punch, calculating the outcome for as much harm as possible. Then, he let go with a thunderous right hook.

Turning my head to the side, the impact caught me on the cheek. I felt a crack, and a searing wave of pain enveloped the side

X

of my head like a mini explosion. I tried to shake free, but the two thugs, one on each arm, were bloody strong. I looked back at Monroe through watering eyes as he prepared to take another crack. This time though, just as he was about to release the next missile, and using the strength of the two thugs, I leaned forward at the waste then launched my upper body backwards, kicking out with my right foot.

Easily, the best part of being a footballer is that feeling when your foot connects perfectly with the ball. You're in the middle of a game. You're under pressure, and you need to think quickly. When kicking a six pointer from fifty metres, there's a sweet spot, almost like you've released a bullet from a giant gun. That's how it felt when my foot connected with Julian Monroe's balls. There was a crunch, like I'd just kicked a bag of mincemeat.

Monroe gave out a high-pitched squeal. He immediately cupped his hands to his groin, dropped to his knees and shrank into the foetal position.

The two thugs let go of my arms and rushed to his aid. 'You alright, Jules?'

Julian couldn't speak. His face was puckered and pale, and his breathing resembled the rasping motor of a Holden HK on a cold morning. Then he threw up.

I hastily made my exit, headed outside the front of the club, and took up position near the carpark so I could see when Mum arrived. Once again, I didn't feel guilty, even when I found out Monroe was out for the rest of the season due to an 'injury he'd sustained during the game' that evening.

'Hawthorn under 15s star, Julian Monroe, showing true grit, playing the entire second half with a double hernia,' the *Glenferrie Times* reported.

That's how Monroe continued to live his life, capitalising on situations whether they be good or bad, always coming out the other end a hero. Only the two thugs, Julian and I knew what really happened that night. On reflection, I couldn't give a toss, it was self-defence. All Monroe knew was that I was eyeing up his girl. How angry would he have been if he'd found out I'd lost my virginity to her? I still wasn't sure to this day if he knew about that, but even though he acted as if he didn't know me, he must have remembered his old nemesis Scotty Stephens – the cocky shit who played for the opposition, eyed up his girl, and kicked him in the balls so hard it hospitalised him for a week.

Or was he just so arrogant and self-centred that he'd blocked out that night altogether?

I had a feeling time would tell.

18

Gardner, Ripley and I were heading for the stairs. Gardner was in front of me. I grabbed him by the arm.

'I need you to tell me what you know.'

He shook his arm free and continued down the stairs. 'I'll fill you in on the way over there.' He didn't make eye contact.

After signing out of the armoury, we made our way to the garage. As always, I found the bulletproof vest restricting on my chest. Like a tight wetsuit, only heavier. The Glock 22 semi-automatic handgun never felt comfortable either. Unlike I imagined a gunslinger's gun to be, it was heavy and cumbersome.

There was a black Special Emergency Response Team (SERT) van with its engine idling, behind it a police cruiser, then a paddy wagon and more cruisers. Apart from an army of faceless uniforms, I picked out the members of my team.

We headed for the first cruiser. Bradley was at the wheel. Gardner jumped into the passenger seat, and Ripley and I got in the back. The black van in front pulled away and we followed in a procession. Once we'd turned on to Ferny Avenue, we increased speed and turned on the sirens.

'Okay,' Gardner said, turning in his seat and facing Ripley, 'Lawrence Binks, white male, thirty-three years old. Lives alone since his mother died last year, at 19 Parkrose Close, Mudgeeraba.'

The car swerved to the right, momentarily knocking Gardner

off balance. Bradley seemed to be having trouble keeping up with the van in front.

'So, what's the tip-off? Does he have previous?' Ripley asked.

'No, apart from a complaint from a neighbour a couple of weeks ago who reckoned he'd been acting weird.'

'And that's it?' I queried.

Gardner ignored me and continued to address Ripley. 'This afternoon, I followed up on a hunch. As we know, the search for anyone purchasing knives recently turned up a blank. Yes, there were sales, but those buying them all had alibis.' He was speaking slowly with a despotic tone. I could tell he was enjoying the attention from his boss. 'The idea that the killer must have worn some kind of protective clothing resonated, so I followed up on sales of fishing gear and outdoor clothing from camping shops and sports stores.'

'And?' Ripley moved forward in his seat.

'Seems our boy, Lawrence, purchased a bunch of showerproof tracksuits, but not from a local store, from a Hong Kong supplier via eBay.'

Purchasing from eBay suddenly made sense as to why we couldn't track any multiple sales from the local stores. It was a good result but not enough for a conviction. 'How do you know this? I asked.

Still ignoring me, Gardner reached into his pocket and pulled out his mobile phone. 'The complaint from the neighbour.' He tapped the screen, brought up a photograph, then handed the phone to Ripley. There was a picture of a young man standing in the middle of a suburban street wearing a black Adidas tracksuit, the PVC kind that athletes and boxers wore when they needed to sweat out a few kilos. 'He's been wandering around the streets, apparently wearing one of these, even in the heat of the day.'

We'd crossed Chevron Island and were now hammering south on Bundall Road.

'What do we know of him?' I asked. 'Is he a sportsman?'

X

Gardner had no choice but to answer me. 'No, he's not anything. He doesn't work, doesn't have any friends. But there's something else, too. If you wouldn't mind, sir?' He took the phone back from Ripley. After jabbing the screen with his finger, he held it up and a voice message played.

'Hello, Detective Inspector Gardner. It's Professor Daniel Cross from Bond University. You left a card and asked me to call if I remembered anything else. Well, there is something I just remembered. On the night of Lisa Wei's killing ... I recall seeing someone walking along Bermuda Street earlier that evening. Look, it's probably nothing. The only reason I'm remembering now is because I remember thinking how odd it was that he was wearing a full tracksuit, one of those shiny types. It was black–Adidas, I think. The only reason I thought it was strange is because it was quite a warm evening. Like I say, it's probably nothing, but I hope this may be of some help.' The message ended.

Still wasn't much, but it was the only lead we had. I wasn't sure of the need for the dramatic chase across town with a tactical response unit, though.

'When did you get this?' I asked.

'About fifteen minutes ago.'

'Is there anything else we know of this ...?'

'Lawrence Binks,' Ripley finished my sentence. He was obviously paying more attention than me.

'No. Weird as shit. Your classic psycho.' There was something about Gardner's narcissistic grin that rubbed me up the wrong way.

We took an illegal right turn into Ashmore Road and continued until we reached the Nerang Southport Road, ignoring red lights while traffic moved to one side to let us through. When we hit the M1, Bradley had to put his foot down hard to keep up with the tactical response van as it crossed into the inside lane and pulled away. Five minutes later, we turned off at the Mudgeeraba exit and circled the small historical town.

'I know Parkrose Close quite well,' Ripley said, 'some big expensive houses along there.'

He was right. Turning into the close, it was obvious this was the affluent part of the township, featuring older style houses next to ultra-modern grand designs. It was the kind of area where doctors, solicitors and politicians lived. Number 19 was one of the older buildings, two-storeyed arts and craft style, very English.

The tactical response van pulled up outside the house. Immediately, the side doors opened and eight SERT officers poured out of the vehicle, wearing SWAT-style armour and carrying Heckler & Koch G36 5.56mm rifles. They raced up the driveway and peeled off around the house. Before Bradley could bring the cruiser to a halt and we had a chance to jump out, I caught a glimpse of one of the SERT guys smashing in the front door with a handheld battering ram.

'POLICE!'

Maintaining the element of surprise, they poured into the building with their rifles raised. As we raced out of the car, I could hear them yelling inside, 'GET ON THE FLOOR! GET DOWN ON THE FLOOR!'

Gardner was way ahead of me, entering the house with his gun drawn while I was still running up the driveway. Ripley, older, was even farther back.

The sound of a gunshot ripped through the air. Almost instantaneously, a barrage of automatic gunfire followed. Too many deafening shots to count, but all over in a matter of seconds. By the time I reached the front door, the entrance hall was filled with smoke.

'What the fuck?' I yelled, lifting a hand to my mouth.

Four SERT officers stood in identical combat pose, like plastic toy soldiers, their rifles at the ready.

Gardner stood in the centre of the room with his gun drawn, as if frozen.

X

Slumped on the floor against the far wall was a young man. He was alive, clutching at his chest while blood pumped from his mouth with each gasping breath.

'Paramedics!' someone yelled.

Two more SERT officers appeared and rushed to aid the young man. 'Get an ambulance NOW!' one of them called out.

Gardner and the others remained in position, as if daring him to move.

Ripley entered, gasping for air. 'My god, what happened here?'

Gardner lowered his gun, returned it to its holster and turned to Ripley.

'Job done!'

19

Lawrence Steven Binks, aged thirty-three, died at the scene from multiple gunshot wounds after resisting arrest. Forensic analysis would later show that the small, hooked knife found at the side of his body matched the knife that had been used on each of the X victims. A search of the property also unearthed six black Adidas showerproof tracksuits hanging in the suspect's wardrobe. The most damning evidence was a third suit, found stuffed into the wheelie bin out the back of the house. It was covered in blood. DNA analysis would later prove it was blood from the last victim, Denise Shaw.

'My God, you've done it Scott. You've caught him!' Ripley said, shaking me by the hand. 'Monroe was right, you really were the right man for the job.'

Things were happening way too quickly, and none of it was under my control. 'What do you mean, I haven't—'

'Still modest. The people of the Gold Coast are going to love that.' It was as if relief was seeping from his pores. 'I'm going to head back. I'll leave you to it.' Before he left, he grasped my hand harder and leaned in.

'Congratulations, Scott. You don't know what this means to us.'
Bradley had tears in his eyes.
'What the hell's wrong with you?'
'Oh, don't mind me. I'm just so proud of you, Scott.'
'For fuck's sake!'

X

The leader of the Special Emergency Response Team, Senior Sergeant Dan Brewer, came over and shook my hand. 'Well done detective, great job.'

'Thanks.'

'We're pulling out. You'll have my full report in the morning.'

'Cool.'

I realised Gardner had disappeared. Once the SERT guys and Ripley had gone, forensics and uniforms swarmed the area. I headed over to the body of Lawrence Binks. He was slim, well-groomed, with a fair complexion. Members of my team were hovering over the scene making notes while a forensic photographer took pictures. I looked down at the knife. It was exactly how Jacob Tyler had described it, more of a hook with a very sharp edge, about an inch wide and four inches long. The handle was stubby with a finger hole just below the hilt. Beside it was a yellow plastic marker displaying the number one.

Markers had also been placed around the body, and throughout the room where bullet cartridges lay.

Once again, there was nothing for me to do. Everyone at the scene was going about their duties. I was left feeling like a spare part.

Thankfully, police had cordoned off not only the house but the entire close, which looped around and back on itself, meaning there was only one way in, and one way out. The barricade was some way from the house, keeping it out of sight of prying eyes. The neighbours were all out on the street though, congregated in little groups. As Bradley and I looked for a car to take us back to the station, I was surprised to see Jenny Radford approaching.

'What are you doing here? I thought you'd be at your mum's.'

'I was.' She nodded in the direction of the house next door.

'She lives there?'

'Yep.'

'Did you know Binks?'

'Did? Is he dead?'
'I'm afraid so.'
'Surely they don't think he was *X*?'
'Looks that way. Did you know him?'
'Sort of. Just to say hi. He was a bit … weird.'
'Was it your mum who rang the police about him?'
'I don't think so. When was that?'
'Doesn't matter. Can you come back in to work?'
'Of course.'

X

'No doubt there'll be a press conference,' Bradley said as we turned back onto the highway.

'No doubt.'

'I've got to make sure you're ready, so when we get back, we need to—'

'Bradley, who are you? Fussing over me like you're me bloody mother.'

'I'm … your partner.'

'No, what I mean is, why are you here? What's your purpose?'

His bottom lip extended, and his cheeks flushed a little. 'What do you mean?'

'I noticed Ripley having a word earlier. What was that about?' I'd noticed this on a couple of occasions.

The blooms on Bradley's cheeks blossomed across the rest of his face. 'He was angry because you weren't prepared.'

'Pull over,' I growled.

'What? We're on the highway.'

'I said pullover, now!'

We were between the Nerang exits. Bradley steered the cruiser over to the hard shoulder and pulled in under the overpass.

X

I undid my seatbelt and turned to face him. 'Right. I need to know what the hell's going on.'

'I don't know what—'

'Skip the bullshit, mate. You're not getting out of this car until I have some answers.'

Bradley took a deep breath and looked straight ahead.

'What did they say to you about me?'

'Just that you were a great detective, but you'd need some help.' My silence prompted him to continue. 'That you may have lacked some of the finer points required for such a high-profile role ... etiquette.'

'Did they say why they'd chosen me?'

He shook his head vigorously, 'No, just that you were the right man for the job.'

'Help me out here, Bradley, because I'm struggling to understand this.' The car rocked from side-to-side as a Woolworths semi-trailer hurtled by. 'Who are we talking about?'

I sensed that after quickly considering his response, he decided to just say it as it was.

'Singleton and Ripley.'

20

'Stop, go around the other way,' I instructed Bradley when the cruiser approached the headquarters.

'There isn't another way,' Bradley said.

I looked over my shoulder. The one-way road was narrower than usual because of the stationary media trucks, and there was a line of traffic behind us.

'We'll have to keep going, just put your head down.' Bradley said driving slowly.

Just before we reached the crowd of journalists spilling off the pavement and into the road, I lowered my head into my hands as if I were contemplating a great mystery. I needn't have bothered, no one was looking our way.

'Oh …' Bradley said.

I glanced sideways.

Singleton, Ripley and Monroe were conducting a press conference. Monroe shone like a jewel in the lights, his champagne-coloured suit a dazzling contrast to the dark uniforms of the officers either side of him. We couldn't hear what he was saying, but he was holding centre stage like a movie star redelivering his acceptance speech outside the Kodak theatre in Hollywood.

'Looks like they couldn't wait for you.'

'Just get us in, eh?' I said, looking back down at my hands.

The entrance to the basement carpark was to the right of the building.

X

'Uhm, don't think so,' Bradley said, pulling the vehicle to a stop.

A news truck was parked over the driveway.

Bradley had already made the turn.

One of the news people nonchalantly turned her head and caught sight of me. 'Hey, there he is!'

To the obvious disdain of Monroe, who appeared to be building up to something, the crowd turned away from him and rushed toward us, surrounding the cruiser. From jostling faces came a volley of questions, muffled through the car's window.

'DI Stephens. How does it feel to be the man who brought X to justice?'

'You cracked the case in only two days. How did you do it?'

'Is it true you gunned down the killer in cold blood?'

'Would you say the police have been incompetent up until now?'

A couple of burly uniforms pushed through the crowd and came around to the passenger door. Two more appeared behind them. One of them knocked on the glass and gestured for me to get out.

'Go on,' Bradley said, 'face your press. They love you.'

Reluctantly, I opened the door. The dampened sound of voices immediately increased in volume and clarity, flooding into the car with the warm night air.

The uniforms made a circle around me as we pushed through the crowd towards the station. When we reached the entrance, they turned and formed a human barrier.

At the top of the steps, Monroe greeted me with his synthetic smile, shaking me vigorously by the hand as if he were my best mate ever. Singleton patted me on the back, grabbed my other hand and launched it up into the air. I'd never seen him smile before, now he was grinning like an idiot. Ripley was actually doing that stupid bowing thing, with his hands in prayer as if paying homage to Gandhi.

Monroe led me to the bank of microphones. 'And here he is,' he paused, skilfully directing a dramatic glance at each of the TV cameras, 'the man of the moment, our hero–Detective Inspector Scott Stephens.'

The crowd applauded and I had to lower my head and squint against a wall of flashing white light.

Monroe squeezed my shoulder and stepped back.

'Uhm ...' after a reminder from Bradley, I'd written down some notes during the ride back from Mudgeeraba. Glancing at them, I realised how little information I actually had.

Ripley stepped forward and whispered in my ear, 'I've already given them a report of the events. If they ask any questions, just say, "No comment."'

The questions started immediately. Blinded by the spotlights and flashes, I couldn't see where in the crowd they were coming from.

'Was it necessary to shoot and kill the suspect?'

I struggled with that question. I wanted to say I didn't know because the shooting had taken place before I arrived at the scene. As if reading this in my saddled pause, Ripley stepped up to the mics.

'There will be a full press conference tomorrow morning at 9.00 am. Thank you.' He placed an arm around my shoulder and led me away. Not wanting to waste an opportunity, Monroe gabbed my hand again, Singleton grabbed the other, and they thrust them up into the air. Off mic, but still loud enough for everyone present to hear, Monroe yelled, 'The saviour of the Gold Coast!'

We entered the station. I lowered my arms, but Singleton and Monroe held onto them as if they were escorting me to a cell.

'I knew it, Scotty, I knew it,' Monroe said as we headed for Ripley's office. 'As soon as I read your profile, saw your photograph, I just knew you were the right man for the job.'

'That'd be right, take all the credit,' Singleton smirked, 'it was me who found this guy.'

When we entered Ripley's office, there was a bottle of Champagne standing in a bucket of ice. Ripley immediately popped the cork and poured four glasses.

X

Monroe raised his glass. 'To the most talked about, admired and loved man of the moment—wait—that's me!' His laugh was more of a snort. Only Ripley smiled respectfully. 'Just kidding. To DI Stephens. Thank you for saving us.'

'To DI Stephens,' they repeated in unison.

We all took a sip of Champagne, except for Monroe, who downed his in one go. I wasn't much of a Champagne drinker, but this one tasted good. Looking at the label, *Louis Roederer*, I suspected they didn't get it on special from BWS.

'There's nothing else for you to do here tonight, Scott. Go home and relax,' Ripley said.

'But I need to write my report.'

'There's no need, Foster will take care of it. You've earned an early night.'

'Here, here,' Monroe said. 'Massive day tomorrow, Scotty.'

I was tired, but not the usual kind of tiredness earned after a hard day of police work. The sapping sensation in my bones felt more like I'd been punched around.

21

All the lights in the place were blazing as we pulled up outside the house. Bradley had driven me straight home in the cruiser. He'd head back to the station, pick up the Range Rover, take it home to his apartment in Main Beach, then pick me up in the morning. He was keen to get back, so I didn't invite him in.

It wasn't unusual for the house to be empty with the lights on and every fan in the place spinning at full speed. We were still like teenagers at home, irresponsible and blithe. I think it was an escape from our daily lives. The house had changed little since we'd moved in.

Opening the Domino's pizza box on the kitchen table, I discovered two leftover pieces of a meat lovers. Good old Elvis, for all his faults, he was a good mate. I took off my jacket and tie, kicked off my shoes, grabbed the slices of pizza and headed out into the back yard.

'Heyyyy, here he is!' Elvis shouted from behind the bar.

Tetley swivelled around on one of the bar stools.

I was surprised to see Johnno, our other mate, rising from the couch. 'Good to see you, bro,' he said.

'Johnno, bloody hell. Did she let you out, mate?'

'You're famous now, eh?' he said, shaking me by the hand.

'No.'

It was good to see my old Kiwi mate. He didn't come around much nowadays since he got married last year. Tetley and I had known him since high school. He was a big lad from Whangārei in the North Island of New Zealand. We'd introduced him to Elvis when he'd moved up from Victoria, and until he started dating Kelly three years ago, the four of us had been a tight-knit group, *Los Cuatro Amigos*.

'It's not every day you get to spend time with a celebrity, mate.'

'Fuckin' celebrity, that's what he is now,' Elvis said.

'He's more than that,' Tetley said. 'He's royalty!'

The three of them nodded vigorously in agreeance. That was a first. I pushed past them, plonked the pizza slices on the bar and got myself a beer from the fridge.

'So, you did it,' Elvis said as the three of them gathered around the bar.

'Did what?'

'You've just solved one of the biggest murder investigations of all time. You've been on every single news channel all night. Look!' Johnno pointed to the muted TV on the wall.

'Mum reckons you're even on the telly in the UK,' Tetley said.

'This is huge, mate,' Elvis said. 'We might need to get a bigger house. A mansion out in Currumbin Valley, perhaps. Graceland!'

'Don't be daft,' I said through a mouthful of pizza.

'Yeah, you're gonna need privacy. I'm surprised the paparazzi aren't here already.'

'You're a rockstar, lad,' Tetley said.

It was odd, but the last two days had gone so quickly I hadn't even had time to gather my own thoughts, never mind think about the investigation. I'd been carried along with a surreal energy that had enveloped me since arriving late for work yesterday.

'They'll give you the keys to the city,' Tetley said.

'My oath,' Elvis agreed, 'Order of Australia I reckon.'

'Knighthood, bro,' Johnno threw in.

'Sir Scotty of Kirra,' Tetley said, holding up his beer.

I was tired. I didn't have a clue what would happen in the morning but I had no doubt it would be another strange day.

'Bullshit!' Elvis yelled after I told them I was going to bed. 'We're gonna party!' He reached under the bar and pulled out a bottle of tequila.

Exhausted, there was no way I was doing tequila slammers. I continued to say this until the bottle was drained and we squeezed the last of the lemon slices into our mouths. Tomorrow morning, after I'd cleared away all the empty bottles and tidied the shed, I'd adopt the usual mantra no doubt, *I will never drink tequila again, I will never drink tequila again.* But as always, after the first couple of shots, tomorrow became just another day. What I was refusing to acknowledge though, was that there'd never be *just* another day in my life again.

X

The next morning was the same old ritual – the sound of snoring from Elvis's bedroom, and Tetley fast asleep on the lounge in the man shed. I padded through the house in just my jocks. For some reason, as usual, and as if it were my duty, I went into the shed and began to tidy the place. Within minutes, I'd noisily placed all the empty beer bottles into the old carton. 'You're kidding me?' I said out loud when I realised there were two empty tequila bottles.

Carrying the carton of empty bottles under one arm, the pizza box under the other, and the two tequila bottles in my hands, I headed towards the front door. I didn't have a clue what time it was, but I sensed it was still early. I'd duck out to the bin without anyone seeing me. As part of the ritual, I'd mastered the art of opening the front door with my arms full. Pressing down on the handle with my right elbow, I'd pull it open just enough to allow me to get a toe around it. Then using my left

X

foot, I'd open it the rest of the way. The door had one of those old fashioned self-closer springs, so there was a need to maintain momentum once it was moving. Like a ridiculously out of shape ballerina, I'd turn with the movement, then hop sideways on the other leg, across the threshold and into the yard. What I didn't realise was that this carefully choreographed manoeuver was the image that would adorn newspaper front pages and TV sets around Australia for the next week.

I was standing in the front yard – in my underwear. The fence around the front of the house was waist-high chain wire.

A uniformed constable stood at the gate, his back to me, holding back a sea of reporters and news cameras.

'Shit!' I turned back towards the door amidst a flood of camera flashes, and although it wasn't locked, it had closed behind me.

'DI Stephens, the eyes of the world are on you,' someone called out from the jostling crowd.

The simplest of tasks can seem impossible when you're anxious, hurried or under a bit of stress. Opening the door was proving this point perfectly. It should have just been a matter of pressing down on the handle and leaning in, but it wouldn't move. The situation was going from bad to worse. I could only imagine how it must have looked – me half-naked, arms laden with empty alcohol bottles, trying desperately but failing to escape.

There was only one thing for me to do. I took a deep breath, turned, and with my chin held high, I marched towards the wheelie bin, which was inside the garden to one side of the gate. Ignoring the barrage of questions, I dropped the pizza box and the carton into the bin with a clank and threw in the two empty tequila bottles. Then, lifting one hand into a wave, I headed back towards the front door.

'NOOOO!' I heard from behind me. I didn't need to turn around to know it was Bradley.

'Get in the house!' He placed a hand on my shoulder and gave me a hefty shove. 'Get in, get in, get in.' He reached around me and opened the front door with his other hand. Once we were inside, he seemed to be having some kind of anxiety attack. 'Oh my god, oh my god, oh my god …'

'What's up, mate?'

'What's up? Are you kidding me?'

Elvis padded into the hallway, still half asleep. 'What's going on?'

Bradley was taking deep breaths like he was hyperventilating. He paced the room, one hand on his hip, the other running manically through his hair.

'Elvis, this here's Bradley.' I didn't know what else to say. I'd fucked up. I should have checked the yard before I went out, should have realised the press would be out there. This celebrity lifestyle was going to take some getting used to.

'What were you thinking, Scott?' Bradley demanded.

'Uhm, don't know. Wasn't thinking, I guess.'

'Wasn't thinking? You certainly *was not* thinking!'

'What are you so upset about?' I asked, heading towards the kitchen, 'I'm the goose.'

'What did you do?' Elvis said, rubbing the sleep from his eyes and stifling a yawn.

'Just went out to the bin.'

'So?'

'So?' Bradley squawked. The hummingbird hand was back fanning his face. 'The world media is on the other side of that door. How am I going to explain this to Ripley, Scott?'

'Ahh, don't worry about it.' I was about to step from the hall to the kitchen when I heard the front door open and close. Elvis had gone bundling out to the garden.

Bradley let out a loud gasp. He froze like a waxwork dummy suspended in motion, staring at the door.

X

X

While I showered, Bradley laid out a dark blue pinstriped suit on my bed, along with a crimson tie and a pair of black socks. When I entered the room drying myself, he was busily ironing one of the new shirts he'd taken from its bag and de-pinned.

'There's toast and coffee in the kitchen. I'll just finish this, then you can get ready,' he said, without looking up.

I padded into the kitchen to find Tetley sitting at the table, eating my toast. I managed to snatch the last piece from the plate before he devoured it all.

22

6 September
I kept my head down as Bradley guided me through the crowd of reporters, towards the waiting car. Closing my defences against the volley of questions, one rogue bullet broke through.

'DI Stephens, is it true you shot and killed an autistic man in cold blood?'

Reaching the car, Bradley shepherded me into the back seat.

'DI Stephens will be making a full statement at the press conference later this morning,' he said, making his way to the driver's side.

'Shit, that's right, another press conference,' I mumbled as we slowly pulled away from the curb, parting the crowd as we went.

'Better get used to it. This is what I keep telling you.'

'What if I don't want this life?'

'Then you shouldn't have taken on the case.'

'I don't remember being given a choice.'

A trace of anger was always present. Anger that I'd carried since I was fourteen years old. Although hidden and mostly ignored, it was always there, stored away in that cupboard in my head. I once read that your subconscious can't determine between what's real and what isn't. It only knows what you tell it, which means whatever data it receives from you, that becomes your belief, your reality. If a person constantly tells themselves they're a loser, the subconscious will manifest that belief, and they will become a loser. The opposite can also be true. If a person truly believes they

X

are a winner, they will become a winner. In my case it was blame. Blame leads to anger.

My anger was the worst kind – anger at myself. There's an old saying, "I got a monkey on my back." I understood this completely. I'd been carrying a monkey every day since I was fourteen years old, and because my anger was intrinsic, I very rarely lost my temper with anyone else. Outwardly I was calm, witty and in control. It was inside where the turmoil could easily intensify to a level six cyclone, if I let it. Thankfully, I'd learned to live with it.

As Bradley and I sat in the boardroom, watching live coverage of the press conference that was happening on the steps of Southport Courthouse, my anger bubbled like an enormous boil ready to burst and spew out its hot pus.

At first, I wasn't sure if I was angry because the press conference was being held without me. I should have been relieved that I didn't have to face the press, but for some reason I wasn't. Was it the way Monroe was speaking about me as if we were best mates? Or was it just the whole charade?

Singleton appeared on the screen, answering questions on my behalf. He explained how I'd followed up on a tip-off, tracked the killer down to an address in Mudgeeraba, and then shot and killed the perpetrator before he had the chance to harm anyone, or himself.

I realised, once again, that my anger was inwardly directed, because I was allowing this to continue. 'What the hell's he going on about?' I blurted.

'You're a hero, Scott,' Bradley said.

'But I didn't shoot Binks.'

Lawrence Binks's face appeared on the screen – young, handsome, smiling, seemingly carefree. Singleton was reading the same report that I held in my hand, word for word.

'Binks was thirty-three years old and was diagnosed with Asperger's syndrome at an early age. He was highly intelligent but lacked the social skills that would allow him to hold down a job.

He was single and had no friends. There was no record of his father. His mother had raised him on her own and continued to care for him until she passed away suddenly, from a stroke, last year. Since then, he'd lived alone, receiving weekly visits from Home Services. He had no police record.'

'So that's all we have?' I said after listening to the report I had supposedly written. 'A young man with a mental illness who was described by a neighbour as weird.'

'It fits the profile perfectly,' Bradley said, sipping from a mug of coffee. 'Socially inadequate, lived with his mother.'

'Yeah, that's what's bothering me. It's too perfect.' The sensation I was experiencing was a new one. It was as if the shadow of anger that had followed me around all these years was suddenly no longer a transparent silhouette hovering in my peripheral vision. It was materialising into a dark spectre that was moving into the monkey house.

Monroe's face returned to the screen. Smiling, he paused for effect. 'We owe a massive debt of gratitude to Superintendent Andrew Ripley for his insistence that we appoint the right man for the job, and to DI Scott Stephens for being that man.'

I'd heard enough. 'Turn it off, for God's sake.'

Before Bradley had a chance to even stand and search for the remote, the news bulletin returned to the Channel 9 studio.

'Shit!' Bradley and I said in unison.

Over the right shoulder of the news reader, Alex Wade, was the picture of me outside the front door of Ruby Street, in my jocks, carrying the empties.

'Hero? Charlatan? Or loveable Aussie larrikin with a brilliant mind? You decide,' Wade said. They played the footage of me trying unsuccessfully to get back into the house. Then things got worse. The image switched to Elvis strutting down the path towards the camera, in his underwear. The camera zoomed in on his hairy man boobs.

X

'Nicholadas Papageorgiou, aka "Elvis," is DI Stephens's closest friend,' a female voice-over said.

'Yeah, I'm Scotty's accountant and *numero uno amigo*.' The shot of Elvis's flared nostrils was way too close. 'I've known him since kindergarten in Victoria.'

'What can you tell us about DI Stephens?' a voice from the jostling crowd asked.

'Oh, he's a great bloke. A good mate.'

'Were you surprised when you found out he'd been put in charge of the *X* investigation?'

'My oath. We all thought he was just a lollypop man or something.'

To my utmost horror, Tetley joined him on the screen. 'Ay up, Mam,' he yelled into the camera, waving.

Bradley found the remote and turned off the TV.

23

You didn't have to be a detective to realise things weren't right. I was living in a bachelor pad with my school mates, purely by choice–possibly because I was scared of commitment, and possibly because it was the only life I knew. I'd been flying under the radar all these years because that's where I was most comfortable. To say that being under the spotlight put me outside of my comfort zone was an understatement. From the moment I'd left the house that morning, I'd been mobbed by reporters and had cameras thrust in my face. When we entered the police station, we received a standing ovation from all the officers on duty. Even some of the offenders in the waiting room applauded us as Bradley and I made our way to the boardroom. Maybe if I'd done something to deserve this kind of attention, then perhaps things would have been different. I was more than uncomfortable.

Needing some privacy, I grabbed the Binks file and went to my office. No sooner had I sat at my desk when there was a knock at the door. It was Bradley. Without waiting for my reply, he came into the room.

'Ripley just called. He's heading back from the press conference. You've got an interview with Channel 9 in an hour.'

'What?'

'Then Channel 7 at lunchtime.'

'You're kidding?'

X

'Hot Tomato radio this afternoon, immediately followed by Sea FM, then ABC National.'

'What the hell am I going to say?'

Bradley took a deep, quivering breath as he pulled out the chair opposite and sat down. 'That's why I'm here. I need to prepare you.'

'Look, I'm putting an end to this bullshit. I'll just tell them the truth.'

'The truth?' He began to gently pat and stroke the side of his short fringe, like he was smoothing it out. His body language betrayed his composure.

'It was Gardner who followed up on the lead, and it was him who shot Binks first.'

'No, no, no, no ...'

Rising to my feet, I leaned forward over the desk, 'Do you know what I know about this investigation, Bradley?'

Like a little bird ruffling its feathers, he wobbled his body from the waist upwards, raised his chin, and pulled down his jacket at the hems.

'Absolutely nothing. Gardner solved this case, not me.'

'You're the detective in charge, you get to take the credit.'

Ignoring Bradley's statement, I asked, 'Where is he anyway?'

'He's uhm ... on leave.'

'What?'

'Sick leave.'

'Well, isn't that bloody handy.'

'I've got to bring you up to speed and get you ready for these interviews.'

Bradley handed me a Manila folder. 'Here's Gardner's full report. Read through it as quickly as you can, Ripley will be back any minute now.' There was fear in his voice when he mentioned Ripley's name. 'I need to make sure you're ready.'

I sat back down and flicked through the file. It was exactly what I expected. Gardner had received a tip-off from one of the neighbours, a Mrs Sheila Roberts. Binks had allegedly been acting weird, but I had to admit, the evidence found after Binks's death appeared overwhelming. The knife had proved positive to traces of DNA from the last victim, and the blood on the discarded tracksuit also belonged to her.

Were it not one of the biggest murder investigations in the history of Australian crime, it would have been an open and shut case, but for me, there were still too many questions. What made me the most uneasy was that there was no mention of Gardner firing the first shot. His report stated that he'd *heard* the shot from behind him, and on turning he saw *me* at the door with my gun drawn. Binks had lurched forward like a mad man, and the Special Emergency Response Team had opened fire to put him down.

That's not how it happened.

Bradley seemed to be reading my thoughts. 'It's okay Scott, don't you see? This is a win-win situation.'

'How do you work that out?'

'The killer's been brought to justice, and the people of the Gold Coast have a new hero. Have you any idea what this is going to do for your career?' His excitement was a delicate veil of anxiety-fuelled elation, 'You're that hero, Scott.'

'I've done nothing. You know it. I know it, and it's only a matter of time before everyone else will know it too.'

'It doesn't have to be like that.'

Ripley came barging into the office.

'What the hell?' he yelled at Bradley.

'I'm so sorry, sir. It all happened before I got there.' Bradley launched himself to his feet.

'You're supposed to be watching him!' Ripley addressed Bradley directly, as if I weren't even in the room. The footage of me in the front yard that morning was obviously on his mind. 'Your job is a remarkably simple one, and you fucked it up!'

X

'Hey, hey …' I jumped to my feet, 'hold on a minute. He's done nothing—'

'Exactly!' he cut me off mid-sentence, his blazing eyes still fixed on Bradley. 'Is he ready for this morning?'

'Uhm … no, not yet—'

'Okay, get out.' Pointing to the door. 'I'll deal with you shortly.' He turned to me, 'I need to see *you* in my office right away.' Then marched out the door, almost trampling over Bradley.

X

Arriving in Ripley's office a couple of minutes later, I wasn't surprised to see Singleton was also there.

Ripley's manner had completely changed. Smiling, he met me at the door and shook my hand, 'Scott, it's great to see you.'

Singleton stood, also offering his hand. Shaking it made me feel somehow dirty.

'Take a seat, Scott, take a seat,' Ripley gestured towards a vacant chair.

I didn't sit. 'With all due respect, sir, what's going on?'

24

Completed in 1991, 50 Cavil Avenue is a twenty-seven storey, circular, blue glass building in the heart of Surfers Paradise. Tenanted mostly by finance, wealth creation, superannuation, and real estate companies, the 17th floor is home to Channel 9's Gold Coast studios.

I'd taken over driving again, relegating Bradley to the passenger seat. Normally, I would have walked the few minutes' distance, but with hordes of media camped outside the station, normality was a thing of the past. So, our only option was to drive.

Bradley was still banging on about the importance of being ready, calm and confident. By the time we turned into Cavil Avenue, all I was hearing was, *'Blah, blah, blah.'*

'Did you do the breathing exercises I gave you?' Bradley asked as I parked in one of the network's reserved spots.

'What breathing exercises?'

'Oh goodness me, Scott.' Even though he was under pressure, and I suspect being bullied by Ripley and Singleton, I knew he meant well. 'It will help with the nerves.' He closed his eyes and began to inhale slowly. 'Do this with me. Close your eyes and just breathe.'

I did as he asked, and we sat for a few minutes inhaling and exhaling. I must admit, it did feel good.

'With each breath, hold it at the bottom of your stomach, then release it slowly.'

X

I could have sat there all day, blocking out the world and hiding from the madness, but the madness was calling me. There was a tap on the car window. I opened my eyes to see a young woman, wearing a singlet and jeans and carrying a clipboard.

'Detective Inspector Stephens, I'm Kelly Davis. We need to get you upstairs right away,' she said through the glass.

The inside of the modern lift was a welcome contrast to the bare concrete basement. During the ride up to the 17th floor, Kelly seemed to be speaking to Bradley rather than me. They were like two minions conferring.

'We'll get him into make-up right away. Bit of powder.'

'Yes, he does tend to glisten somewhat.'

'Then we'll get him straight through to the studio. Alex will be waiting.'

'Is this going to be live or recorded?'

'Live. The show's already on air.'

I closed my eyes and took a deep breath. It did help a little with the nerves. Ripley and Singleton's words were still swimming around in my head, resurfacing every now and again as if coming up for air. 'Everything is riding on you, Scott,' Ripley had said, 'you're the hero the Gold Coast needs right now.'

'Don't stuff it up!' Singleton's manner had been more brash. 'You've been given a once in a lifetime opportunity, detective.'

The Channel 9 foyer was abuzz with personnel. When we stepped from the lift, they all suddenly stopped what they were doing, turned to face me and began to applaud and wolf whistle. I stood there embarrassed, nodding, not knowing what else to do.

'Good on ya, Scotty,' someone called out.

The pretty young make-up artist, who introduced herself as Netty, was as chatty as a lorikeet while she dabbed my face with a make-up brush. 'It's so great to meet you. My mum said I have to say hi for her. Everyone here was so excited when we heard you were coming. I can't believe you're sitting in my chair! Can I get your autograph before you go? My friend, Kylie, wants one too. Is it true they're going to make a movie about you?' She didn't seem to need air – unlike me – I'd switched off with my eyes closed.

My moment of relaxation was interrupted when another young woman came into the small room. This one wore a business suit and introduced herself as Zetta Mallenovic. I'd seen her on the TV before, reading the news.

'Detective Inspector Stephens, it's so great to meet you,' she said, holding out her hand.

'How's it goin'?' We shook hands.

'Alex can't wait to meet you too. We're just about to go into a commercial break. How are we doing here, Netty?'

'Good. Not a lot to do. Just about done.' She was right, she hadn't done much.

'Okay, if you'd like to follow me, detective,' Zetta said.

'Scott, call me Scott, or Scotty if you like.'

Her smile was a refined product of St Hilda's School for girls. 'Scott, follow me.'

The studio was much smaller than it looked on the telly– basically just a room not much bigger than a double garage, with a couple of cameramen and other guys wearing headphones. Alex Wade sat at the news desk in an immaculate suit. He was being briefed by a geeky young bloke in a *Breaking Bad* T-shirt. Alex was a celebrity on the Gold Coast. The clichéd anchor man, ageing, tanned and fit.

The applause thing happened again when I followed Zetta into the studio, and I was surprised when I saw Alex join in.

I was led to the news desk and directed to take the vacant chair at the right of Alex.

'It's great to have you here, detective,' Alex said, offering me his hand.

'It's good to be here, Alex.'

'May I call you Scott?' He must have used the same dentist as

X

Monroe, and now that I was closer, I realised the healthy tan was really a layer or two of tinted Spakfilla.

'Yeah, mate. Or Scotty.'

'Returning from the commercial break,' the geeky guy said, holding up his fingers, 'in five, four ...' He silently mouthed three, two, one while dropping his fingers, and I wondered if this was actual protocol or if he was just a fan of *Wayne's World*.

Alex sat up straight and smiled into the camera. 'Never before have I witnessed such excitement in the studio. Everyone seems to be a little distracted this morning.' He paused and looked around the room.

From my seat, I could see a bank of monitors on the opposite wall. The main one showed Alex how the viewers at home saw him. The one next to it displayed me. I couldn't look at that one.

'Ladies and gentlemen, it gives me the greatest pleasure to introduce our very special guest this morning, Detective Inspector Scott Stephens.'

The theme tune from *Shaft* blared out and my image appeared on the centre screen. The music died down and all eyes, and cameras, were on me.

'Uhm ... good morning.'

'And good morning to you too. And what a morning it is,' Alex said. 'For those of you who may have just returned from Mars, we woke this morning to hear the wonderful news that every single Gold Coaster has been praying for over the last three weeks – that *X* has been captured!'

'Hell yeah!' one of the cameramen called out.

'And it's all down to the remarkable man who is here with us this morning.' His gaze shifted from the camera to me.

'Detective Inspector, I know you can't go into too much detail about the case due to the impending investigation, but how does it feel to be the person who put an end to this horrific nightmare?'

Singleton and Ripley had drummed into me that whatever

I did, I mustn't belittle myself by sharing my view that I'd had nothing to do with solving the case. I was rattled, but I was also in danger of being carried away with the wave of excitement. Was I the bloke who would burst everyone's bubble? For now, I'd have to go along with it, but there was no way I was going to lie. Were I asked the question directly, I'd tell the truth.

'That's not the case, Alex. This was a team effort.'

'Ahh, modest. Just like the Queensland Police commissioner said you would be at the press conference this morning.'

'Well, I don't know about modesty.'

'Scott, right at this moment, you're probably the most famous Gold Coaster of all time. I'm sensing you don't even realise how popular you are. Watch this.'

The main screen changed to an image outside the front entrance to the building, where a crowd was cheering and holding up banners. 'We love you, Scotty!' a woman yelled into the camera, while a banner read, 'Thank You Scotty. You're our hero!'

The footage changed to the line of restaurants at the beach end of Cavil Avenue. The owner of The Beer Garden appeared on the screen. A female voice off-screen asked, 'What does this mean to your business, and businesses like yours, now the killer has been caught?'

'It means everything. The tourists will come back, and my business will be saved.'

'Is there anything you want to say to DI Stephens?'

The young man looked straight into the camera. 'Mate. Thank you so much. You truly are our hero!'

'A free beer perhaps?'

'Free for life!'

'Wow! This is Penny Sellers in Surfers Paradise. Back to you in the studio, Alex.'

'Thank you, Penny.' Alex turned back to me smiling, 'Did you know any of this was going on, Scott?'

'No, I certainly didn't. I'm blown away.' And I was too.

25

To say I was like a fish out of water wouldn't have done the cliché justice. I wasn't flailing around or desperately gasping for breath, I was being handed around and proudly displayed like the prize catches you see at the end of the evening news.

From Channel 9, Bradley took me to the Channel 7 studios for another interview – almost exactly the same as the first one, but with different, yet very much the same, people. The afternoon was basically spent zigzagging across the coast to local radio stations. On arrival at each venue, the routine was the same—everyone stopped what they were doing to applaud me. Talk about a grand entrance. Even when we got a chance to duck into Broadbeach for a bit of lunch, I was constantly recognised and stopped with wild handshakes from the guys, hugs and kisses from the women and kids, selfies and the odd request for an autograph. After deciding on Pizzeria del Spiaggia, everyone present in the restaurant stood and applauded us as we entered. Lunch and drinks were on the house.

I should have been loving this, basking in the glory, but I wasn't.

The radio stations were a bit more relaxed. Some of the jocks came across as normal, down-to-earth people, and we even shared the odd laugh. It's funny though, none of them really wanted to hear my views, especially when I said I had very little to do with cracking the case. It was like, 'Right, so where's your favourite surfing spot?'

Just after 7.00 pm, we finally left the ABC studios and headed back to Kirra. Tired, all I wanted to do was go to bed. 'You've got to be kidding me,' I said as Bradley drove down Ruby Street. There was a group of reporters still outside the house.

'Just ignore them. Go straight in the front door,' Bradley said, pulling up to the kerb.

Easier said than done. I was mobbed as I climbed from the car. The annoying thing was they asked the exact same questions as they had that morning.

'Look guys, I've had a big day. I just need to hit the sack.'

'Are you looking forward to the reception at the mayor's house tomorrow?' someone asked as I made my way towards the front yard.

'Reception?'

'Is it true the mayor will be awarding you the keys to the city?'

'First I've heard.' I made it to the front door, let myself in and closed it behind me. Leaning on the back of the door, I closed my eyes and took a deep breath.

When I finally opened my eyes, I was greeted by the grinning faces of *los tres amigos*. Johnno thrust a beer into my hand. 'Drink it, bro.'

I needed a beer, that was for sure, but I certainly couldn't face another big night on the grog. By the time I made my way to the kitchen, discarding my jacket and tie, undoing my shirt and kicking off my shoes, the stubby was empty.

'I'm going to bed, guys. I'm knackered.'

There were the mandatory protests, but I remained adamant.

Johnno, the mediator, said, 'Okay, that's cool. What time have you got to be at work tomorrow?'

There was no work tomorrow. Ripley had called me during the journey back to Kirra. 'Have a rest day, Scott. You've earned it. But we've got something very special planned for tomorrow night. Bradley will pick you up at six.'

Apparently, Bradley had yet to be briefed, and claimed he knew nothing about it. It was funny how the reporters seemed to know more than we did.

X

After some serious pleading from all three of my best mates, including the argument that I wouldn't have to get up early the next morning, we agreed on a compromise that we'd go to the pub for a couple of schooners and a feed.

X

The packed bar suddenly fell silent when we entered from the side door. For a split second, it was like one of those old western movies when the sheriff walks into the saloon and everyone, including the piano player, stops what they are doing. Then the room exploded with loud applause, whistles and cheers.

'Good on ya, Scotty,' someone called out. And I was mobbed. Local drinkers, tourists, even blokes I'd had the odd run-in with over the years, clambered to shake my hand. Everyone wanted to buy me a drink, but Gaz, the publican, insisted all my drinks were on the house. Once again, I should have been in heaven – but I wasn't.

It was chicken parmigiana night at Kirra Beach Hotel. After what was only going to be a couple of schooners but turned into five or six, the four of us staggered into the large bistro off the side of the bar. It seemed to be becoming a ritual that whenever I entered a room, everyone would stand and applaud. The bistro was no exception. Normally you'd have to queue up for your order, but we were shown to a table by one of the waitresses.

'Four parmies, is it?'

'My bloody oath,' Elvis agreed.

'And a jug of Coopers,' Tetley added.

7 September

Early the next morning, I was running over the events of the previous day while strolling north along Kirra Beach. For some reason, I still hadn't got back into the surf. Wearing a Cooly Rocks baseball cap, sunglasses, boardshorts and a hoody, my disguise hadn't gotten by the old chook at the bakery when I went in to buy a sausage roll for breakfast. She insisted on throwing in a carton of chocolate milk too, both on the house. Strolling past the newsagent, I got a glimpse of the front page of the *Gold Coast Bulletin*. The infamous picture of me in the front garden wearing only my dacks took up almost the full page. The headline read, 'MORE THAN JUST AN AUSSIE LARRIKIN!'

Normally I'd be out in the surf on my days off. Instead, I'd walked to the beach without my board. Kicking off my thongs and stepping onto the sand, I was able to distance myself, breathe and reflect. Only three days ago I was a low-ranking detective constable. So low in fact, that most of the people in my neighbourhood didn't even know I was a copper. I was Scotty Stephens, bachelor, local surfer and your average knock-around bloke. Now I was as famous as God. None of this was sinking in though because none of it was real. I hadn't earned the adulation.

The irony was that I was actually a good detective. My success rate was high. It was just that the cases I'd been assigned until now had been low profile—things like domestic violence cases, low-level fraud, and the odd missing person. For these I'd received no accolades, gained no respect, or even earned a promotion. I'd been simply doing my job, and that suited me just fine.

Sure, I'd been working on the *X* case, but thanks to Gardner my role had been not much more than admin. But the thing is, I *was* a detective. I had an inquisitive mind and a need to uncover the truth, no matter what. If I were to continue this case, I needed to validate myself by doing the job properly and not being dictated to by a bunch of idiots. The only way to do that would be to step off the merry-go-round and delve into the intricate details of the investigation.

If Binks was the killer, there had to be proof beyond a shadow of a doubt. To achieve that, I would need to do what I was good at – flying under the radar and getting on with the job.

26

Even though I'd inadvertently walked all the way to Tugun, it was still early when I got back home. Thankfully, there was no media outside. Elvis and Tetley were still sleeping when I crept through the house. Apart from swapping my thongs for a pair of skate shoes, I decided not to change. One good thing about the new image was that everyone would be looking for a clean-cut bloke in an expensive suit. I was hoping they wouldn't look twice at the old surfer dude in the faded Billabong hoody and shorts.

I'd let Bradley take the Range Rover home the previous night as I hadn't been planning on going anywhere today, not until the mysterious reception at Monroe's house that had been planned for that night. Luckily, I had "the Dub" – my trusty 1967 VW Beetle I'd had since leaving school. My first car, I bought it cheap a long time before the value of these endearing little icons had skyrocketed. The most reliable car ever, back then it would certainly have never been described as cool. In the factory cream colour, it was little more than a rust bucket, but ironically, and thanks to the bandied around term of the day, *patina,* it was the only appreciating asset I owned. Come to think of it, apart from my surfboard, it was the *only* thing I owned.

The house only had a single garage where Elvis's poncy Lexus took residence, while "the Dub" was generally parked out the front of the house.

People were starting to stir when I slipped into the driver's seat, but luckily there was no sign of the press. The engine started with a whistle and whir on the first turn of the key as usual, and within minutes I was heading out towards the back highway.

Parkrose Close was quiet until "the Dub" trundled into the street. An elderly woman walking her dog glanced in my direction but didn't pay too much attention. I pulled into the driveway of number 19, turned off the engine and climbed out of the car. The air felt different from the beachside ozone I was used to – warmer and without breeze, a little dusty. A magpie warbled in the distance. I made my way around the back of the house. The rear entrance was a row of cantilever doors with French-style windowpanes overlooking a pool. A quick jab with an elbow broke one of the panes closest to the handle. Putting my hand carefully through the jagged hole, I was able to flick the lock and quickly slip inside, closing the door behind me.

The open kitchen-diner was tastefully decorated. The quality of the fittings and appliances was of a high standard. I remembered from the report I'd read on Binks that his late mother was a psychotherapist. Each room of the house was immaculate and I wondered if Binks had hired help since his mother had passed away. As I crept through the ground floor, I realised I knew extraordinarily little about this young man who, like me, had been thrust into the limelight. I suspected what I was viewing was the taste of his mother. Apart from a few childhood photographs on a grand piano in the living room, I didn't see anything I would have associated with a thirty-three-year-old man.

In the hallway, the spot where Binks had been gunned down was still apparent. Four holes in the wall, surrounded by sickly blooms of blood from where the bullets had exited his back, were still clearly visible. Dried blood was also present on the highly polished hardwood floor.

X

I had no interest in this area; forensics had photographed, catalogued and analysed every square inch. I needed to learn about Binks *the man*. At the top of the stairs were five single doors and a row of matching closet louvres. A quick scan of each room told me that one had belonged to the mother. And it was still pristine. I presumed a room with a double bed and standard bedroom furniture was the spare room. There was a large bathroom, a separate toilet, and the door at the farthest end of the landing had obviously belonged to Binks.

Inside was a single bed, a bedside cabinet with a flashing digital alarm clock, and a built-in wardrobe with glass sliding doors that filled one wall. A large window, with a tallboy of drawers either side and a matching window seat between them, occupied another. In one corner of the room was an elaborate gaming station, basically a thick tubular workstation with three wide computer monitors side-by-side, plus a keyboard, joystick, and a racing car steering wheel. The computer itself had been removed for analysis. Pushed into the desk was a Ferrari replica racing car-cum-office-chair.

From the ceiling hung six large model aircrafts, which appeared to be identical. The walls featured posters of Guns and Roses, Bruce Lee, and interestingly, an original movie poster of *Friday the 13th*. Apart from being immaculately tidy, at first glance, there appeared to be little out of the ordinary in Binks's room. It was a typical teenager's room – only Binks wasn't a teenager, he was thirty-three years old.

In the wardrobe hung a couple of dress shirts, a black suit and a row of identical black showerproof Adidas tracksuits, which suddenly brought it home to me that this was far from just a normal room. I counted eight pairs of identical black Adidas running shoes along the floor of the robe, all brand new, and at one end was a stack of Adidas shoe boxes. Opening the top one, I discovered a pair of the same runners, also brand new.

In the top drawer of the nearest tallboy, I noticed something odd. There were only five T-shirts—identical, and all folded, but placed in a circle in the spacious drawer. In the next drawer were six polo shirts arranged in a square, and the next held three pairs of identical boardshorts in a triangle. Opening every drawer, I discovered each held items of clothing, including underwear and socks, all positioned in different ways.

A sudden noise from downstairs warned me someone had just let themselves into the house. I quietly slid the last drawer closed and crept from the room.

After tiptoeing down the stairs, I cautiously made my way across the hallway towards the kitchen.

'Jesus Christ!'

27

I'm not sure who got the biggest fright as we almost collided.

'Scott? What the hell?' It was Jenny Radford. I'd forgotten her mother lived next door.

'Hey.'

'What are you doing in here?' She sounded unusually defensive.

'Just having a look around.' I was supposed to be her boss, but I was acting like she was the school mistress who'd just caught me smoking.

'I thought you'd be on *Good Morning Australia* or *Sunrise* this morning.' There was a hint of a grin.

'No, I'm done with all that crap.' Taking off my cap, I ran a hand through my hair. I hadn't spoken to anyone about my feelings towards the case but bottling it all up wasn't helping. I needed someone to confide in, someone to bounce a few theories off. Bradley would have been the obvious choice, but I couldn't be sure he wasn't reporting to Ripley. It hadn't occurred to me before but Jenny was more experienced, more on my level, and we had a lot in common. 'I'm just double checking a few things, making sure nothing's been missed.'

'Good, someone should be.'

'How well did you really know him?'

'As well as anybody could, I guess.'

I'd read the statements that had been taken from the neighbours.

Jenny's mother had said that Binks was a nice, polite young man, albeit a little odd at times. 'Your mother said he was odd?'

Her eyes opened wider, and her face puckered, giving the impression she was impressed. 'You've read the statements?'

'Of course.' I padded around her and back into the kitchen.

Following my lead, we sat on a couple of bar stools at the large granite island.

'What did she mean by odd?'

'He was quiet and shy, but always very polite. He only spoke when he was spoken to, and it was always hurried, like he thought you were going to tell him off for something.'

'Is that odd?'

'Well, you always got the sense you'd just sprung him for doing something he shouldn't be doing. That's how he made you feel. But I never thought anything of it. He was a shy chap who kept himself to himself.'

'And the tracksuits?'

'Well, yeah, that was odd. That must be a recent thing because I wasn't aware of it.'

'Anything else?'

'Just that he was a gamer.'

This I already knew. From pulling apart his computer and sifting through the software and online games history, forensics had determined that Binks liked to play. He was quite high in the ranking of an online gaming community who were followers of a game called *Force of Evil*. Binks's avatar tag was *Dark Boy*. None of this was out of the ordinary. There were millions of gamers worldwide. Bradley told me some of them stuck to a theme and even dressed like their avatars. The black Adidas tracksuits fitted the profile of someone called *Dark Boy*, perhaps that was why Binks had often been seen wearing one.

Jenny peered past me towards the garden as she spoke. 'Sometimes

X

when we were sitting out on the back verandah, we'd see him in his garden. He obviously had some form of OCD.'

'What do you mean?'

'Obsessive Compulsive Disor—'

'I know what OCD means.'

'Right, sorry. We'd see him pottering around in his garden. He'd water the plants, do a bit of weeding. The odd times I'd see him cleaning the pool too.' She stood from the island bench, walked around it and began to open cabinet doors looking for something. 'I noticed he had this habit of doing things a little differently.' She pulled out two tall glasses from an overhead cupboard.

'Water?'

I nodded, watching as she poured two glasses from the tap after checking the empty fridge first.

'One day he was mowing the lawn. It's quite a big block, but it took him a lot longer than it should have. You know how normally you would mow in a straight line, then turn when you reached the end and head back in the opposite direction?'

I was familiar with mowing lawns. We only had a small patch of grass at the front of the house and a bit between the back door and the man shed, but it was my job to keep it tidy. Elvis didn't do gardens.

'Well, he would mow a full line, but then instead of turning, he'd cock the mower up on its back wheels, drag it all the way back, then mow in the same direction.'

This was the kind of detail easily overlooked during an investigation, the seemingly unimportant little traits that witnesses didn't think important or just didn't remember. I'd planned to speak to all the neighbours after searching the house for this very reason, to try and pry out those little splinters of information that could have been missed.

I took a mouthful of water, rose to my feet, approached the

back doors, and looked out over the lawn. Something immediately caught my attention. The grass looked as if it had recently been cut, but it was far from neat. None of the mower lines were even, some weren't even straight. I remembered Binks's bedroom and how he'd arranged all his things. One strength I did have, and one that had been a great asset during my time as a detective, is that I had good recall. I was able to visualise scenes and events and replay them in my mind like I was seeing them again. I wouldn't say I had a photographic memory, but it was pretty sharp.

While Jenny continued to speak of Binks's strange behaviour in the garden, I was visualising his bedroom. Focusing on the image of the T-shirts in the drawer, placed in a circle, I noticed they weren't in a perfect pattern at all. The one at the top was folded with the arms behind it and placed straight. The next one had the arms in front and was placed at a slight skewer. The next one had one arm at the front and one behind, also set at a skewer but at the opposite angle. A quick scan of the circle told me that what my brain originally noted as being a uniformed pattern, was in fact the opposite. The rest of the drawers were similarly arranged, each garment placed in a way that was slightly different.

The contents of the wardrobe were the same. The first two tracksuits hung one with the coat hanger hook facing outwards, one with it facing inwards. The next two faced the same way, but the garments hung in opposite directions. Once again, everything had been placed slightly differently to avoid a pattern. The first pair of shoes was faced toes in, the next toes out, the next pair was one toe in, one toe out, then one toe out, one toe in. The bottom shoe box in the pile was stacked the right way up, the next was upside down, then, end in end out. The model airplanes hanging from the ceiling, which I'd first thought were identical, not only hung facing different directions, but there were details on each that were also different—one had the British target decals on top of the wings, another had them on the bottom, etc.

X

It may not have seemed much at the time, but I couldn't help feeling this information was important. There was a relevance to the case which would either demonstrate Binks was indeed the killer, or it would prove him innocent.

X

The description of Binks from the rest of the neighbours was pretty much the same as Jenny's, except for Mrs Sheila Roberts, who lived next door on the opposite side. It was Sheila who had phoned the police to say that he was acting weird. In her early eighties, her unfiltered view of the 'stupid boy who wandered around the street like a dazed idiot' was delivered with a no-nonsense politically incorrect view, common in many people of her generation. 'I never trusted him, I always said there'd be trouble with that boy.'

Standing in her doorway and leaning heavily on a Zimmer frame, she declared, 'The mother was a fruit loop too. It was all her fault. She was the one who babied him. She got really angry with me one day when I complained about him throwing things over into my garden. Just stupid stuff, like a plastic bag one day with a teaspoon in it, the next day it'd be a fork. He was a bloody nutcase. And I told her so.'

'Was she violent?' I asked.

'Oh yes, she went off. She said if she ever saw my cat in her garden again, she'd wring its neck.'

'What about the father?'

'Never knew him, but I'd bet he was just as daft as the lad. The apple never falls too far from the tree.'

28

Bradley arrived in the Range Rover at 6.00 pm to take me to the reception. When I opened the front door, I thought he was going to faint.

'What? My god, Scott … no. There's no way you can wear that!'

I was wearing my other old *Lowes* suit, the dark green one, complemented by a mustard-coloured shirt, my black and red striped Essendon tie, beige socks, and brown shoes. I was sick of being paraded around like a mannequin. From now on, I was going to be myself. He was lucky I wasn't wearing my thongs.

I'd learned more about Binks by doing an hour of the kind of old-fashioned detective work I was used to and was good at, than the whole investigation had unearthed, or shared, so far. He was a young man with Asperger's syndrome, which was confirmed by Doctor Patricia Paington at Autism CRC that afternoon when I described Binks's symptoms. Although his actions may have seemed strange to most onlookers, his behaviour wasn't that uncommon. It certainly didn't automatically qualify him for the category of serial killer. I wasn't going to let it go. I needed more proof before I could condemn him.

'Picking *who* up?' Even from the back seat of the Range Rover, I could see the flushing blooms on Bradley's cheeks.

'Jenny Radford? But you know about her history with the Monroe family?'

'Yep.'

X

'Oh, my goodness,' the fanning hand was back. 'What's happening to you, Scott?'

'What do you mean?'

'Well look at you. I had you looking like Chris Hemsworth. Now you've slipped right back to Colin Carpenter.'

That made me chuckle. I loved old 'Col,' but Bradley hadn't meant it as a joke.

'After all the hard work I've put in, I'll be fired in the morning after Singleton sees you.'

'Lighten up, Bradders. See, that's the problem. You're getting caught up in it all.'

'Caught up in what?'

'This bloody circus!'

That day had been an exceptionally good one for me. Since the long walk to Tugun and back that morning, I'd had time to clear my head, breathe and take stock. Over the last couple of days, I'd been shepherded around as if I'd just won *The X Factor*, being treated like something I wasn't. I'd done nothing to earn any of it, nor did I want it. When I'd stepped off the beach in front of the Kirra Beach Surf Club that morning, my mind was made up. I was Scott Stephens from Kirra Beach. If that didn't sit right with anyone else, then stuff 'em.

I wasn't angry with Bradley. In fact, I liked him a lot. He'd been given a job to do. I was a little concerned he might get in trouble though, so a word with Ripley to make sure he didn't, wouldn't go amiss.

Jenny came straight out to the car when we pulled up outside her apartment. She looked pretty good in a not too formal, while not too casual, floral summer dress. I was relieved to see she hadn't overdressed. A ball gown would have been embarrassing.

'Oh shit,' she quipped as she climbed into the back seat. 'You didn't tell me it was fancy dress.'

Bradley's laugh was more of a nervous squeal.

'What do you mean?'

'The clown suit. Or is there a homeless theme?'

There was something about this girl that I liked. She was tough, intelligent and cute. She gave the impression she could handle herself, but she also had a sense of humour not unlike my own. I could imagine that even Tetley's refined art of banter would bounce right off her.

'Bloody cheek,' I said, straightening my lapels, 'this is me best suit.'

'What happened to the *Anthony Squires*?'

'They're not mine. They're Bradley's.'

'What? You borrowed them?'

'No, they were bought for me.'

'You're seriously going to a civic reception held in your honour at Julian Monroe's multi-million-dollar mansion, wearing that?'

'My oath.'

29

Two enormous date palms with white fairy lights spiralling around their thick spiky trunks, stood either side of an ancient reclaimed, bleached timber gateway. A six-foot-high white stucco wall surrounded the double frontage block, protecting what a layman could only imagine from the outside world was a utopian interior. The floodlit sky above the property swayed and throbbed in time with the electronic beat of David Bowie's *Fashion,* and the chatter and laughter of what sounded like a substantial party rolled over the walls as we climbed from the car.

Bradley didn't turn off the engine or get out.

'What are you doing?' I asked, tapping on the driver's window. 'Aren't you coming in?'

'No. I'm not invited.' There was a slight tremor in his voice.

'Of course you are.'

'No. You guys go. Enjoy yourselves.' Before allowing me to object, he pulled away from the kerb and drove away.

'He can be a queer bugger sometimes,' I said, turning to Jenny.

'Uh, you might want to rephrase that.'

'What?'

'Not very politically correct.'

My use of the word 'queer' wasn't meant as a stab at Bradley's sexuality, it was merely a term the amigos and I fired at each other when one of us was acting like a sook. The only difference was, we'd usually modify it, substituting 'bugger' with the C-bomb.

Jenny threaded her arm in mine, and we walked across the grass verge towards the large double gates, one of which was ajar. Inside stood two burly doormen wearing white tuxedos. I suddenly felt like I was eighteen again, approaching the entrance of The *Playroom* and expecting to be refused entry by the bouncers because of my mullet, or because Tetley was blind drunk, or Elvis had his leery sway on. The older of the two doormen, his hair cropped close to his head, was holding a clipboard and a pen. On it I suspected was the guest list, but he didn't even look at it as we approached. Instead, both men lowered their heads and stepped aside.

'Welcome, sir, madam,' the older one said with a sweeping gesture.

'Thanks,' I said, allowing Jenny to step through first.

The second doorman was a big strapping lad with the face of a street fighter, a nest of black hair on the top of his shaved head. 'It's a great honour to meet you, sir.' He held out his hand.

'Don't I know you from somewhere?' I asked, fixing him with my best policeman stare, while shaking his hand. It was a copper joke that never got old.

'No, sir, I don't think so.' He pouted his lips and his neck jutted like a cockerel.

The older guy got it and smiled. 'If you'd like to make your way up the steps and through the front doors, someone will meet you there.'

Arm in arm once more, we slowly made our way towards the house. Marble steps led up to a single door that must have been eight foot high and wide enough to fit "the Dub" through. Two life-sized bronze tigers sat on either side of the entrance, while a Hollywood-style spotlight illuminated the stone façade.

We climbed the steps to be met by a glamorous young waitress holding a tray of Champagne glasses.

'Don't mind if I do,' I said as I grabbed one.

'Uh, hmm,' Jenny cleared her throat.

X

'Oh, sorry. Here ya go.' I gave her my drink just before it reached my lips, then grabbed another one for me.

Standing in a marble-clad foyer, sparsely furnished, with a large, modern chandelier hanging from a high vaulted ceiling, I could see beyond what appeared to be an enormous living room, filled with mingling people dressed to the nines. I looked down at my suit. A rental tuxedo had been delivered to the house that afternoon. There were even instructions on how to tie the bowtie. About now I was regretting the decision I'd made not to wear it, wondering what the reasoning for my stubbornness had been. I'd decided I was going to make a stand, and that I wasn't going to be told what to do or be bullied around anymore. I'd show them. But instead, the words of Tetley came to mind. *You fuckin' twat.* I looked at Jenny and her expression seemed to be mirroring Tetley's words.

'If you'd like to go through,' the waitress said, 'everyone's waiting for you.'

The party seemed to be in full swing as we approached the living room. Although we'd made a slight detour picking up Jenny, I doubted we were late – Bradley wouldn't have allowed that. When we passed through the double doors, right on cue, everyone stopped and began to cheer and applaud. Men I'd never met before greeted me with warm handshakes, patting me on the back as their wives or girlfriends hugged and thanked me for being their hero.

We were led through the house to an enormous waterfront pool area and a second crowd; some were dancing, most were congregated in groups. Wait staff slowly threaded through them, carrying trays of food and drinks. I immediately spotted Julian Monroe and his glamourous wife, Gladys. They shone like jewels amongst a sea of coal. No black tuxedo for Monroe. His was a sparkly gold, very Duran Duran. Gladys wore a tight-fitting evening gown made from the same material, showcasing her ex-model body nicely. After another mandatory bout of applause, the hosts met us at the doorway.

'Scotty,' Monroe yelled, like he'd known me forever. He paused for a moment when he realised what I was wearing. A flicker of shock blended into a slight smirk as he grabbed my hand and shook it violently. Luckily, I'd already sculled the Champagne, or it would have gone everywhere. He threw his other arm around me and pulled me in close under his armpit. A photographer captured the moment in a bright flash. 'Scott, this is my wife, Gladys,' he said, letting go of me.

'It's lovely to meet you at last, Scott,' she said, offering a bejewelled hand.

Everyone on the Gold Coast, and possibly Australia, knew who Gladys Monroe was – ex-supermodel, wife of golden footy hero Julian Monroe, high-profile businesswoman, philanthropist, and all-round celebrity. As I shook her hand, our eyes met, and I wondered if she also remembered me. They say you always remember your first time. I certainly remembered mine. I guess for her, I wasn't her first though, all those years ago in the ladies' toilets of the Hawthorn footy club.

The handshake seemed to linger, and I realised Monroe was watching me closely.

'Nice to meet you too, Mrs Monroe.'

'Gladys, call me Gladys, and this is?' She withdrew her hand and turned to Jenny.

'This is Jenny, Jenny—'

'Detective Jenny Radford,' Monroe interjected. 'Interesting choice of guest, Scott.' He didn't shake Jenny's hand.

'Nice to meet you, Jenny,' Gladys offered, her smile faulting momentarily as she realised who Jenny was.

'Hi,' Jenny smiled back awkwardly.

'Come on in and meet everyone,' Monroe said, almost turning his back on Jenny. 'We've got a special night planned for you.'

X

It was the reaction I'd been expecting. I wasn't sure if I'd invited Jenny because I liked her, or if I'd done it just to piss off the Monroes. Of course, I knew Julian would remember her, because she had famously busted him for drink driving when she was still in uniform. Video footage from a passer-by had hit social media almost instantly, then appeared on TV news Australia-wide, of a drunken Julian aggressively jumping from the car and verbally abusing the young female cop. Unfortunately for him, he hadn't realised how tough the girl was until he ended up with his face on the tarmac and an arm twisted up behind his back.

But it didn't end there. Two months later, a similar scenario took place, but this time with Monroe's daughter, Haley. Jenny had pulled her over for speeding on the M1, close to the Dreamworld exit. There was no footage on that occasion, but Haley had gone to the press claiming the family were being victimised by the Gold Coast police.

30

I've always been an observer. I guess part of being a good detective is having the ability to read people. As I glanced around the crowded pool area, my first impression was that everyone present were what Tetley would have described as tossers. Sycophantic, self-centred, plastic people with lots of money, which was reflected in their clothes, their fake smiles and body language. Superintendent Ripley stood out from the crowd, not quite as badly as me perhaps, but I could see that both he and his wife were also uncomfortable and not engaging in the same way as everyone else. Mrs Ripley was genuinely courteous when introduced to me by her husband. She laughed at my suit and asked if I'd just come from the op shop. Jenny laughed too, but it wasn't delivered with bitchy intent, more as friendly banter, which put me at ease.

Monroe and his wife insisted on introducing me to just about everyone at the party, parading me around like a lucky charm. Angela Brigano, the premier of Queensland, was gracious and curtsied when we shook hands. 'It's great to finally meet you, DI Stephens, and I want to personally take this opportunity to thank you on behalf of the people of Queensland. You truly are an Australian hero!'

'Oh, I don't know about that.' I introduced her to Jenny.

Police Commissioner Singleton wasn't married. There were rumours surrounding his personal life, and I suspected the reason he was hanging around the premier was purely professional.

X

I was introduced to a couple of veteran stars from the long-running Australian soap *Neighbours,* and a young actor from *Home and Away*. I didn't have a clue who they were, but I didn't let on. It was weird because everybody knew me. Elvis would be impressed when I told him I got to shake hands with Johnny Burns, and he'd love the fact that the ageing rocker was hammered.

I was surprised to see a few shady characters among the guests. Don Kinley lost his fortune a few years ago after being accused of running one of Australia's largest fraudulent real estate schemes right here on the Gold Coast. Benny McGuire was well-known to the police as a racketeer and a leading component in the Coast's underbelly scene. Jean (Totty) Mitchel used to run most of the brothels from Tweed Heads to Beenleigh, and here they were, mingling with the rich and famous.

One person I was interested to meet was Dillon Monroe, Julian's son, and the current full forward for the Gold Coast Suns. Like his parents, he was also a Gold Coast celebrity, but not always for the right reasons. Young, tall and handsome, he was your typical playboy type, milking everything the coast had to offer, without apology. I hadn't met him before, but I was aware of his reputation for being a spoiled brat. His body language as we shook hands immediately told me the rumours were true. The blonde glamor who hung off his arm like a stoned beauty queen seemed incapable of speech, and simply giggled. Dillon didn't bother to introduce her, nor did he pay any attention to Jenny.

'So, I hear you used to play?' he said.

'Yep, full forward, just like you and your dad.'

He laughed. 'Hardly the same.'

Both mine and Jenny's eyes suddenly opened wide as Dillon's double pushed through the crowd and joined us.

'Oh, this is my brother, Troy,' Dillon hastily explained.

Although identical in appearance, it was immediately obvious that Troy was very different to his twin brother. His clothes were simple. Wearing an open-necked shirt, plain trousers and pigskin moccasins, he held his head low like he didn't want to be seen. His handshake was reluctant and weak. He didn't speak.

'You'll have to excuse my brother, he doesn't mix too well.' The voice was female.

Jenny and I turned to see another Gold Coast socialite smiling at us. Haley Monroe. A year or two older than the twins, she was all about business. It was well-known that her father had put her in charge of the family's affairs when he became mayor, and like her brother, although in more of a networking sense, she'd used her position to the greatest advantage. Haley was always in the news, not so much as a darling like her mother, more of interest due to some of the ruthless business deals she'd been involved in. She was also married to, arguably, one of Australia's greatest movie stars.

She didn't offer her hand to Jenny. 'Constable Radford, what the hell are you doing here?' Her smile had disappeared, replaced by a scathing, snake-like sneer.

'That's Detective Radford, and I was invited,' Jenny said.

Haley supressed a humourless laugh, then looking to me, her expression changed as if to say, *Of course, she's with you.* She brushed past Jenny and took my hand. 'Now *you* need no introduction at all.'

'How's it goin'?'

Her smile was more of a *how-very-quaint* gesture. After the photographer snapped an impromptu picture of us, Haley noticed someone more important in the crowd and swanned towards them. I realised the twins had slipped away too.

From the hundred or so glittering people present at the party, the person intriguing me the most was Jenny. Although small in stature, her presence seemed to bring people in line, like she was wielding a big stick. Even Benny McGuire looked uncomfortable when she fixed him with her stare.

X

'Stop it,' I whispered when we got a moment between introductions.

'Stop what?'

'You know.'

'You mean watching the scum squirm.' She grinned. 'I thought you'd enjoy it.'

'That's the trouble, I am.'

Two more glasses of Champagne were thrust into our hands. 'Is there any chance of a beer instead, mate?' I asked the young waiter.

'Sure, what would you like?'

'What have you got?'

He reeled off a list of beers, none of which I'd ever heard of. Noticing my unimpressed expression, he added, 'Four X?'

'That'll do.' I handed him back the Champagne.

'Make that two,' Jenny said, doing the same.

A tray of puffed pastry things floated by us but wasn't going to stop, so I gently tapped the waitress's arm, grabbed a couple and a napkin. 'Uh ... is there any ketchup?'

'No, sorry.'

'Alright, listen, when the sausage rolls and pies come out, make a beeline for me, eh. And don't forget the sauce.'

The music had been surprisingly good, a mix of eighties and more modern stuff. Jenny and I were trapped in a one-sided conversation with the Goldsmith brothers. Surrounded by the three men, we were learning all about their growing real estate empire, the success of the racehorse they owned, and the specs of the new multimillion-dollar boats they had on order. Typical of the evening, really. Thankfully, there was a welcome distraction when the music died down. Everyone turned to see Monroe standing on a raised platform at the far end of the pool, a microphone in his hand.

'Ladies and gentlemen, I'd like to thank you all for being here for this very special occasion on this wonderful, wonderful Gold Coast evening.'

Loud applause and wolf whistling followed.

'Of course, we all know why we're here.'

All heads turned in my direction.

'We're here because of one man.'

More applause, but this time directed at me. Jenny joined in, but I could tell from her smirk that her admiration was tongue-in-cheek.

'Ladies and gentlemen, I'd like you all to join me in welcoming on stage the person we will be forever indebted to, the saviour of the Gold Coast, Detective Inspector Scott Stephens.'

What?

The applause was wild, with cheers and grunting cat calls. Jenny's smirk was spilling over into a full grin. I headed towards the platform, but realising I still had a beer in my hand, I turned back and handed it to Jenny.

'Go get 'em, detective,' she said sarcastically.

The crowd parted for me, hands patting me on the back as I made my way through. Stepping up to the platform, I was relieved when I realised Monroe wasn't about to relinquish the microphone.

'Now as we all know, he's a man of few words, so I'm not going to embarrass him. Scott, we just wanted to show our gratitude tonight and give thanks to you.'

More applause.

'There will be an announcement to the press tomorrow, and in a week's time there will be an official ceremony.' Experienced at working a crowd, Monroe paused for effect.

'But tonight, I'm delighted to inform you in advance. Detective Inspector Scott Stephens, I hereby grant you the Key to the City of the Gold Coast.'

This time the applause seemed to go on and on.

Monroe thrust the microphone into my hand.

A sick feeling took over my stomach. How long was I going to allow this to continue? In hindsight, I should have ended it right there and then. I should have asked the question that if this party

X

was in my honour, how come none of my friends were present? The growing pit in my stomach was from a realisation far greater than that. All talk that evening, and for the last two days, had been about the Gold Coast and its grateful inhabitants, but not a single person had asked me about the investigation tonight. Nobody was spending a thought for the victims, and no one was interested if Binks was innocent or not.

I needed to end this.

31

There was no need to make a scene, I just needed to get out of there. Jenny didn't have a problem with us leaving. It was her who called the Uber. Three minutes later, we were climbing into a Toyota Camry outside Monroe's house.

'OAM. Really?' she said as the car whisked us away.

When Monroe had handed me the microphone, all I did was thank him politely, and thank everyone for coming – the best man speech yet again. Then I'd paused, as my mind negotiated the idea of just coming clean in front of everyone, telling them what a joke this whole thing really was. As if sensing an impending scene, Police Commissioner Singleton stepped onto the platform, took the microphone from my hand, and announced he'd be putting me forward for the Australian Police Medal. As if not to be outdone, Premier Angela Brigano joined us to declare she'd be campaigning the prime minister and the governor-general on my behalf to receive this year's prestigious Order of Australia Medal. I was numb. This was me, Scott Stephens. The last thing I'd won was the meat tray at Kirra Beach Hotel.

Jenny had set the destination for Cavil Avenue, and with little traffic it took only a few minutes to get there from Sovereign Island.

Surfers was busier than I'd seen it in a long time. It seemed the night life was back already. We realised we were both

X

starving. The sausage rolls had never appeared. Some party. 'Fancy a kebab?'

'Gee, you really know how to treat a girl, don't you?'

'What do you mean? I just took you to Elton John's party.'

'I can't believe that place, those people. The backbone of the Gold Coast. God help us.'

We decided we needed something a bit more substantial, so ended up in line outside El Restaurante de Mexicano. When the mostly young couples in the queue saw me, they insisted on letting us go to the font of the line, shaking my hand, patting me on the back and thanking me. Miguel, the maître d', welcomed us with open arms.

'*Buenos Notchas Senor, Senora*, come, come inside,' he said, shaking my hand vigorously. '*Es mucho honourably me Amigo.*' He showed us to a table for two. We ordered two bottles of Dos Equis. While we waited for our drinks, a stream of kitchen staff, including the chef, approached our table, shaking my hand one-by-one. A part of me was starting to get used to this. Would it end when people found out the truth? Would the coast return to lockdown if it were made public that the killer could still be out there? Could I really be responsible for that happening?

'Penny for them,' Jenny said across the table.

'Oh, I was just, you know ... contemplating.'

'Is there anything you want to tell me?'

I took a sip of my beer. 'Maybe.'

A pretty waitress interrupted and took our order.

'I'm sensing you've got something to get off your chest,' Jenny said after the waitress breezed away.

I nodded thoughtfully. 'Maybe.'

She narrowed her eyes. 'But it's more than just the investigation, I'm guessing.'

'What do you mean?'

'You've got me intrigued. You're a good-looking bloke, early forties, no relationship that I know of?'

I gave a dismissive little shake of the head.

'You're living in a house with your school mates. A bachelor pad, really? You're not twenty years old, Scott.'

'So?'

'I've done a bit of digging.'

'You've checked me out?'

'Of course, I'm a detective, remember?' She took a sip of her beer. 'You're from Essendon. A promising footy player at school and for the Essendon Bombers under 15s. Your coach reported to the local rag that he expected you to go all the way. So, with a promising career in front of you, you arrived in Queensland at the age of fourteen and never played again.'

'So? It happens.'

'That's right, it does.' She took another sip of beer, 'but usually down to an injury. I couldn't find any record of you being injured.'

Our food arrived and soon the table was filled with plates of steaming hot Mexican food delivered by not just our waitress, but all the staff. The chef had decided to supply us with every dish on the menu.

'Wow, I could get used to this,' Jenny said, randomly tucking in.

'Have you been here before?' My attempt at changing the subject was a bit lame.

'No, must be new,' she spoke with a mouth full of food. 'I can't remember what was here before. Can you?'

I couldn't, but that was because it had been many years since I'd seen Surfers Paradise as a place for socialising. Like most locals, I stayed away.

'So, you were about to tell me why you gave up the footy.'

'Was I?'

'The last game you played was against the Hawthorn under 15s, it was the night …'

X

I was glad she didn't continue. Nobody had ever asked me about that night before. Even Elvis knew it was taboo.

But then she did. '… the night your mother died.'

I suddenly lost my appetite. I waved over the waitress and asked for the bill.

'No, no, *Senor, la comida es del Casa.*' The food was on the house.

'Scott, I'm sorry. I didn't mean to upset you.'

Miguel appeared, his face beaming. Seeing all the leftover food, he insisted we take it home.

'All right.' There was no argument from me. Forget saving the Gold Coast from financial ruin and bringing Australia's most feared serial killer to justice, this one act would raise my status higher than that of Superman's with Elvis and Tetley.

'Scott?' Jenny said as we headed towards the beach, me laden with doggy bags.

'Look, my private life has got nothing to do with anyone. It belongs to me.'

'I was just trying to get to know you.'

'You're working, that's what you're doing, Jenny.'

'I'm sorry. Old habits.' She placed a hand on my shoulder, and we stopped walking. 'Do you forgive me?'

The machoism, the chauvinistic disposition and being 'one of the boys' were just pieces of the same mask I wore on a daily basis. Only I knew it, or at least I hoped so. I thought I'd done a pretty good job of hiding my true feelings over the years, but the charade I'd been unwillingly party to over the last few days wasn't so different to the sham I'd been living for most of my life. I'd been in the police force long enough to be familiar with the science of psychology, and although I'd never felt the need to enlist the help of a shrink, I knew exactly what the diagnosis would be after the first session. I had bottled up issues I was unwilling to face, and I'd been carrying them around with me all these years. Perhaps it would have been different if I'd had family to share the burden with. I'd never know. I'd been estranged from my dad and my brother for years. But I couldn't blame them, I was the one to blame.

I guess I'd always subconsciously known I needed someone to confide in, but was Jenny Radford that person? Was she a friend or just a colleague? There was something, however, beneath that tough façade that excited me. Something familiar. Something that put me at ease when I was in her presence. I'd never felt like this before. I needed to regroup, pull myself together and decide what I was going to do.

32

9 September
I'd always been interested in the local area and its history. Kirra Point is still regarded by many as one of Australia's premier surf breaks. Although, against the protests of local surfers, conditions changed dramatically in 1972 when Gold Coast City Council decided to build a groyne between Kirra and Coolangatta to prevent sand erosion on Coolangatta Beach. It was a disastrous decision and saw the breaks shift two kilometres south to Snapper Rocks. Until then, there'd been a surf culture in the Kirra area like nowhere else in the world. What is now Musgrave Street was little more than a dirt track with house blocks fronting the shoreline. In the 50s and early 60s, the campsite that used to run along the beachfront, heading north from the surf club to Haig Street, would have been populated by young hip surfies living in VW Kombis, panel vans and tents, spending everyday surfing, drinking, getting high, and living the dream.

All that was gone now, but you could still get a good wave off the point most days. Perhaps not quite the World Surf Championship standard you could expect at the overcrowded Snapper, but good enough for yours truly.

Padding around the point in bare feet, just on daybreak, surfboard under one arm and wetsuit peeled down to my waist, was once a daily ritual, but not so much these days. I didn't get out as much since moving up from uniform to the detective division. There was a time when my boards were religiously replaced every six months. The one I had now was three years old.

As I walked past the old pavilion, one of the only three surfers already out there raised his hand and waved. It was Chilly, my barber. A few minutes later I was alongside him, both sitting on our boards, gently bobbing up and down waiting for the next set.

'Here he is. The man of the moment,' Chilly said, leaning off his board and offering a wet hand.

I didn't even know his real name, but I got on all right with Chilly. He was laid back, chilled – hence the nickname. I often imagined him as how the surfy dudes in this area would have been back in the day. But I wasn't really looking for companionship that morning; I wanted to be alone, I needed to think. I reluctantly shook his hand.

'Didn't think you'd be slumming it down this end of the coast now, mate.'

I ignored him as the first wave of a new set rolled in. We let it pass under us.

'What with all your new buddies.'

'Leave it out, Chill.'

'The Gold Coast's newest socialite.'

The second wave of the set rolled in. Chilly wasn't going for it, so I did, lying on my board and launching myself forward. Not the perfect wave, but I caught it just right, and boy did it feel good.

X

I'd decided to get into the office early. There was something I was missing, something unseen that was bugging the crap out of me – like the piece of apple stuck between your teeth that you just couldn't get rid of. With a cup of takeaway coffee, I began to sift slowly through the photographs of the victims at the crime scenes, pulling out the full-body frontal shots of each. When I had all eight, I spread them out side-by-side.

Whoever had done this had gone to great effort to ensure each scene was identical. He'd obviously derived a system that began

X

from the moment of leaving his house to arriving at the scene, waiting in the shadows for his victim, committing the horrendous act, then making his escape without once being seen.

Sitting back in my chair, sipping lukewarm coffee, I pictured Lawrence Binks. Had he driven to each scene in his mother's Nissan? Would he already be wearing the tracksuit? Was the knife stored in his pocket, or in the glove box perhaps? Did he park the car the same distance to the next location as he had the previous one, lock it, then head quickly off with his head down, but not too rushed as to bring attention to himself? If so, both he and the vehicle would have been picked up on CCTV from at least one of the scenes. And yet, after scanning all the footage in the areas, there had been no sign of him or the car.

Although I suspected the killer didn't know the victims, he knew it was just a matter of time before they came along because he'd familiarised himself with the areas and the comings and goings. Each confrontation took place like clockwork. The victim would be startled, but before she had a chance to scream, she'd already be bleeding out. Clutching at her throat, her legs would buckle, and she'd fall in on herself – not backwards like the photographs would suggest, but down on her knees. The blood patterns on each scene suggested this. Then she was laid out with the pools of blood at her feet. Once again, the act would be exactly the same every time. Always the same.

Prior to the attempted arrest of Binks, the scenario put forward by profilers was that this was the work of an individual suffering from a common form of OCD. Post arrest and *hey presto*, the weird young man with Asperger's syndrome fits the bill, and it's an open and shut case. Or so everybody, especially the Gold Coast mayor, the police commissioner and my boss would like to believe.

The image of Binks's bedroom came to mind. The model aircrafts hanging from the ceiling – each the same, but a little different. The broken patterns in the way the T-shirts had been placed in his drawers, the shoes in the wardrobe, the tracksuits hanging back-to-back, inside out, nothing was the same.

Swallowing a mouthful of coffee, I hastily sat forward in my chair and looked down at the photographs of the crime scenes. Identical – purposely so. This was the absolute opposite behaviour to Lawrence Binks. His disorder didn't allow him the comfort of uniformity in any way or form. If he'd killed those girls, each scene would have been slightly different. That would have been his MO. I scanned the photographs for what must have been the twentieth time, looking for anything at all that would differentiate them – but there was nothing. The killer who had committed these horrendous crimes had OCD, not Asperger's.

I needed to speak with Ripley immediately.

33

'Good morning, Scott.' Ripley rose from his desk. 'What happened to you last night? I didn't see you leave.' He shook my hand and showed me to the vacant chair.

'Oh, I slipped away. Tired.'

'Yes, it can be overwhelming.' He sat back down. 'OAM eh? Goodness me. Well deserved. I'll be seconding the nomination for the Australian Police Medal and—'

'Let me just stop you there, sir.' I shifted butt cheeks. Bradley had insisted I wear one of the new suits. He'd suggested the tan one. I'd decided on the black. It was made from wool and was a little itchy. 'Binks wasn't the killer!'

'What?'

'In the 120 hours since I was promoted and put in charge of this case, I've only spent about an hour of that time actually being a detective. I've used that hour productively.'

'The case is closed. Surely you're wasting your time?'

'No, sir. The case isn't closed, as you well know. The investigation is still very much open.'

'But you've found the killer.' His voice was raised and a little shaky. 'All the evidence led us to him. And he's dead, end of story.'

'I found nothing of the kind. It was Gardner who brought us the tip-off. Where is he, by the way? I haven't seen him since we left Binks's house.'

'He's on vacation. Don't worry about him.' He was shaking as he changed the subject. 'Now we've got you scheduled to fly down to Sydney this afternoon for your interview with *60 Minutes*.'

'What? Nobody told me anything about going to Sydney?'

'Bloody Foster. He was supposed to give you the itinerary. That boy really isn't working out, is he?'

'Bradley's doing all right.' He'd probably forgotten to mention the Sydney thing due to being overcome with anxiety when I'd told him what I was going to do. Like everyone else, he was sure Binks was the killer and the case was closed.

'I'm not so sure about that. So what time are you leaving for Brisbane?'

'Brisbane?'

'ABC Queensland? He didn't tell you about that either?'

'No?'

He inhaled loudly through his nose, 'You better get going. Your interview is scheduled for 11.'

'I'm not going anywhere. I'll be staying here and continuing with the investigation.'

'No, you will not!' His tone, an octave lower, was more of a growl. He fixed me with a headmaster stare. 'You'll be going to Brisbane where you'll be interviewed by ABC before going to lunch with Joe Collins, the Brisbane mayor. Then you'll be back down the coast for 5.00 pm to catch a flight to Sydney from Coolangatta Airport.'

'Okay. I'll continue with the interviews. In fact, that might be a good idea.'

Now it was Ripley's turn to shift in his seat.

'I'll be able to get the word out that the killer is still at large.'

Ripley's face turned as red as the feature wall in his office. 'Why are you doing this?' he yelled.

'Doing what? My Job? The role you forced on me? Being a detective?'

'All you have to do is exactly what we—' He faltered, then

corrected himself. 'What *I* say. The case is closed, and everyone is grateful to you. VERY GRATEFUL!'

'Do you know the thing that's worrying me the most, sir?' I remained calm and respectful.

'No, what's that?' There was no curiosity in his question.

'I've informed you of my belief that Binks was an innocent man, but instead of asking me to elaborate my findings, you've gone on the defensive. Why is that?'

'How dare you?' He jumped up and circled his desk until he was standing over me. Leaning into my ear he said, 'Five days ago, you were nobody.'

Like slowly revving an engine, I could tell that my calm, agreeable nods were pissing him off.

'You're going to Brisbane, and then you're going to Sydney, and you're going to tell everybody that Binks was the killer, and the case is closed. Do you understand?'

'No, I don't understand.' I stood and turned until we were face to face. 'I don't understand why you aren't concerned that we've shot and killed an innocent man and that the killer is still out there. Don't you realise he could strike again at any time?'

'Binks *was* the killer,' he replied, slowly and deliberately, like he was trying to drill his words into me. 'The case is closed. You're a hero. How ungrateful do you want to be?'

'Ungrateful for what? I've done nothing, except be paraded around like a prize pony. Is this what you wanted? A puppet?'

'Don't put yourself down.' His sympathetic tone told me he was changing tack. He wandered back to his chair and sat down. 'You're a good detective, Scott. I wouldn't have recommended you if I didn't believe that.'

'Well thank you, I appreciate that. Which is why I'm hoping you'll understand I'm only doing what you hired me to do.'

'You've done more than we could ever have asked.' He kept inadvertently slipping into the 'we' tense.

I imagined the little group of conspirators – Monroe, Singleton and Ripley, possibly alone on Monroe's boat moored off South Stradbroke Island – scheming ways to put an end to the crisis that was gripping the Gold Coast. Would framing an innocent man be on the agenda? In a way, it wasn't just Binks who'd been framed, it was me too. All I had to do was act grateful for the opportunity I'd been given, appreciative of all the accolades and wonderful experiences coming my way, keep my mouth shut and go with the flow. But that wasn't my way. Still calm, I remained standing. 'Okay. I'll do the interviews.'

A wave of relief seemed to undulate through him, working its way down from his head and softening the tension in his neck and the rest of his body. 'Good man, I knew you'd see sense.'

'So, do you want me to go through my findings with you first, before I share them with the media, or …?'

As if I'd flicked a switch, the tension returned. 'What? Have you not listened to a word I've said?'

'Loud and clear, sir. Loud and clear!'

'What's that supposed to mean?'

'It means I'm in charge of this case. And with all due respect, it means I'll be the one to decide when it's over.'

'But you—'

I was bordering on insubordination but was past caring. 'I've instructed Bradley Foster to get the team back together for a meeting.' I checked my watch, 'They should be in the incident room about now. I'd also like yourself present please.'

He appeared stunned, so I continued before he had the chance to argue.

'I'll also need you to recall Gardner back from his "holiday" as soon as possible please.' Another source of gnawing frustration had been Gardner's report. I hadn't even had a chance to interview him before he'd disappeared.

'Do you have any questions, sir?'

34

Detectives Roper and Bannister had returned to Sydney. I didn't request they be recalled. In fact, there wasn't really a need for the team at all. If the case hadn't been so big, I would have preferred going it alone, or maybe just having Jenny as my partner. I certainly didn't want Gardner working with us, but I needed him back so I could question him. Don Mason and Steve Bishop were good detectives, but basically all they'd be doing was going over the same details of the case, checking every witness report, medical reports and everything else associated with the investigation, looking for anything that may have been overlooked.

There'd been no evidence against Binks apart from Gardner's tip-off. Then, as if by magic, we'd suddenly had everything we needed to convict him. As much as I didn't want them wasting too much time on Binks, having them out searching for clues for the real killer would have been my preference, I'd instructed them to start with him anyway, just so I could prove his innocence. The information we required was there in one form or another, I was sure of it. We just needed to find it.

'Document everything, double-check witness reports and speak to everyone involved again.' The lack of enthusiasm was obvious by their what-the-fuck expressions. They didn't take notes. I wasn't sure if this was due to the lack of motivation or because they were just so familiar with the case. Constables Dee Forester and Wayne McDonald, on the other hand, still at that early stage of their careers, keen to impress, motivated by the possibility of promotion if they did good, scribbled down everything I said. A lot of superiors would look down on them, give them the menial jobs and treat them like gofers, but not me. I appreciated their enthusiasm and would tap into it.

Dale Mason was an experienced detective and worked well on his own, so I was happy to leave him to his own devices.

When Jacob Tyler returned to Sydney, we'd lost our profiler. Bradley was a first-year psychology student using home study, so I expected Ripley to object when I suggested he take Tyler's place, but he didn't. Instead, he sat at the back of the room, quietly scrutinising me through narrowed eyes.

It was a double whammy for Bradley. He blushed like a schoolgirl and lowered his head when I informed him that not only would he be the new profiler on the case, but he'd also be partnering with Jenny and myself. Although our personalities were polar opposites, I enjoyed his company, He was intelligent, and like the two constables, eager to please.

Jenny Radford put up her hand. 'I understand the theory of Asperger's syndrome having the opposite symptoms to OCD, but is that all we have?'

It was a question I should have been prepared for. There was some medical information to back up my views, but my theory was still thin. 'It's enough to shine doubt over the case, and it's important enough for us to continue asking questions until we're absolutely sure of Binks's guilt.'

'But with all due respect,' Dale Mason interjected, 'we pretty much *are* sure that Binks was guilty.' He scanned the room as if rallying the troops.

'What does "pretty much sure" mean?'

'A hundred per cent sure then.'

'I don't think you are, or you would have said so.'

X

'But what about the evidence?' Dale continued. 'The victim's blood on the tracksuit, the knife?'

There was a part of my theory that I had yet to share with anyone. It was certainly out there, and without any proof whatsoever, it was going to be difficult for me to push. 'I believe the evidence may have been planted at the scene!'

A communal gasp erupted. Ripley rose to his feet and marched towards me. Leaning in close, his whisper was that familiar growl. 'Wrap this meeting up and be in my office in two minutes.' Red-faced, he stormed out of the room.

The onlookers sat wide-eyed and quiet until Dale Mason said, 'Surely even *you* wouldn't throw up an accusation like that without any proof?'

I wasn't quite sure what he meant by 'even you,' but it was obvious the question was a loaded one. I didn't have any proof, and everyone in the room knew it. I guess they just needed to hear me say it to be sure. 'No, I don't have any proof yet. It's just a theory.'

'Just a theory?' Jenny said.

In my mind, everything had made sense. Binks was a patsy. The evidence had been planted to bring the case to an end. But when I put it into words, it sounded exactly how it really was – an unsubstantiated theory that probably should have been tested more before being shared.

'So, who planted the evidence?' Jenny asked.

'That's for you guys to find out.'

X

When I knocked and entered Ripley's office, he was on the phone.

'Okay.' Lowering his voice, he turned away. 'I've got to go. Don't worry, I'll sort it out.' He put down the phone and rose from his desk.

'You wanted to see me, sir?'

'What the hell do you think you're doing?'

'Not sure what you mean, sir.'

'You know exactly what I mean. Why are you making trouble?'

'Are you asking me why I'm doing my job?'

'Your job. Ha! Your job is to be grateful for what fate has bestowed upon you.' He gave a sickly chuckle. 'We're certainly not going to reopen this investigation on this ridiculous hunch of yours.'

'I'm the detective in charge of the case.'

'You were never in charge of this case, you *idiot!*'

I wasn't shocked by his outburst, it just confirmed what I'd known all along.

The chuckle advanced into a patronising laugh. 'Do you really think you'd be able lead a case like this?'

'No, I don't. That's what I've been trying to tell everybody since you put me in charge.'

This seemed to stun him.

'I've known what you bastards were up to right from the beginning. I'm not the dumb cunt you think I am.'

'Oh yes, you are. That's why we chose you.'

'We?'

'Me. *I* chose you.'

'Binks was innocent, and you know it.'

'Binks was the killer.' His anger was high pitched and irate. 'The case is closed!' He sat down at his desk, his shaking hands betraying his spurious calmness. 'You're not having the team back. You're being reassigned. I'll have details of a new domestic case for you shortly. There'll be no more interviews. I've cancelled everything for today and everything that was scheduled for the next few weeks. You're forbidden from talking to the press in any form or manner.' He momentarily paused, as if anticipating my reaction. 'Officially, you'll be wrapping up the finer details of the

X

investigation over the next two days. Obviously, you'll be called for the court hearings, whenever they are, but that will just be a formality. I'm sorry to say you fucked up, son. You had the world at your fingertips, and you blew it.'

There was another awkward pause as we locked eyes.

'Now get out of my sight.' He averted his eyes to his desk as if he had more pressing engagements to attend to.

'Thank you, sir.' I spoke calmly, but my angry mind finished the sentence. *We'll see about that, dickhead!*

35

By lunchtime, I was beginning to question my motivation. With no new evidence and no leads to follow, all I could do was sift carefully through the intel we already had in the hope that something had been missed the first time around. It didn't take long to realise there was nothing. There'd been no new instructions yet from Ripley, so until there were, it was business as usual. I was desperately hoping the team would find something new, but in my gut, I knew that wasn't going to happen. What the hell was I going to do?

At 2.30 pm, I was sitting in the office of Binks's shrink, Doctor Miriam Shard. At first, she remained reserved, hiding behind the patient confidentiality clause, but when I shared my theory about Binks's habits being the opposite to the killer's, she became interested and started to open up.

'That's correct,' she leaned forward in her chair, 'Lawrence would never arrange anything in that way. He couldn't.'

'Would you testify to that in court?'

'Of course!' There was no hesitation. 'If that poor young man was innocent, which I'm pretty sure he was, then I'll make sure the authorities know about it.'

At last, I had someone who believed me. The relief replenished a little of my waning confidence. The evidence was still thin, but it was a start, and I had a credible witness at least.

I'd only been able to manage a quick meeting with the doctor

X

during a break between patients, but the few minutes she'd allocated me were plenty. As I strolled back to my car in the basement of the Southport Park Shopping Centre, my mobile phone rang. It was Ripley.

'The mayor wants to see you right away.' No salutations, just business. 'You're to go straight to his house. He'll be waiting for you there.'

'No worries.'

'This is probably your last chance to put things right, detective. For your own sake, don't stuff it up.'

X

Monroe's street was deserted and quiet. Although the property had a high wall built around the front and sides, in daylight I got a much better view of the largest house on the island. I'd also done some research. The hacienda-style seventeen-bedroom mansion, built in 2008, sat on a triple waterfront block. Its easy access to the seaway, fifty-five-metre boat jetty, and even a helicopter pad, went some way to fuelling the initial gossip from the surrounding neighbours of its true purpose during its construction. The fact that its mystery Central American owner purchased the land and built the house without even setting foot in Australia ensured that the increasing gossip soon ripened into folklore. Even though Pablo Escobar was long dead and El Chapo behind bars, this only fed the rumours as to why it had sat empty until Monroe bought it for thirty-six million dollars in 2017. It had been on the market for forty-five million. Back then, the property was open to the street. The first thing Monroe did was have the perimeter wall built.

I approached the antique oriental doors that had been repurposed for the gateway. There was a plaque over it that I hadn't noticed the last time I was there, it read *Palazzo del*

Falco – Palace of the Hawk. I pressed the bell icon on the intercom touch pad to the right and a voice came from a small speaker almost immediately.

'Yes?'

'Detective Inspector Stephens to see Mr Monroe.'

There was an electrical buzz, followed by a clunk as the concealed lock slid to one side. Although the solid timber door was heavy, it opened effortlessly when I turned the handle.

In daylight, the front garden looked small and sparse, just a lawn, a border of lilly pillies planted inside the perimeter stucco wall, and a path leading to the grand marble entrance.

The front door was open and a short Asian woman, who was obviously the housekeeper or the maid (if there was such a thing nowadays) stood waiting at the top of the steps. She greeted me with a simple bow and gestured for me to enter the property.

Once again, in daylight and without the party goers, I was able to see the property in more detail. The hallway had the clichéd sweeping staircase and marble-clad floors. The space was quite bare except for the chandelier. I followed the housekeeper through the expansive reception room, furnished tastefully with simple bleached timber pieces. The walls were adorned with expensive Australian works of art; I spotted pieces by Brett Whiteley, and a Sidney Nolan. The floors were now a light bleached oak to match the furniture.

A row of glass bifold doors that extended across the entire back wall was open, allowing a gentle easterly breeze to enter the house.

We went out to the back of the house. In the bubbling water of a large circular spa at the end of the pool, sat Julian Monroe up to his chest, sipping a large whiskey. Wearing sunglasses and looking every inch the ageing playboy, he was staring past the forty-plus-metre yacht that sat to the left of the large jetty, and across the Broadwater towards Stradbroke Island.

'Detective Inspector Stephens, sir,' the housekeeper announced.

X

Momentarily startled, Julian turned to face us without getting up. 'Ahh, Scotty. It's great to see you.'

'Good to see you too, sir.'

'Come on in, join me.' He patted the top of the bubbling water with his free hand. 'Two more of these please, Rosie.' Jingling the half empty glass.

'Not for me, thanks. I'm on duty.'

'No, you're not. Two more, Rosie.'

Rosie backed away, her head lowered like she was being dismissed by the Queen of England.

'Come on, don't be shy.' Monroe grinned. 'The water is amazing.'

'I'll pass, thanks.' I decided there and then that calling him 'sir' wasn't working for me.

'Okay, pull up a pew.' He pointed to one of the outdoor chairs a few feet away.

I grabbed one, dragged it across the terracotta tiles and plonked myself down at the side of the spa.

'What's on your mind?' I needed to treat him as an equal and stay in control, because I knew exactly why I was there.

'Ripley tells me you're still interested in the case.' His expression exhibited curious amusement.

'That's right. There are a few loose ends—'

'No, there aren't!'

'Yes, there are!'

'No! I'm telling you, there *aren't!*' The politician grin didn't hide the anger in his voice.

Not feeling the need to respond, I left him hanging.

'You just don't understand what's at stake here, Scott.'

Rosie arrived with two more double scotches. She handed one to Monroe, then offered the other to me.

'No, thanks. I'm on duty.'

She shot Monroe a sideways glance.

Monroe nodded and waved her away. While sipping his drink, he considered me for a few moments.

'Did you know that after all these years, Council has finally approved the cruise terminal and a new casino, as well as a hotel and holiday resort complex that will make Barangaroo look like Redland Bay?'

'How could I not? Your daughter was on the news this morning banging on about it.' The redevelopment of the Gold Coast spit was already underway. The COVID-19 pandemic hadn't really affected construction of the multibillion-dollar development – slowed somewhat in the planning stages perhaps, but it had continued to move forward.

The familiar sound of a jet ski bouncing across the water, its engine throbbing with each skip, brought a frown to Julian's brow. He took another sip of Scotch and we watched as the first of two identical crafts approached. The one in front had a large rooster tail spraying from its back end. As well as the rider, there was a young girl on the back wearing a yellow bikini, screaming with each bounce of the craft. It turned and headed straight for Julian's jetty, but just before impact, veered sharply and pulled up on a tiny strip of beach. The second jet ski followed, only without the dramatic approach, and a lot slower. On it just a single rider.

Julian sat very still, as if he were hoping they wouldn't see us. The spaced-out girl I remembered from the party did. After climbing from the jet ski, she headed straight for the pool, dived in and swam to the edge of the spa.

'Mr Monroe.'

'Cindy.'

'Hey Dad, where's Mum?' asked Dillon as he approached. He wore boardshorts and retro Ray-Bans, his torso glistening with ocean spray, his blond hair, yellowed by the salt water. Noticing me, he frowned.

X

'G'day, mate,' I said casually, 'good to see you again.'

I was ignored as if I wasn't there.

'I don't know. Where would she usually be this time of the day?' Monroe replied, looking away into the distance.

The girl smirked.

We were joined by Troy, Dillon's identical twin. My first impression of him when we'd met at the party proved correct. Unlike Dillon, he was shy, his body language slow and unsure. Wearing a quarter-length wetsuit, he didn't speak when he reached the side of the spa. I did notice him look at the chair I was sitting on though, then glance at the table where it belonged. When I'd dragged it over, I'd knocked the other two chairs that were either side a little. Troy marched over to the table and straightened them up.

'Get me another drink, will you, Troy Boy?' Julian held up his empty glass.

Troy took the glass and padded towards the house.

'Get me one too, eh mate?' Dillon called after his brother. 'What would you like, babe?' he asked the girl.

'A Negroni,' she said, loud enough for Troy to hear. Then she lifted herself from the water, slid over the partition wall and into the spa. Dillon jumped in too.

'Do you mind, you two? We're having a private discussion here,' Monroe complained.

'Don't mind us, old man,' Dillon grinned. He shot me a smirking glance, like a mischievous child who was showing off. 'Are you taking the boat out this weekend?'

'What?'

'If not, can I take it over to Tipplers?'

Julian stared at his son in disbelief and seemed to forget I was present. 'Are you fucking kidding me?'

Dillon shook his head and smiled. The girl's giggle was beginning to get on my nerves.

'You seriously think I'd let you take my nine-million-dollar boat out on your own?'

'Yeah. Why not?'

'You're delusional, boy.' For a moment, I thought Julian was about to reach out of the water and deliver a backhanded slap across the girl's cheek as she continued to snigger. Instead, he rose to his full height. The water level was now lower than his waist. He was naked. He climbed from the spa and reached for a silk kimono that lay on the ground.

'We'll continue inside, detective. This way.' He marched towards the house, just as Troy appeared with a tray of drinks. Julian grabbed his glass and I followed him into the house. Glancing over my shoulder, I noticed Troy place the drinks by the spa, then hastily replace the chair I'd been sitting on.

36

In the southern wing of the house, contemporary style gave way to dark wood and plush, deep-red carpets. Through a double Art Deco-styled doorway with a brass frame and smoked glass, I spied rows of leather recliner chairs that led down a sloping floor to a decent-sized movie screen. We were in a space that resembled an old-fashioned theatre lobby. There was a circular, tube-shaped, glass elevator in the corner.

'Kids, eh?' Monroe said. We were now in the lift, which rose at a terribly slow rate.

'How old are the boys now?' I continued the conversation casually, attempting to avoid an awkward silence.

'Twenty-one this year.'

'They're both very different.'

'Troy's slow, stupid, while at the same time intellectually brilliant. Dillon's the opposite – fast, flash, not intelligent by any means, but still clever, if you know what I mean.'

Just like his dad, I thought. 'And Haley?'

'Ah, she's the genius of the family.'

Monroe's study occupied the top floor of a square turret that stood one floor higher than the building's southern end. The tower's footprint was about the size of an average family home. We stepped from the lift into what appeared to be an office/rumpus room with a bar. Monroe's footy memorabilia and trophies adorned the walls and cabinets.

'Sure you won't have a drink, Scotty? There's really no need to be so formal here,' Monroe said as he slid behind the bar.

'I'm fine, thanks.'

'Suit yourself.' He gestured with his free hand for me to take a seat on one of the bar stools.

I checked my watch. It was 3.30 pm. 'So, what's this about? I haven't got much time.'

'Of course you have. You've got all the time in the world.' He sipped his drink and watched me again through guarded eyes.

'I haven't. I—'

'Oh for God's sake, man. What are you trying to do?' He slammed his drink down onto the bar.

'I'm not sure what you mean.'

'Look around you, Scott.' He waved his hand through the air like a magician. 'Do you like what you see?'

Rather than answering, I gave him my attempt at the unnerving detective stare.

'This is all in your league now. You've made the bigtime!' He finished his drink in one gulp, reached for a bottle of Glenfiddich from a shelf, and poured another. 'You want a million-dollar boat? You've got it. A beachfront house? A Porsche, girls, travel? It's all there for the taking my friend because you've earned it.'

'What if I don't want any of that?' I said, keeping it calm and in control.

Monroe's patronising chuckle was a series of short bursts from his nose. 'Of course you do! Everybody does.'

'Binks was innocent.'

'Binks was a vicious serial killer who not only murdered eight young women during an unprecedented three weeks of terror, but he almost single-handedly brought the coast to its knees.' He came around the bar, placed a hand on my shoulder and gently squeezed it. 'And you put an end to all of that, my friend, for which the people of the Gold Coast are very grateful.'

X

'It's a sham. I've known it from the start and I'm kicking myself for allowing it to continue this long.'

His grip tightened on my shoulder.

'You're just not getting it, are you?'

He shook me slightly before withdrawing his hand and returning behind the bar. 'Let me spell it out for you—'

'How about I spell it out for *you*, eh?' I rose from the stool and stepped backwards. 'This is what's going to happen. Not only am I going to prove Binks was innocent, but I'll be requesting an inquiry into why he was framed, and *who* was responsible.'

'Requesting an inquiry? You? You're a clerk. I could have you back in uniform by this time tomorrow.'

'Oh, it'll all come out. Why you needed the case to be solved so quickly. Your daughter's shady dealings over the cruise terminal and everything else you've got your finger in.'

He was openly laughing at me now.

'It won't be too difficult to prove she's only acting on your behalf.'

'Oh dear, Scotty. What a shame. You could have had it all.' He came back around the bar and fronted up to me. 'I didn't get where I am today by dealing with insubordinate little shits like you. Bad enough we've had to even tolerate you over the last few days. You're a joke. Pulled out of the gutter. You were given the golden ticket and you threw it away. Now get the fuck out of my house!'

'No worries.'

I turned and headed for the lift. As the door slowly opened, I looked back at Monroe over my shoulder. 'And thanks for confirming my theory, by the way. You've been extremely helpful.'

X

I was back at the station in plenty of time for our team meeting. A takeaway burger and a coffee had replenished the energy I'd wasted with Monroe.

At 6.00 pm, the team filed into the incident room. It came as no surprise they'd unearthed nothing new. The detached expressions told me the biggest question they'd been asking themselves all day was, 'Why the hell are we wasting our time with this?'

Once again, Ripley sat at the back of the room, listening, not engaging in any way. However, I did notice him shuffle uncomfortably in his seat when I shared the doctor's opinion with the group. When I added that she would testify in court as a witness for the defence, he stood up and left the room.

'So, what now, boss?' Dale Mason asked. 'There's not a lot for us to do tomorrow?'

'Let's regroup in the morning. Something'll come up. It's just a matter of time, I'm sure of it.'

37

After a busy twelve-hour shift, Tracey Porter headed towards her car as quickly as her weary legs would allow. Like most staff at Robina Hospital, she didn't use the expensive hospital carpark, choosing instead to find a free space as close as possible in the surrounding suburb. She'd been fortunate that morning, finding a place in the Cbus Super Stadium overflow at the back of the hospital. It was 8.00 pm by the time she left her ward after a long-winded handover, but at least she didn't have to walk far. She had five days off now until her next shift and she was looking forward to doing very little.

Tracey lifted her pace and opened her bag as she walked, searching inside for her car keys. Still rifling through her things when she reached the car, she was startled by a voice.

'Hey babe.'

She looked up from her bag, alarmed.

A blow to her neck, like a slice of wind, was followed instantly by another from the opposite side. For a split second there was no pain, only heat in her neck as she squinted to see a dark figure standing in front of her. Suddenly her head jolted backwards, and she felt a massive surge of pressure from either side of her neck. Hot, metal-tasting liquid filled her mouth and spewed from her lips. She let go of her bag and lifted her hands to her neck, but it was like clutching at flumes of gushing hot water. She couldn't breathe, couldn't even gasp. Her head began to throb as the blood drained quickly from her body. A wave of dark crimson lowered over her eyes like a matinee theatre curtain. Dropping to her knees, still clutching at her neck, she fell forward.

By the time she hit the tarmac, she was dead.

X

I'd stuck my neck out. There'd always been an underlying stubbornness within me, apparently something I'd inherited from my dad. During the drive home, the familiar feeling that I was missing something niggled at me again. It was obvious why Monroe wanted to sweep this all under the carpet, his multiple investments were under threat. Regardless of what type of developments were proposed – hotels, casinos, resorts, the cruise terminal, or even the one-billion-dollar football stadium Monroe was pushing for at Carrara – without the tourist dollar, none of it would happen. The coast would shrink and die.

Although Monroe had officially, and very publicly, taken a step back from his development companies after becoming the mayor, by handing the reins over to his daughter he'd ensured the business remained in the family. Perfectly legal on paper. No doubt the mistakes of his infamous predecessors, Alan Bond and Christopher Skase, had taught him a great deal. But nobody seemed to care, and the Gold Coast was flourishing once more. Over the last few decades, it seemed to have developed its own economy, continuing to grow regardless of what was happening in the rest of the country or the world. COVID-19 had slowed things only momentarily, but the *X* killings had been likened to the dreaded second wave.

Commissioner Singleton was obviously in on it. Meeting the guy didn't dispel for me any of the rumours that he was a dodgy character. His self-important arrogance only reinforced them.

But it was Ripley who had me stumped. Did he really believe

X

Binks was the killer, or was he acting purely on loyalty toward the agenda of his superiors? Or did he too have reasons to make sure the investigation was closed as soon as possible, no matter what? My mind buzzed with questions as I drove down Ruby Street on autopilot. It was the sight of Tetley's Vespa parked outside the house that brought me back to the moment. I pulled up behind it, climbed out of the Dub and headed up the front path. The place was quiet.

Loosening my tie as I padded through the house, I was surprised to see Tetley sitting alone, nursing a stubby in the kitchen.

'Hey, mate.' I threw my car keys on the table and noticed there was another beer, a full one. 'What's going on?'

'It's Elvis. I think there's something up.' He took a nervous swig of his beer.

'What do you mean?'

'He's gone to the pub.'

'Alone?'

Tetley nodded.

'Oh!' A bloke going to the pub on his own wasn't anything unusual, nothing to worry about. But this was Elvis. For him to go off alone meant something was wrong.

'What's happened?'

'I met him here after work. He checked the mail and there was a letter addressed to him. He was fine before he opened it. His usual self, you know.'

'Where's the letter?' I asked, scanning the kitchen.

'D'know. Must have took it with him. He didn't even drink his beer look, or change out of his suit. Just said, "I'm going to the pub."'

Something was definitely wrong. The contents of the letter had pushed all thoughts of Monroe and his entourage from my mind. I grabbed the extra beer, skulled it, and slammed the empty bottle on the table. 'Come on, let's go.'

When we walked around the corner onto Sadie Street, we were met by a welcoming ocean breeze. Normally, this would carry with it the bar chatter and laughter that wafted around the curved Kirra Hotel from the open concertina doors at the front of the building. Tonight, it seemed quiet. We entered the side door as usual. Not only was it quiet, but the bar was empty. I knew where Elvis would be. Sat at one of the pokies, mindlessly feeding it coins. With Tetley behind me, I headed for the bar.

'SURPRISE!'

At the far corner was a small TAB area, not much more than an alcove, its walls adorned with flat screen TVs displaying racing of various kinds from around the country – horses, the trots and dogs. A sea of smiling, bubbling faces spilled from it and surrounded me. Elvis was the leader of the pack.

'Eh mate, I thought you'd never get here!' he yelled over the din, thrusting a beer into my hand.

I was hugged, patted, kissed, and slapped on the back. It took me a moment to work out who all these people were. The bar had instantly gone from silence to a full-on party. As I began to adjust after the initial shock, faces morphed into familiar forms. Johnno, Chilly, all the boys from the morning surfs and the lads from the footy club were present – all the locals of course. Proprietors from the surrounding restaurants – Brian from St Tropicano, Georgio from Pizzeria Magnifico, Des from the chip shop, and Min Shin and Ray from the Thai restaurant were there. Even Beryl and Stan from the surf club had popped over. Bradley and Jenny were the only people present from work. The biggest surprise was when Jenny threw her arms around me and plonked a drunken kiss on my lips.

'She was the first here,' Elvis said in my ear. 'Jeez, she can put it away!'

'Hey, Scotty,' Jenny grinned mischievously.

'Hey Jenny, how's it going?'

X

'Let me get you another drink,' Johnno led her away towards the bar.

'You bastards!' I turned to Elvis and Tetley.

'What?' they said innocently.

'You guys know I don't like surprises.'

'Mate,' Elvis put a hand on my shoulder, 'you've been working hard. You're the king now. I relinquish my crown.' He lowered his voice into a Southern drawl and added, 'Baby ...'

'We knew you'd hate it, of course,' Tetley joined in, 'but seriously, we all just wanted to spend some time with you before you got too important for us, whisked away to the land of bollocks.'

'That's bullshit!'

'I know. So drink ya drink.'

Elvis lowered his gaze to the floor. 'Listen mate ... there is uhm, one thing.' He looked up cautiously and shot a tentative glance towards Tetley.

'We've got another surprise for you,' Tetley said.

'It's not our surprise,' Elvis interjected, 'in fact, we had nothing to do with it.'

'You guys better not have organised a stripper.'

'In the bistro. Go and get it over with now before we get on it,' Elvis said.

38

It took me a while to wade through the crowd of well-wishers. Another drink was thrust into my hand as I passed the bar. Carrying two untouched beers, I finally made it into the bistro. Scanning the room, my eyes were drawn to a small table for two.

The surrounding world suddenly melted away.

Almost dropping the beers, a throb beat at my forehead like a Bali gong, and my chest constricted as if in the grip of a giant python.

Sitting at the table, staring back at me, were my father and my brother.

It was Todd who stood, his smile forced and wary. Dad remained seated, his stare a mixture of biopic squint and caution. He didn't smile.

I was torn between turning and heading back into the bar or making a quick exit out the front of the pub.

Todd approached me. 'G'day, mate. Long time, no see.' He grabbed the two beers. 'Thanks, that's really thoughtful.'

Words didn't come.

Nodding back over his shoulder, he gestured for me to follow him to the table.

Without taking my eyes off my dad, I reluctantly obeyed.

Dad slowly stood and nodded in my direction. 'Son,' was all he was willing to offer, not even a handshake.

The tightness in my chest increased like the snake was constricting.

X

I was fourteen again. Everything I'd achieved, or the lack of, suddenly meant nothing. I was once more that kid who'd fucked up. 'What do *you* guys want?'

Todd placed the drinks on the table and slid one over next to Dad's half empty pot. 'Look what Scotty bought us, Dad.'

The jaw remained fixed as those cold, grey eyes, still locked onto mine, narrowed and probed.

'We thought it was about time we caught up, see how you're getting on,' Todd continued.

'Yeah? Why now?' My words were as hard as my father's stare.

'Come on, mate. We haven't seen you for ages.'

I broke eye contact with my dad. It was achieving nothing. Instead, I switched my attention to Todd. 'That's right. I haven't heard bugger all from you blokes in years. So why are you showing up now?'

Dad pushed away the schooner and took a sip from his pot.

'We've missed you, Scotty. We reckon it's time to put the past behind us.'

My laugh was an automatic response, like a nervous kid in the headmaster's office. 'Like bury the hatchet, you mean? You buried that years ago, mate – in my bloody head.' From my peripheral vision I noticed Elvis and Tetley join us.

'Everything all right, bud?' Elvis asked.

'All good here. Go back to the bar. I'll be there in a minute.'

'You sure?' Tetley asked.

'Yep. Go on.'

They retreated to the bar.

I picked up the beer Dad had slid away from him – my beer – and took a sip. 'So, you just suddenly thought, jeez, we haven't seen old Scotty for a while, I wonder what he's up to these days?'

Todd shrugged, raising his eyebrows, 'Yeah, pretty much.'

'Nothing to do with the fact that I've been in the news over the last few days?'

My brother deflated a little. 'I know what it looks like, mate, but it's not like that.'

'No? What is it then?'

Dad grabbed Todd's arm. 'You're wasting your time, son. I said it was stupid coming here, and I was right.'

'But Dad—'

'He's still just as selfish as he ever was.'

'I'm selfish? Are you kidding me?' I'd never raised my voice to my father before. Even though I was a grown man now, it still felt strange.

Dad rose to his feet.

'Dad, wait.' Todd scooted around the table. 'Scotty, there's something we need to–'

'Forget it, Todd. We're going.' Dad finished his drink, slammed down the glass, and marched towards the exit.

Todd appeared genuinely shaken. 'We need to talk, patch this up.'

'We don't need to do anything of the kind. You can go now. Your daddy's waiting for you.'

'Seriously, mate, we need—'

My mobile rang. The number was Dale Mason's.

Todd shrugged and shook his head in defeat.

I left him standing there and answered the phone as I made my way out into the beer garden.

'Scott, where are you?' His voice was anxious and rushed.

'I'm in Kirra, why? What's up?'

'You're not pissed, are you?'

'No!' I'd only had one stubby earlier and a couple of sips in the pub.

'Get yourself out to Robina Hospital right away. Come off at Exit 79. You'll see the lights.'

'Lights? What are you talking about?'

'There's been another one, Scott. *X* has killed again!'

39

Bradley drove me in the Range Rover. We'd slipped away from the party, leaving Jenny at the pub as she was a little bit wasted. Turning off the highway, we headed down the dark road towards Robina Hospital. A sea of flashing blue and red lights illuminated the sky in the distance like a fairground. We didn't have to show our badges to the two constables manning the roadblock. They waved us straight through, but we had to park some distance from what appeared to be the epicentre because every unit on the Gold Coast, or so it seemed, had been dispatched. There were also three ambulances for some reason, and a fire engine.

'Get this circus cleared,' I instructed Bradley as we marched towards the carpark at the back of the hospital.

In my mind's eye, I could already see what lay ahead. That same expression on the previous victims' faces appeared before my eyes, and I knew I was about to experience it again. The body would be laid out flat, the skin devoid of colour. When I eventually pushed through the crowd of uniforms, that was exactly what I found.

The team was already there – Surfers was closer than Kirra.

'You were right, sir,' Constable Dee Forester said as I knelt by the victim, 'it's definitely *X*.'

You didn't need to be a detective to work that out. Our friend had signed his artwork as usual. Forensics arrived and did a good job of taking over and clearing the scene. Within minutes, the usual tent was erected over the body and the uniformed personnel were replaced with ant-like creatures wearing white hooded jumpsuits and masks. Only my team was allowed to stay within the new boundary of about ten metres squared.

It was important to let them get on with their job. I wasn't one of those cranky old-timers who resented their presence, and I didn't need to spend any more time at the scene. The findings would be exactly the same as on the previous occasions. There'd be no clues and no signs leading us to the killer, but on the very unlikely chance that something had been left behind, these guys would find it. I instructed the team to return to the station immediately for a meeting, but told Constable Wayne McDonald to remain, record everything and report back to us when the scene was eventually cleared, which would be some time yet.

'You were right all along, Scott,' Bradley said as we drove through Robina Parkway.

'I kind of hoped I was wrong.'

'You're amazing.'

'Nah, just a bit stubborn, mate.'

'But everyone else thought it was an open and shut case. Binks was the killer, end of story,' Bradley continued.

'None of that matters. The killings would have continued regardless. I just wish Binks hadn't had to have died.'

'Be killed you mean.'

'Whatever.'

'But what's going to happen now?'

'The case resumes.'

'Will the coast need to go into lockdown?'

'Should do.'

'Hell!'

X

My first point of call was Ripley's office. I was surprised he hadn't been at the scene but seeing him sitting at his desk wearing the same tuxedo he'd worn the night before, I realised he'd obviously been called away from yet another 'very important' function of some kind. His face was grey with scattered scarlet blooms, and he was sweating. His worried expression gave me the impression he was contemplating going up to the roof and jumping off.

'Scott, come in, come in. Take a seat.'

I didn't have time to sit down. I was keen to get back to the team, but I obliged anyway.

'So, we've got a copycat killer now!' It was more of a statement than a question.

I shook my head in disbelief, a nervous smile quivering over my lips. 'No, no copycat. *X* has struck again!'

Ripley jumped to his feet. 'But Binks is dead! This is quite common. A one-off, I'm sure of it.'

Lips pursed, I sat shaking my head slowly as he continued.

'That's what we'll be putting out to the media. You'll tell them there's no need for panic. This was merely the work of an attention seeker who you expect to apprehend very soon, the way you did Binks.'

'Not going to happen, sir.' I rose from the chair and joined him at head height. 'I didn't apprehend Binks, we both know that. I wish I had because he'd still be alive today.'

Ignoring me, while trying unsuccessfully to remain calm, his tremble was more of a low frequency vibration as he rambled on. 'I'll organise a press conference for first thing in the morning. Singleton, yourself and the mayor. We'll make sure—'

'Sir, stop ... look at me.'

He blinked and shook his head erratically as if snapping out of a trance.

'I'm going to be here all night. I've called a meeting with the team.

When the expedited forensic reports come in, they will completely back up my claims, I'm sure of it.'

He remained quiet, and for the first time since being assigned to the *X* case, I felt in control.

'However, if I'm wrong and it *does* look like this could be the work of a copycat, then yes, I'll be happy to report the situation as so.'

His eyes twitched as he tried to comprehend my words.

'But that's not going to happen, so you need to brace yourself for the worst.'

'What do you mean?' His voice had wilted to a pitiful whisper.

'*X* is still out there, and he will kill again!'

40

10 September
It was 5.00 am by the time Bradley dropped me back at the house. There'd be little time for sleep. The plan was to have a shower, grab some breakfast and change into a clean suit. By the time we'd received the forensic findings, it was the early hours. I'd sent the team home after waiting around half the night, with the idea of regrouping in the morning. Brainstorming may have seemed pointless, but there was a need to get them together, motivate them, and basically start again as if this was the first murder. The forensic report concluded that the MO was identical to the previous killings, but I wanted the team to focus solely on this one. More than that, I needed to take control, to make sure everyone realised I really was in charge. I didn't mean that in a narcissistic way, but it was important for them to understand I was no longer the puppet who had been chosen and manipulated by Monroe and his gang – I was a detective proper.

'Oh no …' Bradley said as we approached the house. The media was back.

'Bugger, they've got wind of it.'

Bradley slowed the car as we approached. 'What do you want me to do?'

'Just pull up as normal, drop me off.' I checked my watch. 'Be back here for 7.00.'

Lights from a couple of shoulder-held TV cameras illuminated the Range Rover as we pulled up at the kerb. The little group of reporters jostled towards the passenger side.

'See you soon, mate.' I opened the door and climbed out.

'DI Stephens, can you confirm there's been another killing?'

There was a new energy pulsing through my veins, kind of like the feeling when I caught my first wave as a teenager. Leading up to that moment, I'd been a little scared of the surf, anxious perhaps. After a few months, I'd begun to move away from the group of novices. Tentatively, at first, the waves got bigger. I persevered, until that fateful August morning at Kirra Point. It was a championship level wave, rolling towards me and rising into the perfect crest just at the right time. My performance was nothing compared to that of Mick Fanning's of course, but it meant everything to me. I'd mastered my fear of the surf, and I was in control.

That's how I felt approaching the press – no longer being carried along by the wave, but riding it. I wouldn't be hiding behind the 'no comment' answer Singleton and Ripley had demanded. I'd answer the questions I wanted to answer. I *was* the detective in charge of the *X* investigation. 'Yes, that's true, there has been another killing.' I didn't push through the crowd as on previous occasions, but remained planted, facing them head on.

Another voice from the faceless crowd asked, 'And does the MO match the previous killings?'

'Yes, it does.'

'So, Binks was innocent?'

'It certainly looks that way.'

'Is it true you planted false evidence to convict Binks?'

'No, that isn't true,' I responded, remaining calm.

'What do you say to the rumours that you set Binks up as a patsy?'

'Rumours? What rumours are they?' My instinct was to start moving towards the house, perhaps I should have gone with the 'no comment' card after all, but I stood my ground.

'I have it from a reliable source …'

I focused in on the voice – the girl from *The Bulletin*.

X

'That you were under so much pressure that you—'

I held up my palms to stop the surge.

'Look, there's going to be an official press conference later this morning, but I'm happy to quell all rumours right now.' I paused for a moment, making note of the faces for the first time. 'There has never been any suspicion towards my practices as a detective. What happened to Lawrence Binks was very, very unfortunate. There will be a full inquiry, but for now, I'll be concentrating on this new killing with the knowledge that *X* is still at large.'

'Is it true you shot Binks dead before the allegations against him could be proved or disproved?' It was a man's voice.

I realised the group was only interested in what they wanted to hear. Still in control, I replied calmly, 'No, that's not true.'

'Do you feel guilty for accepting all the accolades you've been awarded over the last few days?' the *Bully* girl fired again, '... and the way the Gold Coast community has embraced you. Are you a fraud, detective?'

'No, I'm not a fraud, and I'm going to prove that when I bring this killer to justice.'

'Isn't that what you said only a few days ago?'

'I've never said that before.' I placed my hands on my stomach. 'Now, if you'll excuse me folks, I need some breakfast. I'll see you all at the press conference later.' I headed for the front door, ignoring the questions in my wake.

X

The usual sound of Elvis's muffled snores reverberated through what would have otherwise been a quiet house. Passing through the living room, I stopped and looked down at the couch to see Jenny, covered up to her neck by a doona, fast asleep.

'Hey,' her voice was groggy and heavy with sleep as she opened her eyes.

'Hey. Didn't make it home, eh?' I'd purposely left her behind last night.

She sat up and scanned her surroundings, obviously not knowing where she was or how she'd gotten there. 'Is this your house?'

'Yep.'

'How did I?' She sat up and immediately raised her hands to her forehead. 'Oh, that's right.'

'You were wasted.'

'What happened to you? I seem to remember you disappearing.'

'So, you obviously haven't seen the news this morning?'

She threw off the doona and swung her feet onto the floor. She was fully dressed. 'What's happened?'

'Get yourself ready. I'll put the jug on.'

41

Once again, Ferny Avenue was blocked off to accommodate news vans and members of the press. Only this time, the crowd seemed twice as big. Ignoring the questions hurled at me, I carefully negotiated the Dub through a narrow path that was cleared by a group of uniformed officers.

The team meeting wasn't scheduled for another thirty minutes but I knew, like me, they were anxious, and would all be there early too, which they were. When I walked into the incident room, the atmosphere was the opposite to what I'd expected. There was no sense of motivation, no energy. Batteries, instead of being recharged and ready to go, were flat. No one made eye contact with me. Quick glances, followed by falling eyes to the floor, were my only welcome. This was unusual behaviour for Constables Forester and McDonald – they were usually eager regardless. Was Dion Gardner's presence in the room making them feel uncomfortable?

Apart from Jenny, Dion, who had returned from his holiday in the Maldives, was the only person who made eye contact. His expression was the usual analytic, patronising glare. Jenny had driven home, showered, changed, and come straight to the station. I noticed concern in her expression. With my objective of remaining in control, I addressed the group. 'Okay, guys. I understand you might all be feeling a bit down, but we need to continue with the job. Everything we discussed until the early hours of this morning is in place now. Is anybody still not clear of their role?'

Gardner stuck up his hand. 'Please miss, I wagged the last class and my dog ate my homework.' Nobody laughed.

'That's really funny, detective, but irrelevant because you'll no longer be needed.'

'What are you talking about?'

'I'm relieving you of your duties. Go and see Ripley, he'll assign you something else. But don't disappear. I need to question you about the Binks shooting.'

Gardner grinned and rose to his feet. 'You really are a complete *idiot*, aren't you?'

Expecting him to head for the door, I wasn't about to stand in his way. But he didn't, he walked straight towards me at the front of the room.

'It's you who needs to go and see Ripley.' He fronted up to me like a schoolyard bully.

'I certainly will be doing that.' *Remain calm, in control.* I pointed to the door. 'Now if you don't mind.'

'I don't mind at all.' He held up his hand and walked his fingers in mid-air like the old Yellow Pages ad. 'Off you trot. They're waiting for you.'

It was an embarrassing situation. I was being bullied in front of my team – some leader. 'How about we go and see him together?' was the only response I could muster.

Gardner chuckled, 'Brilliant idea. After you.'

I made my way towards the door, speaking to the team over my shoulder, 'No need to wait around. Let's get to it. Good luck.'

No one moved.

X

I was only half surprised to see Monroe and Singleton waiting with Ripley in his office. Gardner followed closely behind me as if preparing to block my escape.

X

At my knock, Ripley gestured for me to enter. The three of them stood and turned to greet me, but not in a jovial or even professionally polite manner – their expressions were grave. Monroe looked different without the sycophantic smile. The laugh lines were still visible, engraved into his face like weathered canyons, but the scowl was something I hadn't witnessed since I'd kicked him in the balls.

'Detective,' Ripley said.

The office wasn't that big. Apart from Ripley, who was shorter and thinner, the rest of us were quite burly, so the space was cramped, made worse by Gardner's insistence on standing so close to me.

'I'm not going to beat about the bush,' Ripley glanced sideways at Monroe and Singleton before continuing, 'you've not just let us down, but you've let down your community, your country in fact.'

My searching frown prompted him to continue.

'Our trust in you has proved to be fool-hardy, detective.' He directed his eyes to Gardner.

My right arm was suddenly grabbed from behind and forcefully twisted up behind my back.

'Detective Inspector Stephens, I am arresting you for perverting the course of justice and falsification of evidence resulting in the death of an innocent man.'

'Are you kidding me?' I growled at Ripley through clenched teeth.

'You have the right to remain silent,' Gardner bent me over Ripley's desk, produced a pair of handcuffs, and skilfully placed them on my wrists while reading me my rights.

Realising my rights meant nothing at that moment, I waived them. 'Are you really going to let this happen?'

'If we feel there is enough evidence, the charges may be increased to manslaughter, or even murder,' Ripley said.

'What?'

'Take him downstairs, detective. Let him sit for a while, then go and organise your team.'

Singleton patted Gardner on the back. 'At last, the right man for the job.'

Monroe leaned forward and whispered into my ear, 'Now who's kicking who in the balls, eh?'

Gardner wrenched me up straight.

'Not so smart now, are you?' Monroe continued.

It was the heat of the moment, childish perhaps, but it was the only response I could think of as Gardner pulled me backwards from the room.

'Give my regards to Gladys, eh.'

42

I was obviously familiar with the procedure. Some detainees were put into communal holding rooms, some placed straight into cells, while others (usually the low-risk VIP types) were placed in an interview room. I was the latter. Seated at a table in a nondescript grey room with no windows, it was now a waiting game.

I'd had the phone call that all detainees were allowed. Never having had the need for a solicitor, my only choices were to either call one of the Public Defence lawyers, whose cards were taped to the wall by the public phone, or ring someone to sort one out. I rang Elvis at his office in Coolangatta. For all his faults and carefree nuances, when at work he was a talented accountant and a dedicated businessman with contacts and some clout in the southern Gold Coast community. He wouldn't let me down.

I had some time to reflect over the surreal episodes of the last week. Seven days ago, I was a detective constable, enjoying the job for what it was – a career not driven by hunger or a need to change the world. I was happy with the daily routine of clocking on and off. Basically, my motivation had been that of a standard factory worker – go to work, get the job done, go home. Also, being single meant I had no responsibilities other than providing for myself – no dependants, no stress, just living by the beach with my mates.

The door opened, yanking my thoughts back to the present. To my utter surprise, Craig Nash, the high-profile defence lawyer, breezed into the room carrying two takeaway coffees and a Manila folder under his arm.

Placing the cups on the table, he slapped down the folder and with a wide grin, held out his hand.

'Scotty. How are they treating you?'

I shook his hand and before I could reply ...

'I'm Craig Nash. I'll be defending you.'

'Wow, Nashie!'

Nash was another one of those annoying personalities who popped up on the evening news from time to time. He'd also written a couple of books a few years ago – novels, courtroom dramas, that kind of thing. According to Elvis, they weren't that bad. Of course, being a detective, defence lawyers weren't my favourite people. I'd never worked opposite Nash, though. His cases were way out of my league, but I was well aware of his reputation. His past clients had included the bikie king and suspected drug lord, Aden Mitchel, and former TV personality-come paedophile, Rex Harrison.

And now he was here.

'You're a detective, you know the procedure. We've only got a few minutes, so is there anything you want to tell me?'

'Mate. There's a hell of a lot I can tell you.'

He pulled out the chair opposite me, sat down, opened the folder, and produced a pen from inside his jacket. 'Okay, before we get going, I have one important question.' He looked me straight in the eye. 'Are you guilty of any of the charges they've laid against you?'

'No.'

'Great. We'll have you out of here by lunchtime.' He scribbled down notes erratically, recording my details. 'Full name? Date of birth—'

'Mr Nash?'

He looked up again, his well-trained stare locking onto mine.

'I can't afford you, mate.' It was true, I was poor. Just because

X

I was famous, it didn't mean I was making any money. The truth was, although I'd been promoted, the pay wasn't that much higher, and I hadn't even seen any of it yet. My last pay packet was for the measly detective constable rate – enough to pay the utilities, food and drink for the week, fuel for the Dub and a little bit put aside for a rainy day. As for all the interviews and appearances, I was yet to see a single dollar, and probably never would now.

'Don't worry about that. We'll make those bastards pay for everything.' He continued scribbling down notes. 'Now they're going to start questioning very soon. I need you to practise a new mantra.'

My silence prompted him to stop writing and look up.

'Recite these two words over and over in your mind. "No comment." And until further notice, I want you to deliver them whenever you're asked a question. Got it?'

'Got it.'

'We need time to prepare. We need time to work together to build our defence against the case they're going to throw at us. Any questions?'

'No comment.'

He laughed and held out his hand for me to shake once more.

43

Gardner's patronising grin was the polar opposite to Dale Mason's grave expression as the pair of them entered the interview room. Charges were yet to be laid, but it was obvious by the way Gardner took his time that he was enjoying himself, savouring the moment. Under the advisement of my brief, my answer to each of his questions was, 'no comment.' This didn't sway him. Nothing was going to spoil his fun.

'So, even though there was little evidence against Binks, you felt it necessary to call in the Special Emergency Response Team?'

I wanted to respond by yelling that it wasn't me who organised the raid.

'No comment.'

'Why did you shoot Binks in cold blood?'

'No comment.'

'Is it true you planted the evidence in Binks's house?'

'No comment.'

'Is it true you were in negotiations with *60 Minutes* to release your story even before the Binks shooting?'

'No comment.'

'A book deal, I heard.' He glanced over at Mason as if they were having a private discussion. 'Lining his own nest.'

'Is that a question, detective?' Nash asked.

'Oh, you bet it is.'

'Can we stick to the facts please?'

X

'Sure.' The grin returned and Gardner fixed his dark eyes back on mine. 'We have a witness who will testify there was an old Volkswagen Beetle seen circling Parkrose Close on a couple of occasions – a rusty old cream thing. You don't see many of them nowadays, do you, Dale?'

Dale shook his head. I could tell he was uncomfortable by his lack of eye contact with me.

'Was that you, Scotty? Casing out Binks and his house?'

'No comment.' It was getting hard. Gardner was a pro, an expert at wearing down his victims. The use of fabricated intel obviously wasn't beneath him.

'Okay, after the shooting, did you return to the crime scene and enter the building unlawfully?'

'No comment.'

'Is there anything you would like to add in your defence, DI Stephens? Anything at all that could prove your innocence?'

'No comment.' I hoped Nash knew what he was doing.

Gardner turned towards the recording machine. 'For the record, the defendant has refused his right to defend himself in any way. End of interview.'

Dale Mason turned off the machine.

Gardner chuckled, 'Basically, you're fucked, Scotty.'

'You'll be fucked mate when the truth comes out,' I spat back.

'If that'll be all, detective?' Nash said, rising to his feet.

'All for now.' Gardner also rose, but then leaned across the table until our faces were close. 'Don't get too comfortable, mate, in your little gay boy pad with your bent little surf buddies. There's gonna be a knock on the door when you least expect it.'

'Oh yeah?'

'Oh yeah, and it'll be me. Come to take you out for a ride.'

I stood and matched his glare. 'No comment.'

X

Charges pending, I was released, but suspended indefinitely with pay and ordered not to leave Queensland. Walking from the interview room with Nash, I got a glimpse of the office that was briefly mine. Now it was Gardner who sat at the desk, that ever-present grin boring into me.

'Go straight home. Don't go out tonight. Don't talk to anyone,' Nash ordered, 'and be at my office, 9.00 am tomorrow. Do you understand?'

I nodded and we shook hands.

'Don't worry, Scotty. They've got nothing against you.'

'Oh, I'm not. It's them who should be worried. I'm gonna—'

'No, no, no, no.' Lowering his voice, Nash put his arm around me and guided me towards the stairs. 'I don't want to hear any of that. Just keep your head down. Let me do my job, okay?'

'Okay.'

'All this will blow over. Trust me.'

The Dub was parked in the station basement, so I would have to drive through the crowd of media still camped out the front of the building. Nash, ever the pro and ever the showman, left via the front door, approaching the horde of journalists with open arms like an evangelist preacher while creating a little decoy for me to escape.

I was surprised to see Elvis in the waiting room. 'Scotty! Shit mate, are you alright?' he asked, rushing towards me.

'Yeah, all good.'

'All good? How the hell is it all good? They're saying you killed Binks and falsified evidence. It's all over the news!'

'What?'

'Come on, let's get you back to Kirra. I've parked near the beach. Meter's gonna run out anytime now.' Elvis glanced at the clock on the wall.

'Thanks mate, but I've got the Dub downstairs. And listen, thanks for organising Nash. How the hell did you pull that off?'

X

'I didn't. I rang old Reg Barker from Cooly. Poor bugger came all the way up here only to be told you already had representation.'

'Really? That's interesting.' I peered out the window to see Nash still holding court, and I wondered what he was saying. No doubt I'd see it on the evening news.

'Okay, I'll see you at home.'

X

Predictably, the media was at Ruby Street. My only option was to park and make a dash for the house with my head down. There were no constables assigned to assist me. The crowd of reporters surged, pushing, jostling, and bombarding me with questions. Before I could reach the front gate, however, my path was blocked.

I looked up to see a middle-aged woman, who I immediately recognised as the mother of Stella Simpson – victim number six.

'You lying, heartless bastard!' she snarled, her bloodshot eyes drilling into mine. 'How could you?'

'Sorry love, what?' I leaned in so I could hear her above the chaos of the press.

She slapped me across the face. 'You lied to us.' She was yelling now. 'Gave us false closure. How could you do that?'

'I've done nothing of the kind, I can assure you.'

The members of the press had fallen silent. All eyes, cameras and recording devices were directed at me.

'You'll rot in hell for what you've put us through!'

It would have been pointless to stand there and argue my case. I was under the spotlight, and whatever I said or did would have been turned around and thrown against me. My only option was to push past her and continue to the house. No doubt this would be reported as DI Stephens showing little regard for the victims' families. Regardless of the approach I took, I'd be damned.

44

11 September
Before I could introduce myself, the receptionist, who could have moonlighted as a Gold Coast Meter Maid, asked me to take a seat. 'Mr Nash will be with you shortly, Detective Inspector Stephens.' It no longer came as a surprise that everyone knew my name.

'Would you like a tea or coffee?'

'No, I'm fine thanks.' There'd been no drinking the evening before, but I'd laid awake most of the night. The grogginess that made my brain heavy that morning was from the lack of sleep.

'He won't be long.'

'Thanks.'

I could hear Nash's muffled voice through the door to his office, and although the words were inaudible, it was obvious he was talking on the phone. After a few minutes, there was silence, broken only by the gentle clickety-click of the receptionist's typing. The door to Nash's office flew open and out bounded the man in an invisible shroud of expensive cologne.

'Ahh, Scotty. Thanks for coming.' He took my hand and grasped it hard. 'Did you manage to get some sleep?'

'No.'

'Didn't think you would. Come on through.'

His office was exactly what I'd expected – flash and contemporary with a glass desk, white Eames chairs and a bookshelf full of law books. Nash's barrister wig sat askew on a brass bust of Lord Byron.

X

'Do you want a drink or anything? Tea? Coffee? Something a bit stronger?' He showed me to one of the chairs at his desk.

'No, I'm fine thanks.'

Nash slammed himself down into his chair like he'd just finished running a marathon. 'So, you've obviously got a lot on your mind. I just want you to know there's no need to worry, I've got your back.'

'I'm not worried at all.'

'You're not? The sleepless night, though?'

'Just my brain whizzing with the past few days' events going over and over in my mind.'

'That's perfectly normal.' Nash leaned over his desk and pressed a button on an intercom. 'A couple of lattes, Kelly, please.'

He sat back in his chair. 'Good to hear none of this is getting to you. Things will soon be back to normal.'

'No, they won't.'

'They will, mate. Trust me.'

'They won't because I'm going to make sure of it.'

'What do you mean?' Nash frowned.

'They're not gonna get away with this.'

'Who? What?'

'Monroe and his gang. The bastards set me up, not to mention Binks.'

Nash leaned forward again. 'Scotty, come on, let's not be hearing any of that.'

The door opened and in walked the receptionist, precariously carrying two tall lattes. She placed them down in front of us.

'I did say I didn't want a drink.'

Nash waved away my protest. 'Taste it. Kelly makes the best lattes. Go on, trust me.'

The words 'trust me' seemed to roll off Nash's lips in the same way some people inadvertently added 'you know' or 'okay' to the end of their sentences. It was an automated response.

'Why?'

'Well, we only use fresh coffee beans—'

'No. Why should I trust you?'

Nash looked up from his cup, a moustache of froth on his top lip. 'Okay, fair point. I guess we haven't even really been introduced. I just waltzed in and got you out of jail. What's to trust?'

'I never hired you.'

'You didn't have to.' He sat back in his chair again, nursing his mug like it was hot chocolate at bedtime.

'The choice would have been good.'

At first Nash's frown was one of mild annoyance, the kind you'd associate with someone dealing with an unexpected situation, like he couldn't figure out how to get the top off a jam jar, or why the new toaster kept burning his toast. This was replaced by a flicker of anger, which was then professionally adjusted to one of *I've-got-this*.

'My apologies, I did kind of burst in like Batman and take over …' He took another sip of his latte, 'Let's start again. I'm Craig Nash. I—'

'I know who you are.'

'Good, of course you do. That's probably because I'm the most famous defence lawyer in Australia.'

As much as he was a pro, he was no match for my detective instincts. The gritted smile, the bead of sweat on his forehead, and the slight shuffling in his seat told me he was rattled. My guess was he'd had his head so far up his own arse for so many years, dealing with celebrities and wealthy businessmen, he'd forgotten what it was like to deal with real people. I couldn't imagine him coping with the same daily workload as old Reg Barker down at Coolangatta Magistrates Court. The scum Nash dealt with were of a higher class. 'Let's just cut the bullshit, eh?'

'I'm really struggling to understand your lack of gratitude. I got you out of the watch house yesterday.'

X

'And I thank you for that, but I feel like I'm on a rollercoaster, approaching the top of the first climb. Scared shitless, but thinking *oh well, nothing I can do now, just got to go with it*.'

Nash nodded and continued to sip his drink.

'Then afterward, you think *never again*. Well, that's me right now, only I'm heading back up.'

'It's been one hell of a ride, I get it.'

'But who hired you?'

Nash smiled, placed the mug on his desk and nodded as if to say, *oh-I-see-where-we're-going*. 'I didn't get where I am today by waiting around for something to happen, hoping for the next client to find me.' He rose from his chair and began to slowly pace the room. 'I stay one step ahead, keeping a close eye on what's happening around the coast. Yes, I'm in the desirable situation where I can pick and choose my clients, but I've worked hard for that. And although I'm known as a defence lawyer, the initial stages of all the cases I take on begin with a very offensive approach, in that *I* find *them*. Most of the ones who come looking for me aren't even considered.'

'Unless they're a Chinese billionaire conducting a shady real estate deal or slapping around some working girl in Surfers,' I responded.

'You don't seem to realise how lucky you are, Scott.'

'Funny, I've been hearing that a lot lately.'

'I chose to represent you. You're now part of a very elite fraternity, my friend.'

'You chose me because you know this is going to be one very high-profile shit fight, the kind you relish.'

Nash nodded in agreement. 'All that's true, of course. Look, a big part of my success is taking on the cases that require a big personality like me at the helm.'

'So far, this seems to be all about you.'

He took a deep breath and sat back down. 'This is all about getting you off.'

'But no charges have been laid.'

'It's just a matter of time, we both know that. Why, Ripley's probably reading through the transcripts of yesterday's interview at this moment and considering Gardner's recommendation for your arrest.'

'So, what do you reckon we should do?'

'That's easy. I can make this all go away. All you have to do is forget everything you said earlier. Forget Monroe, Singleton and Ripley. In fact, forget about the case entirely.'

'How the hell am I supposed to do that?'

'Easy. Go back to the life you had. Forget about stirring the pot. I'm not only going to get you off and back to that carefree life in …' he looked down at an open file on his desk, 'Kirra, I'll also get you some compensation.'

'And how are you going to achieve this?'

'It's already happening. There'll be an inquiry, which should last around six months. All this time you'll be on suspension with full pay, after which the findings will prove that you had nothing to do with Binks's killing, and that the Gold Coast police were at fault by promoting an unsuitable detective and putting him in charge of the investigation.'

I shifted uncomfortably in my seat.

Sensing my discomfort, Nash continued, 'They'll issue a full public apology and reinstate you to your former role as a detective constable.' He leaned back in his chair again. 'All will be forgiven, my friend.'

'That all sounds very nice and easy.'

'It could be.'

I sensed a caveat in his tone.

'All you'll have to do is keep quiet. No speaking to the press whatsoever, and no more mentioning your feelings and beliefs towards Monroe and his cronies.'

'I can't do that.'

X

'Okay ...' Nash nodded his head like he truly understood my moral position, 'if you can live with the alternative.' He didn't have to spell it out, but he did anyway. 'You'll go to trial, and you'll be convicted, all of which will be watched and enjoyed by millions of Australians via live TV broadcasts. And I don't have to tell you what it would be like for a bent detective spending time in jail, do I?'

'So, you're saying if we go to court, you won't be able to defend me?'

'That's the situation, yes.'

45

Like most blokes, stubborn pride was a trait I possessed, but one I'd supressed for most of my life. Prior to that fateful night back in my teens, I'd been brash and bigheaded, life had been all about me. Since then though all those emotions had disappeared as if that part of me died with my mum. It wasn't pride that was gnawing at me as I drove back to Kirra; my sense of pride had been replaced by the need to do the right thing. Part of being a detective was doing whatever was required, within reason, to attain results. If that meant bending the rules a little to ensure the 'right thing' was achieved, I had no qualms.

There was no need to read between the lines–Nash had made it perfectly clear. If I kept my mouth shut, there'd be no charges laid against me. All I'd need to do was keep my head down, stay away from the press, get on with my life, and the world would eventually move on. In a couple of months, I'd be old news, then forgotten about altogether.

On the other hand, if I went to the press with the allegations I'd spelled out to Nash, charges would be laid against me. Not only would I be squashed by the full force of the law, but my fate would be bolstered by public condemnation. Binks may well have been the Lee Harvey Oswald in this case, but I'd be the Jack Ruby. This meant I could be facing years in jail. Once again, Nash was right – that was no life for an ex-cop.

But my pride wouldn't allow this, right? My need to do the right

X

thing would prevail and I'd fight those bastards in the courts until the end. I was right, they were wrong. Justice would always triumph over evil. But I didn't have any pride, remember? Common sense was the dull blade I brandished.

I needed someone to talk to, someone to confide in. Elvis was my best mate, followed closely by Tetley, then Johnno. Although we shared regular discussions, including the deepest intimate details of our not-so-exciting love follies, philosophy, politics, sport, and putting the world to right, these were debates fuelled by alcohol, and lots of it, the outcomes of which dissolved the next morning with a couple of Aspro Clears.

Loving those guys as much as I did, on this occasion I needed more than *The World According to Elvis*. I needed proper advice.

There was no way I could face the gauntlet of reporters still camped outside the house. On the street behind and backing on to our property was a two-storey block of 1960s units. A cracked bitumen driveway led along the side of the rectangular building to a row of undercover parking spots, beyond which was our back fence. I parked the Dub on the back street and strolled down the driveway. The carports were basically just a rusted corrugated iron roof on heavily dinged steel legs. The structure creaked and swayed as I climbed on to it. As if trying to limit my weight, I skipped across it like I was tiptoeing over hot coals. The bitumen roof of the man shed on the other side of the fence looked just as precarious, so when I jumped onto it, I made sure I remained close to the edge where the support of the outer walls was. From there it was an easy jump down into our garden.

Entering the kitchen, I was surprised to see Elvis sitting at the kitchen table, but I was more shocked when I realised the person sharing a coffee with him was my brother.

'Where the hell did you come from?' Elvis squawked.

'Over the back.'

'Don't blame you. They're all still out there.'

I didn't acknowledge my brother. 'Why aren't you at work?' I asked Elvis.

He slid back his chair and stood. 'Heading back now. I'll leave you to it.'

'There's no need to go, mate,' I frowned, 'you bloody stay put.'

'No mate, you need to hear this. I'll see you later.' He breezed out of the room, and the mayhem outside seeped in for a split second when he opened the front door.

'How's it goin' Scotty?'

'I've got nothing to say to you, Todd. I thought I'd made that clear.'

'You did, and I get it. You think we crawled out of the woodwork because you're a famous detective now.'

'I'm not a famous detective.'

There was a flicker of a smirk. 'Infamous perhaps.' He sat up straight in his chair and began turning his coffee cup with his fingers. 'We're not here for any of that. Dad just thought ... *I* thought ... there was something you should know.'

'Yeah? And what's that?'

He took a sip of his drink, and I could tell he was preparing the words he was about to deliver.

'Thing is mate ... he's dying!'

'What?'

'Prostate cancer. Silly bugger had the symptoms for ages, didn't tell anyone. By the time the pain got too much, it was too late.'

Fuck me, another paradigm shift. I wasn't sure what the emotion was that I was experiencing. Shock, sadness or anger. Maybe it was a combination of all three. One thing I did know though, when I inadvertently ran a hand through my hair, it was trembling.

46

I'd arranged to meet Jenny at Burleigh Heads Surf Club because it was close to where she lived. It was a weeknight, so the club wasn't packed. Jenny was waiting for me, sitting on a stool at one of the high tables, two schooners of beer in front of her.

'How's it going?' I asked, climbing onto the stool opposite.

'Good.'

I took a sip of beer. I'm not a connoisseur or anything, I just know what I like and what I don't. I had no idea what I was drinking, but it tasted good.

'So ...' Jenny raised her eyebrows, prompting me.

'So ... indeed.' I placed the glass back on the beer mat. 'I uhm ... I just need someone to talk to.'

Now it was Jenny's turn to sip her beer.

'But not as a colleague, more ... more as a friend.'

The distinctive opening bars of the Channel 7 News theme rang out and we both instinctively turned our heads towards the TV on the wall.

'Breaking news tonight,' Alex Wade said, staring intensely into the camera. 'Could the latest killing on the Gold Coast be the work of a copycat killer?'

'Is this what you wanted to talk to me about?' Jenny asked.

'No, well ...'

After reading a list of other stories still to come, then switching briefly to a sports correspondent, Wade returned to the main story.

'In a press conference this afternoon, Gold Coast police revealed that what at first appeared to be the latest in a series of killings by the infamous killer known as *X*, was in fact a copycat killing.'

The scene switched to the familiar female reporter standing outside Surfers Paradise Police Station.

'Do we have any more information, Penny?' Wade's offscreen voice asked.

'None at all. Speculation is that an arrest is pending, but there's been no confirmation yet.'

The screen returned to Alex Wade. 'New concerns regarding the blown-out costs of the M1 upgrade between Varsity Lakes and Tugun ...'

My exhalation was a heavy one. I took a mouthful of beer and allowed it to swill around my teeth. 'So, this means Binks will still be convicted for the other killings.'

'But Lawrence was innocent.'

'That's why I'm no longer a part of the investigation.'

Jenny nodded. 'We've been briefed. Gardner's in charge now. Hate that guy!'

Sipping beer became our instrument for pause. 'Look, I want to talk, but what I have to say could have implications.'

'Okay.'

'I've decided I'm going to continue digging.'

'On the case you mean?'

'Yes.'

'Like a private detective?' Her tone was a little patronising.

'Binks was a patsy. I'm sure of it.'

Her eyes widened and she was suddenly serious. 'A cover up?'

'Yeah. He was set up.'

'But ... who?'

'Monroe.'

'Because?' She squinted, furrowed her brow, then answered her

X

own question. 'Because he was worried that the negative press was going to kill the coast. No tourists, no investments, no Monroe developments. Still, it's one hell of an allegation.'

'It is,' I nodded, 'and I don't think it's just Monroe.'

'The commissioner? Not the premier, surely?'

'I don't know yet, but I need to find out.'

There was a heavy pause as Jenny digested the information. 'So, what do you want me to do?'

'I just need you to listen.'

47

And listen she did. She even ordered two more drinks while I continued my story. Relaying the events of the last few days to someone I hardly knew almost seemed to have a therapeutic effect. A sense of relaxation began to spread through my body, like one of Bradley's meditation exercises. Narrating my story made it feel like it had happened to someone else.

'Wow!' Jenny said when I'd finished. As if understanding the importance of the moment, she'd sat quietly and not interrupted once. 'So, you definitely think Monroe is behind this?'

'Yep. Even down to enlisting Nash to take my case.'

'But that's the bit I don't understand. How is having Nash as your defence lawyer going to help Monroe? Nash has got a pretty good reputation of winning the cases he takes on.'

'It's just another example of how Monroe's brilliant scheming mind works. It's a win-win for everyone involved.'

'How so?'

'Nash taking on my case was merely a continuation of the charade. Monroe won't have lost, he'll be the winner. In fact, I wouldn't be surprised if he was the one paying Nash. As far as the people of Australia and the media know, Nash will get me off. My name will be cleared, the Gold Coast will go back to normal, and Monroe will continue making money through his developments and whatever else he's got going on.'

As she processed the information, Jenny exhaled slowly, letting

X

the air vibrate through her lips as if blowing a slow-motion raspberry. 'That's one hell of a conspiracy theory.'

'What do you think?'

'Why would you take the easy way out. Why not fight them?'

Until now, answering this same question in my head the way I had over and over hadn't really solidified it. There was still a fair amount of doubt, reinforced by that little voice in my conscience—*you're selling out, you're selling out*—but putting it into words seemed to dispel those doubts, as if it had manifested my resolve into a living thing and sent it out to the universe. 'I'm going to fight them in my own way. I can't do that while I'm sitting in a jail cell waiting for a farcical trial.'

'But you've signed a statutory declaration to say you won't say or do anything regarding the case.'

My shrug may have appeared as a nonchalant gesture, but it wasn't meant to be. 'Thing is, there's a lot more at stake here than just me lifting the lid.'

'Right. Because if what you're saying is true and there has been a cover up, it means X is still out there, not a copycat killer, and it's only a matter of time before he strikes again.'

'That's right.'

'So why are you telling *me* all of this?'

Shuffling my butt cheeks on the hard stool, I confessed, 'I may need your help.'

'Is that what this is all about?' Her brow lowered into a tight knot. 'You want me to, what? Get information?'

My vigorous head shaking was all that was required to interrupt her. 'No. Well, maybe a little, but that's not why I asked to meet you.' A sip of beer created another loaded pause. 'I asked you here because I needed someone to just ... to off load everything to. I needed to talk to someone. I mean talk properly, like I used to with my ...'

Jenny was nodding slowly with each word. When I stopped

speaking, she was left hanging mid-nod. 'Go on, like you used to with whom?'

'With my mum.'

'Right ...' Her tone was a mixture of hard-nosed detective, empathy and surprise, tinged with a little sarcasm. She was hard to read.

'Perhaps I've made a mistake talking to you.' Another horrendous error in the life of Scotty Stephens.

She placed her hand on mine. 'No, you haven't. I'm sorry, I'm here for you. Fancy another drink?'

'I better not. I've got to drive back to Kirra.'

'My place is just a short stroll from here.' Was that a flutter of the eyelids?

'Okay.' For a detective who prided himself on being able to read body language, I was failing miserably.

'Great.' She rose two fingers to the barman to indicate two more beers.

That feeling of being a shy schoolboy was back, but everything about Jenny Radford seemed familiar. It was like I'd known her forever, whereas I knew nothing about her at all. 'So, you know all about me. Tell me about you.'

She shrugged matter-of-factly. 'Nothing to tell, I'm a Gold Coast girl born and bred.'

'Really?' One thing I loved about living on the Gold Coast was that most of the people you met were from somewhere else, which meant you immediately had something in common with them. To find someone at our age who was born and grew up on the coast was rare indeed.

'Yep. Born in Burleigh. My parents bought an acre block out at Tallebudgera and built a house when I was about six. I went to Burleigh State School then Elanora High. I have one older brother, Bobby, who is a police sergeant in a tiny coastal town in Far North Queensland.'

'Boyfriend?' I thought it only right to check.

X

'Nope. Not at present.' This made her shift a little uncomfortably in her seat. 'What about you?' she asked after the barman breezed back and forth with two more beers.

'Huh?'

'Girlfriend?'

'No,' I grinned, 'but you were telling me about *you*, remember?'

'Went to Griffith Uni after high school and got a Bachelor of Criminology and Criminal Justice degree. Did a gap year in the UK before graduating.'

'Yeah, whereabouts?'

'London. Got a job as a barmaid in a pub in Shepherd's Bush.'

'Sounds great.'

'Not really.' The sipping pause again.

I followed suit.

'Came back to Australia, finished my degree and joined the police force. That's pretty much it.'

'There's got to be more to your life than that?'

She grinned.

48

12 September
It was early the next morning when I left the beachfront apartment at the top of Goodwin Terrace. Jenny was fast asleep, so I didn't wake her. Sneaking out instead, I left a note that said: *Thanks for a great night. I'll call you later.*

My car was still parked close to the surf club in Mowbray Park, a pleasant two-minute walk away.

I hadn't felt this way since … ever! There'd been the odd casual relationship, but nothing serious – certainly nothing to bring on this unusual giddiness. We hadn't messed around. As soon as the front door closed behind us, we were at each other. It was passionate and exhilarating, but it felt right.

It was a strange feeling driving south on the Gold Coast Highway towards Kirra. Normally the day ahead would be dominated by work. I needed to fill the void, get busy and start making my own enquiries, but there was one very important thing I had to do first.

X

Unfortunately, attending funerals is part of the job for a detective. I'd been to too many over the years for victims of crime, and colleagues killed in the line of duty. As part of my detective constable role on the *X* case, along with a young social worker, and a WPC, I'd been the family liaison officer after the first two deaths, which meant it was my role to break the news to the

X

victims' families. When the killings continued and the profile of the case increased, I was replaced by Ripley for the third and fourth victims, after that it was the Queensland Commissioner. At the sixth victim's funeral, Monroe was in attendance – either because it was the right thing to do, or just another opportunity for prime time exposure.

Detective Inspector Des Williams' memorial was different. The highest official who attended was Ripley, more I suspect from a sense of duty rather than a sign of respect. Des's daughter and her husband had flown up from Batemans Bay in New South Wales with their young son. The rest of the congregation was made up of his work colleagues, which I was happy to see were many. In fact, the only face missing was Gardner. As for me, I sat at the back of the chapel and managed to avoid everyone. Even Jenny didn't see me.

The service was inspiring. The celebrant spoke of a good father, a good copper, and a good bloke.

I didn't go to the wake.

X

During the drive home, my attention was suddenly piqued by a short blast of a police siren. I looked in my rear-view mirror to see a patrol car flashing me down.

There was something familiar about the gait of the young police officer who strolled towards my car. I'd pulled up outside the Centrelink building in Palm Beach and remained in the driver's seat. The old crank groaned and grated as I rolled down the window of the Dub. The police officer bent down and leaned in close to the window. His smile was a mixture of caution, sympathy and embarrassment.

'Hi Scott.'

'Bradley?' I jumped out of the car. 'What the hell?' I embraced him. It was good to see his friendly face. Like a parent, I gently pushed him backwards and held him at arm's length as if admiring him in his new school uniform. 'They've put you back on patrol?'

'Yes.'

'Ah, mate, I'm so sorry.'

'Don't be. It's not your fault.'

'Well, it kind of is.'

'No, none of this was your doing. I might be in uniform, Scott, but I'm still a detective. A rooky maybe, but—' Bradley cocked his head to one side and listened as his radio crackled. The message wasn't for him. 'I've given this a lot of thought. Everything that happened to us was orchestrated. There was a Plan A and a Plan B. If everything went according to Plan A as expected, cultivating two pawns – Lawrence Binks, the killer; and you, the hero – the Gold Coast would have returned to normal and everyone would be happy.'

'And plan B?'

'If Plan A didn't work out, Plan B would see the blame fall entirely on your shoulders and the outcome would be the scenario that we now face.'

'That's right.'

'Plan A failed because they hadn't banked on you actually being the detective you are, so they were forced to revert to Plan B. This was just as cleverly masterminded as Plan A. They've thought of everything.'

'You really are a detective, Bradley.'

'Better believe it.'

X

Although I lived on the back street, which is closer to the highway, I often drove the long way home for the thrill of cruising down the beach front. I turned right into Lord Street. Ironically, the new building where the old bottle shop used to be, was called X.

X

I was fairly sure the house would be empty at this time of the day. Tetley's Vespa was still parked outside, but it wasn't unusual for him to leave it here and walk home after a night on the grog.

I had the habit of slightly nudging the vintage scooter that had once belonged to Tetley's dad, Mick. I'd done this so often there was a slight fold and a chip of red paint on the Dub's bumper.

At least I'd have the house to myself. Silence didn't suit the place though.

The bedrooms of the old fibro building weren't big and there were none of the usual luxuries taken for granted in today's buildings. The one bathroom in the house, as you can imagine, was a very overused and under-maintained amenity. The house was clean though, thanks to Tetley's mum, Carol. She came around twice a week, did the washing and ironing, and cleaned the place from top to bottom. Bless her.

My room was a little over a three-by-three cube with peeling paint and a stained carpet that was once beige. I had a double bed, a bedside cabinet, an old Op Shop wardrobe, and a chest of drawers hand painted in yellow gloss. On the way home, I'd stopped off at Officeworks and purchased a wall-mounted whiteboard, a pack of erasable markers, a ream of paper, yellow Post-it notes, a roll of Sellotape, and a couple of Manila folders. Within minutes I'd hung the whiteboard on the wall above the chest of drawers.

Elvis had a computer and a printer set up in his room and didn't mind if I used it. Luckily, it was easy to find pictures of the X victims by doing a Google search. Not the graphic versions of course, only the headshots that had been used by the press, all of which were still available on various news archives. I printed them and stuck them side-by-side at the top of the whiteboard, their names scribbled underneath. Physically, this was all I had, but mentally I had every single detail of the case stored away. I didn't need to see any of the crime scene pictures again. What I'd witnessed first-hand at the last three killings would remain with me for the rest of my life. All the other murder scenes had been identical, which meant staring at pictures of them in the hope of finding something new was pointless. I needed the headshots, however, as a reminder that these innocent young women were real people who deserved justice.

I'd also purchased a map of the Gold Coast – the pre-Google fold-up type – and pinned it on the wall next to the whiteboard. After clearing the top of the drawers, I removed the ream of paper from its wrapping, sat it next to the Manila folders, then set out the pens in a row with the roll of Sellotape.

My incident room was ready.

49

13 September
Whenever possible, I'd go for a surf before work. Even though I was on suspension, I decided there was no reason my routine shouldn't remain the same. The reactions towards me from the boys out in the waves when I paddled out from Kirra Point varied. Chilly waved as usual, as did most of the guys, while a couple seemed to ignore me completely.

The thing I liked most about being out in the surf was that it gave me time to think, while sitting on my board between sets, bobbing gently up and down, gazing back at Kirra. Many a life decision was made in those moments.

The second part of the daily routine was whisking around to the bakery for a carton of flavoured milk and a sausage roll for breakfast. Sometimes, usually on my days off when I had more time, I'd stand at the waist-high bench outside the bakery and eat there before heading back home.

On my third official day of suspension, I decided I had time, so I propped up my board in the corner. Of course, I knew that flavoured milk and a sausage roll, or a steak and bacon pie, weren't the healthiest choices for breakfast, it just seemed to be a part of the uncaring lifestyle. But over the last year or so, I'd begun to notice a burning sensation in my throat and the sour taste of indigestion after most meals. *Was I getting too old for this?* I knew I was.

An old timer sat on a stool next to me, eating a croissant and reading the front page of the *Gold Coast Bulletin*. The headline blared out at me: COPYCAT KILLER CHARGED!

This was big news. The old guy noticed me looking over his shoulder.

'Can you believe it?' His voice was deep and phlegmy.

'Who have they got?'

'Some bloke from New South Wales. Up here on holiday.'

I couldn't read the small print, which was something else I'd noticed recently too. I finished my breakfast and headed home.

The arrogant, self-important smirk of Dion Gardner seemed to be directed solely at me when I turned on the TV. He was standing outside an apartment block in Mermaid Beach with questions being fired at him from off-screen reporters.

'Detective, what can you tell us about the man you arrested last night?'

'Early thirties, white, single …'

'What evidence do you have against him?'

'I'm not at liberty to disclose that information yet.'

'Can we get a name?'

'Adrian Paul Stamp.'

'You said he was from New South Wales?'

'Yes, Wagga Wagga.'

'What was he doing in Queensland?'

'As far as we know, he was up here on holiday. That's the only information we have.'

'Does this mean Lawrence Binks was innocent?'

'No, it does not.' He paused for effect. 'Pending the enquiry, we have enough evidence to prove that Binks was rightly convicted for the eight previous killings. This last death was a copycat killing by a deranged individual.' Gardner was giving little away.

After a shower, I put on a pair of jeans and a casual polo shirt, made a cup of coffee and retired to the incident room. I wasn't sure what I was looking at, there was no new information

X

there. I just stared at it, almost as if I were paying homage to a shrine. The previous evening I'd marked all the crime scenes on the map, and that was it.

During my surf that morning I'd planned out my day. I couldn't be sure if this Stamp guy had been set up in the way Binks had, but my hunch told me he had. The only way I was going to find out the truth was by starting my own investigation. To do this, I'd need to go back to the very beginning.

X

The first killing took place on the evening of August 13th at the building site where the Iluka Resort once stood in Surfers Paradise. It was secured by construction fencing, but I didn't need to go in. All I wanted to do was stand and observe the surroundings.

Where would the killer have waited?

How often had he visited the site prior to the killings?

I strolled the perimeter of the empty lot, imagining the scene of that terrible night. The site was overlooked by the twenty-two storey Surfers International Apartments. *Surely somebody had heard something.* The residents and tenants, mostly holiday makers, had all been canvassed. No one remembered hearing or seeing anything. At that time of night, Trickett Street on the southern end of the block would have been the quietest of the three sides. That had to have been the killer's escape route.

The other scenes were pretty much the same. Once again, all I could do was stand and observe, which I did, making note of the surrounding areas, possible escape routes, etc.

Arriving at the Home of The Arts complex (HOTA) on Bundall Road, the scene of the fifth killing, I parked the Dub in the left-hand side of the expansive carpark and strolled to the cordoned off area. Flowers and teddy bears were placed around the bottom of the tree where the body of waitress, Julie Staniforth, had been found.

For a moment, I just stood looking out from the trees where I guessed the killer would have waited. The old wooden church, relocated there some time ago, stood quietly, nestled amongst peaceful gardens. The apex of the main modernist auditorium jutted upwards like a slab of discarded Lego. Temporary construction fences and a crane were the signs of ongoing development. In my mind, I was mentally reconstructing the night of the killing. Julie had finished her shift and was making her way to the carpark at the northern side of the complex. Just before she got to her car, she was startled by someone who appeared behind her. When she turned, her throat was slashed with the killer's signature *X*. As with the rest of the victims, she'd bled out and died in a matter of minutes, before being laid out and left there.

I attempted to replay the scene from the killer's perspective—from waiting beforehand in the trees, knowing exactly what time the staff finished work and where they parked their cars. Knowing too, that there were no security cameras on this part of the carpark, with very few people around at that time of night as theatregoers and patrons would be long gone. Most of the staff broke the company rules and parked at the southern end, closer to the exit. Did this mean that, unlike the Bond University killing, the killer had picked his victim beforehand? Watched her movements perhaps?

The victim: female, early twenties – tick.

The location: quiet, yet in the heart of things – tick.

Easy get away – tick.

The only vehicles captured on CCTV leaving the complex that night were accounted for, so the killer must have fled the scene on foot. Heading out over the carpark would have been too risky. Even that late at night, there was traffic on Bundall Road and the complex was wide open. The obvious thing to have done was to make his way back through the trees and onto the bank of Nerang River. I did just that, and after reaching the water it was an

X

easy trek to the new footbridge, and then over to Chevron Island, where he'd probably parked his car.

The exact scenario was the same for each of the sites I visited that day, one after the other, in the order they took place. Walking, watching, listening, I was trying to put myself in the killer's mind.

At the end of the day, I was no closer to being able to prove Binks's innocence or bringing the real killer to justice. There was no new information to add to the whiteboard that night, but I didn't feel the day had been totally wasted. I'd had time to examine each scene closely, and although there was nothing new, I'd been able to put myself in the killer's shoes. It was just frustrating that they didn't fit.

50

Jenny was supposed to have come down to Kirra that evening after work, but due to the arrest of Stamp she'd had to stay back late.

In our semi-drunken state the previous night, we'd made a pact – whatever information one of us might unearth about the case, we'd share it with the other. This was risky for us both. For Jenny because she could lose her job, and for me because I was on suspension and forbidden access to the case.

I also suspected Bradley would be willing to help if called upon. Although PCs weren't always privy to the intel shared between the detectives, they were usually the first responders and got to see quite a lot.

Jenny had been called into a meeting that morning that went on for most of the day. She'd phoned me at lunchtime. After being questioned all night, Stamp finally admitted to the murder of Tracey Porter, the nurse. The only details Jenny could share was that Stamp had a history of mental health issues, including symptoms of OCD, he was on medication for a mild form of schizophrenia, and he had been arrested in the past for harassing young women at the Oasis Aquatic Centre in Wagga Wagga.

I was home in time to watch a live press conference scheduled for four o'clock that afternoon. The old gang were there: Ripley, Singleton, Monroe, and Gardner. I was surprised to see Jenny in the background, along with Dale Mason. Ripley fielded questions

X

from the press. They didn't divulge much information I hadn't learned from Jenny's call, just a little more on Stamp's history and his recent activities.

Singleton took the podium and didn't waste time in praising the work of DI Gardner and his team. I was about to turn off the TV when the front door opened and slammed. Elvis came padding into the room.

'Ah ... this is what you're gonna do now, is it? Laze around all day watching the telly?' The top button of his shirt was already open, and he was pulling off his tie. Heading straight for the fridge, he pulled out three beers.

'Not for me thanks.'

He thrust an icy bottle into my hand regardless. Before I could ask who the third one was for, the front door opened, slammed shut, and in breezed Tetley. I might have known.

'Fuckin' 'ell, look at him laying around on the settee drinking beer all day. Alright for some, Elv.'

Elvis handed him the other beer. 'I know, that's what I said.'

'For your information, I've been working all day.'

'Yeah right.' Elvis took off his suit jacket and hung it over the back of a kitchen chair. 'What you been doing then?'

I took a swig of beer.

'He's got to think about it, look,' Tetley said, plonking himself down on the couch.

'Listen, before you blokes get on the piss, I want to talk to you both.' I stood up.

Tetley had a lazy eye that twitched when he was nervous, while Elvis's lips would moisten and inflate when he was serious, causing his jaw to hang open. Tetley referred to this as being gormless. Like on the very rare occasions in the past when I'd had to remind them I was a police officer – the time Froggy produced a bag of weed at one of our parties, and when Elvis wanted to drive home from Burleigh one night when loaded – the boys had reverted to the naughty-schoolboys-standing-in-the-headmaster's-office mode. There was a flicker of this now, as if they were expecting a lecture.

'It's alright, you're not in trouble,' I hastily added.

They shook their heads nonchalantly.

'Never thought we were,' Tetley said.

'All I wanted to say is, I'm still going to be working the case.'

'Isn't that illegal?' Elvis asked, concerned.

'Yes, well, no.'

Tetley grew excited. 'You can be a private detective.'

'But wouldn't it be a breach of your suspension terms?' Ignoring Tetley, Elvis was serious now.

'Well yeah, but—'

'But what? Do you want to go to jail?'

'Look,' I wandered around the kitchen counter, 'I can't just be controlled like this and let an innocent man take the blame for murders he didn't commit.'

'Binks, you mean?' Tetley said.

'Yes.'

'But what about this new bloke?' Elvis sat on the couch next to Tetley. 'What if he isn't a copycat?'

'He isn't.'

The boys frowned and looked at each other.

'So ...' Elvis searched the floor with his eyes. 'He's *X*?'

'No. Neither Binks nor Stamp are *X*.'

51

15 September
Two days passed. Over that time, I'd studied the difference between Asperger's syndrome and OCD. The identical arrangement of each scene made it clear that X either had the latter—or was cleverly making it look that way. Binks, on the other hand, was diagnosed with Asperger's syndrome when he was only five years old. His symptoms were the opposite to a person with OCD, and according to his doctor, he couldn't fake it if he tried. This was enough proof for me that he wasn't the killer, but I had nothing else to back up my theory. My only hope, although morbid, was that if, or *when* X struck again, he'd slip up and leave at least a tiny clue. This left me with an inner conflict I could never speak of to anybody. Of course, I was hoping that no one else fell victim to this vicious fiend, but a small part of me was also left with a selfish yearning for him to strike again.

I hadn't heard from Jenny for over a day. She'd been super busy with the mountain of admin tasks she'd been assigned. Things had quietened down. Adrian Stamp had been charged and remanded in custody until his trial in six weeks' time. The media was now focusing on other things.

The world had moved on. The big topic of the moment was a potential scandal over the cruise ship terminal and resort complex that was due to begin construction at any time. Monroe's daughter, Haley, was under the spotlight amongst allegations she'd enticed prominent investors to the scheme by inventing false buyers to bump up interest. In doing so, she'd cleverly created a pack desire to get in quick before the good deals ran out. Monroe fervently denied all allegations on her behalf, as she was in China for discussions with potential backers. My first impression of Haley Monroe was that of a manipulating narcissist, a sentiment shared by many, especially the media of late. Monroe though, ever the charming pro, stood up for his daughter every chance he got. Jeez, I was sick of seeing that guy's face on TV.

One thing that half surprised and half worried me though, was that X was yet to strike again. The killings had all occurred over a period of a little longer than three weeks. Until now, the longest time between them was three days, and it had now been six days since the Robina Hospital death. This could mean only two things – either the killer had stopped, which was highly unlikely, or he'd been captured.

X

I'd never knowingly broken the law in my life. Part of my bail terms was that I must remain in Queensland. I'm afraid on this occasion, that would be impossible. My overnight bag was packed. I owned one coat, which I only ever wore this time of year when I went down to Melbourne. It was a time I dreaded the most – the anniversary of my mother's death. Regardless of whatever else was happening in my life, it was a pilgrimage I'd made without fail every year since leaving school. The two-and-a-half-hour flight meant I could leave from Gold Coast Airport at 6.00 am and be back by early evening the same day. I doubted anyone would be looking out for me at the airport, but at the same time my face was so well-known, I could easily be recognised. Hopefully a pair of sunnies and a baseball cap would help me slip through unnoticed. The convenience of checking in online was the key.

I had no friends or family down there, so there was no need

X

to stay any longer. Walking around the city killing time would just bring back bad memories of a kid who used to think he owned the place.

Mum was buried at Keilor Cemetery in East Victoria. Her headstone was a small, simple marble tablet bearing the inscription: Katherine Stephens, taken from us so tragically, September 15th 1993.

X

I stood before the grave with my eyes closed, head bowed, my fists clasped as if in prayer. A cool Victorian breeze rustled through the trees, carrying with it the far-off warble of a magpie, and the haze of a smouldering bonfire. Suddenly aware of someone standing behind me, I turned, and was surprised to see my brother, Todd. His eyes met mine and didn't let go.

'Didn't expect to see you here?' I said.

He shrugged. 'I come down here a lot.' There was a quiver of emotion in his voice. He broke eye contact and directed his gaze at Mum's headstone. 'Just need to be with her sometimes.'

I'd never heard him speak like this before – sensitive, vulnerable. The only time we spoke was when we were having a go at each other, and his tone was usually fuelled by blame. This was different, like we were sharing something we had in common for the first time—our grief. I suddenly realised I knew absolutely nothing about my brother. Was he married? What did he do for a living? I didn't even know where he lived. The two years difference between us looked more like ten now. He was overweight, his hairline receding, with a tinge of grey around the edges. The day or so of stubble on his blotchy chin was also grey.

'Dad comes too.'

'Yeah? Where is he then?' I exaggerated a scan of the cemetery as if expecting to see Dad standing in the shadows.

'Scott.'

'I've been here on this day every single year since I was nineteen. I haven't seen him here once, or you for that matter.'

'We've been here. Every year …'

I shook my head, frowning.

'You just don't understand, Scott.' He looked down at the ground, 'and I haven't helped. I've … I've been a terrible brother.'

'Uhh, yeah.'

'Dad comes down the day before the anniversary and celebrates that time – the last day she was on the earth.'

My instinct was to shoot back with something bitter and smart, but my arsenal was suddenly depleted.

'He loved her so much, Scott. Don't you see that?'

I turned back to the grave and squinted at the stone as if struggling to read the inscription.

'He's still in mourning after all these years.'

'But he never loved her when she was alive.'

'Of course he did! What the hell do you know?' he raised his voice.

'You guys did everything together. Never included me or Mum in anything.'

'Is that how you remember it?'

'That's how it was.'

He stepped forward so he was standing beside me. 'It wasn't that way at all. Mum wasn't interested in fishing or footy, you know that.'

'But she came to *my* games!'

'She never went to any of your games, Scott.'

My frown deepened as if I were wringing out my brain like a sponge, trying to find a memory of Mum standing on the sideline.

'She was happy to be the stay-at-home mum. She loved us all, that was the main thing.'

Was it true? I continued to stare at Mum's headstone in silence.

'Sure, Dad may not have shown his feelings in front of us kids, old-school generation and all that, but she was the love of his life.'

X

Mum did love Dad. I knew that but could never understand why. Had I been so caught up in my own selfish ways to see what was really going on? Todd hated me when I was a kid, but I'd hated him just as much, so who was right and who was wrong? My only memories of Mum and Dad together were vague, but there must have been more than that.

'Believe it or not, Dad's done a lot of soul searching over this last year.'

'Soul searching?' I didn't lift my gaze.

'We both hated you on that night.'

'It was long before that night.'

'No. You never showed any interest in the things Dad wanted to do with us, the fishing, the camping trips.'

'I was never asked.'

'Yes, you were. Constantly.'

More wringing out of the sponge failed to squeeze out a single memory to back either claim.

'Dad tried and tried, Scott, but each time you shunned him. Us. You just wanted to do your own thing.'

The only recollections I could find were of the teenage me strutting around Melbourne with Elvis, kicking goals for Essendon, hanging around outside Lowther School for girls, having a great life. The memories were all about me. This was getting a bit deep. I instinctively steered the conversation back to my defensive disposition. 'So where is he now then?'

'On the Gold Coast, at the Hopewell Hospice.'

'Hospice?'

'Yep. This is the first year he hasn't been down here. He's too sick to travel.'

I turned to look at my brother. His eyes were swollen and red.

'He hasn't got long left.'

'What do you mean?'

'Probably only days.'

Only thirty minutes earlier, this news wouldn't have bothered me in the least. Dad was dying, so what? Good riddance. But now, as if remnants of the memories I'd supressed were finally dripping from that twisted sponge, an icy tightness returned to my chest. *Had I really been so blind all these years?*

'I tried to tell you the other day at your house, but ... I knew the one place I'd be able to get you alone was here.' He placed a hand on my shoulder and continued, 'I'm sorry for the way things have worked out, Scott. We're both pig-headed idiots. I guess we get our stubbornness from Dad.'

I nodded and exhaled slowly.

'We can't change the past, but is there any way ...?'

I turned to look at him.

'Would you visit him? Let him make his peace?'

'Make his peace?'

'He wants to apologise. He knows he'll never be able to make things right between you. He wants to lay to rest the bad feelings.'

I was unsure how to respond. My mind was a whirl with disjointed memories and a whole set of new emotions.

'I want to apologise too, Scott. I've been so hidden behind my defensive barriers that the only offensive available was to be a complete dick towards you.' As he held out his hand for me to shake, I grabbed him by the shoulders and pulled him in close.

'It's me who should be apologising, mate. If it wasn't for me, Mum would still be here.'

We embraced as brothers should. Hot tears I hadn't experienced since the day the doctors turned off Mum's life support stung my eyes.

'No, that's all in the past now.'

Todd was crying too. 'It's time to look to the future.'

52

16 September
The flight back the previous night had gotten me into Gold Coast Airport for around 8.00 pm. After literally a three-minute Uber ride, I was home for 8.30. As I tiptoed through the house, I could hear Elvis and Tetley in the back shed in a heated debate about something, while Michael Hutchence sang 'Need You Tonight' in the background. I'd gone straight to my room. My exhaustion was of the mental and emotional kind. The thought of the banter and the dumbing down didn't appeal to me at that moment. *Was that what I did? Dumb down when I was with those two?* It was something I'd never considered before, but if it were true, it meant I'd spent most of my life doing just that.

The problem with going to bed early is that you wake up early. It was 3.30 am when I realised I was wide awake, lying there thinking about my dad.

It was still dark when I stepped outside the front door. The street was quiet except for the distant rumble of the ocean, carried on an easterly wind. The surf was up, I could tell purely from the sound of the waves, but I wasn't planning on going for a surf just yet. Maybe later.

I headed towards the beach and crossed Musgrave Street. A solitary light glowed in one of the apartments of the Iconic building, while the odd car, a delivery van and a police paddy wagon were the only traffic at that time of the morning. The children's playground looked eerily sinister in the shadows. A homeless person was asleep under the triangular-shaped barbeque area, cocooned in a scabby sleeping bag. There was a shopping trolley full of bags and soft drink cans parked close by.

Illuminated by spotlights, the century-old surf club building with its distinctive red tin roof glowed up ahead in the hazy salt-filled air. The sound of the surf grew louder as I drew closer to Kirra Point. The curved esplanade was a modern walkway, lit by a row of lights set into a stainless steel balustrade. Access to the beach there was via a wooden staircase leading down to the sand. Arguably the best part of the Gold Coast, *the real part*, there was a sprinkling of rocks at the southern curve of the bay. In the distance, just far enough away, Surfers Paradise glistened in a cloudless night sky like the Emerald City or fabled Eldorado.

I continued around the point a little, eventually taking a seat on a knee-high rock. From there I had a great view of the entire Gold Coast: Currumbin, Palm Beach, Burleigh Heads, and as far as Runaway Bay and Stradbroke Island to the north.

The easterly was breezy, but not cold. There were no surfers out yet, so I had the beach to myself – the perfect place to think.

The personal situation with my father and brother had pushed back the events of the last couple of weeks to the recesses of my mind. On my phone I had a picture of my mother, without which I probably would have forgotten what she looked like. Whenever the image of her face started to fade, I'd bring up the picture and stare at it as if reloading it into my memory. Sitting on that rock, I wasn't interested in the beautiful view and the calmness of my surroundings, I was focused fully on the screen of my mobile phone and the beautiful smiling face that looked back at me. Even her eyes seemed to smile. Her very being was one of happiness and comfort. That's how I remembered her. In fact, I couldn't recall a time she wasn't happy. So, if that was the case, how come I'd grown up with the belief that my father had treated her so badly?

A realisation struck me. Everything I remembered about my childhood was from the perspective of a different person–a cocky,

X

selfish kid who rebelled against anything he didn't agree with. My opinion of the world and the people around me at that time was if they didn't fit in with my agenda, they weren't worth knowing. I was more than selfish. Was it really me who shunned my dad and my brother, rather than the other way around as I'd grown up believing? The smile, the raised eyebrows, the laugh lines around my mother's eyes almost seemed to animate into an encouraging nod as if she were saying, 'That's it. You're finally getting it.'

I wasn't sure how long I'd been sitting there, but when I looked up, the skyline had changed from a star-filled darkness to a gradient band of pink. A golden flame suddenly appeared on the horizon, and I watched as a giant orb of shimmering fire slowly revealed itself. As it continued to rise, the tall buildings around the distant shoreline seemed to ignite from its glare.

A sprinkling of surfers was now paddling out the back, waiting for the next set of waves to roll through.

At that moment, I realised I needed to see my dad. It would be difficult. An apology would be too little – pointless and meaningless. I had no idea how I was going to handle the situation, but I had to face it head on.

I hadn't given Todd a definite answer when he'd pleaded with me to visit. Instead, I'd said I'd consider it. Apparently, there were no set visiting times at the hospice. I checked my watch, it was 5.00 am.

After a leisurely stroll back into Kirra, I continued past the bakery and went into the 7-Eleven 24-hour store. Searching the aisles, I found a small section of breakfast cereals. Muesli had to be healthier than a sausage roll with ketchup, right? In reality, there was probably more nutrition in the cardboard box than its contents, but at least it was a start. It was time for Scotty Stephens to grow up and get his act together. My health would be a good place to start.

After a bowl of cereal, a shower and a cup of herbal tea, which had probably been in the cupboard for years, I turned on the TV. Amazingly, there was no mention of *X*, or Adrian Stamp, or even of that all-time loser, Scotty Stephens. The relief I breathed was purely for myself. Although it would be a long time before the people of the Gold Coast forgot about me entirely, if they ever did, it felt good to finally be left alone. It was a double-edged relief though. Knowing X was still out there and would likely strike again, added a bitter aftertaste.

It had been seven days since the last killing. This went totally against my perception of the killer – perhaps I was wrong about that too.

I'd decided not to go to the hospice too early, so called Todd and told him I'd be visiting Dad that morning. He insisted on meeting me there. We agreed on 11.00 am.

Elvis rose, showered noisily, and appeared a few moments later, immaculate as always in his business suit. 'Been for a surf?' he asked.

'Nah.'

'What time did you get back last night?'

'Late,' I lied, 'house was quiet when I got home.'

'How'd it go?' This was an annually asked question that was just within the bounds of a topic Elvis knew we never discussed.

'Good.'

'What you got on today?'

I couldn't tell him about what had happened with my brother. That wasn't the kind of relationship we had, or was that just me again, pushing people out, keeping them at arm's length? 'Nuttin …'

'Alright, well, I've got to go. Don't lay around here wanking all day.'

My mobile phone rang. It was Jenny.

'Scotty, something's come up. Something really important!'

'What is it?'

'Not on the phone. Meet me at Janie's in an hour.' She hung up.

I could tell by the shaky tone in her voice it was serious. Had X struck again?

Traffic that time of morning would be pretty heavy, so I set off right away, figuring I should still be able to make it to the hospice in Ashmore for eleven. The coffee shop was in Marina Mirage, only a ten-minute drive from Dad.

53

Janie's was a small, licensed coffee shop overlooking the marina. Jenny was seated at one of the outside tables, but she wasn't alone. Sat with his back to me was a uniformed cop. Approaching them along the timber walkway, I glanced out over the water, which was even more blue than usual due to an influx of blue bottle jellyfish.

Jenny saw me and stood. The cop also stood and turned. Of course, it was Bradley.

'Hey guys,' I said, 'what's up?' Their expressions were grave.

Jenny glanced dramatically from side-to-side, as if making sure I hadn't been followed. 'Take a seat.' She was in detective mode.

I slid out a vacant seat and plonked myself down.

A waitress immediately appeared with a bottle of tap water and three glasses.

Jenny took charge and ordered three coffees.

'You guys alright?' I asked after the waitress had left.

'Uhm ...' Jenny glanced at Bradley then back at me.

Leaning forward, I lowered my voice, 'Has there been another killing?'

'No, no, nothing like that.' Jenny poured three glasses of water as she spoke, 'There's been a development.'

I raised my eyebrows.

'We've found some evidence,' Bradley said.

'*X*?'

They nodded in unison.

'What kind of evidence? Prints? DNA?' I'd inadvertently moved to the front of my seat.

The waitress arrived with our coffees. 'Can I get you anything to eat today?'

'No, thank you,' I replied abruptly, causing her to retreat. 'Come on guys, bloody hell!'

'Not prints no, but something that's probably just as good,' Bradley said. He went to sip his coffee, but I grabbed his arm.

'Don't leave me hanging, mate.'

The two of them seemed to be playing a mental game of table tennis. Bradley returned the serve with his eyes, as if giving Jenny a prompt.

'Better I show you.' Reaching under the table, she pulled out a laptop, opened it up and turned it on.

Bradley gently shook his arm free of my grip and sipped his coffee.

After a flurry of fingers and clicks, Jenny turned the screen to face me. On it was an open video window with a dark, frozen image. 'This is at the back of Robina Hospital, close to the stadium carpark on the night of September 9th.'

'The night of the last killing?' I leaned in and squinted at the screen.

'Watch,' Jenny instructed. She rolled the end of her index finger over the touchpad and clicked play.

It was brief, only a few seconds. Like a silent black and white movie, a dark figure moved across the screen, then vanished into the dark. I remained staring at the screen, expecting more. One thing I did notice was that the movement, although quick, wasn't fluid. There seemed to be a very slight pause when the figure was centre screen.

'Play it again.'

Yes, there was a definite pause and a blurred flicker.

'Can you slow it down?'

'Yep.' Jenny played it again in slow motion.

X

'Holy shit!' I couldn't get any closer to the edge of my seat. 'He looked at the camera!'

Jenny and Bradley grinned at each other, but I still sensed a tinge of nervousness in their behaviour.

'Can we freeze it?'

Jenny gave me an anticipated nod. Playing the video again, she skilfully paused it right at the moment when the figure looked up at the camera.

My nose was now almost touching the screen. It was impossible to tell who it was, but the image was surprisingly clear.

Looking at Jenny, I could tell she already knew what my next question would be.

'Can you zoom in on it?'

She turned the screen back to face her and went to work on the keys with her speedy fingers. 'I've been working on this at home until the early hours of this morning. I've not only managed to zoom in on the figure's face, but I've been able to enhance it.'

'You're kidding.'

'Nope. Brace yourself, mate. This is going to blow you away.'

X

Had anybody walked along the Marina Mirage gangway that morning, they'd have been forgiven for thinking that the couple and the copper sitting outside Janie's Coffee Shop, had been frozen in time. Jenny sat leaning on her elbow, chin resting between the thumb and index finger of her right hand, while Bradley sat upright, staring at the screen. I was slumped back in my seat as if I'd just been whacked with a baseball bat. I couldn't pull my eyes away from the screen. Looking back at me was *X*, in all his glory.

And I knew him.

54

A remnant of the fading offshores whipped up a salty breeze, sending a sudden shiver along my slouching spine. I twitched, slowly straightening up, and dragged my eyes from the screen until they met with Jenny's.

Jenny nodded nervously and said, 'I know, right?'

'Seriously? This was that night?'

'Yep. Fifty metres from the crime scene, around ten minutes after the victim's ETD.'

'So, we've got him ...' I looked back at the screen. 'We've got *you—ya bars-tard!*'

The face on the screen was exactly how it had been the last time I'd seen it, the default expression distant and vacant. Although he wore a hooded tracksuit exactly like the ones found in Lawrence Binks's wardrobe, and the hood was pulled tight with an elasticated tie string, revealing only an egg-shaped window, the features were unmistakable.

It was Troy Monroe!

Once again, Jenny and Bradley exchanged that nervous glance.

'What?'

'Got who?' Jenny said.

'What do you mean?' I pointed at the screen. 'Monroe ... Troy.'

'Is it?'

I grabbed the laptop and pulled it close to my face, then placed it back on the table. 'Yep. Case closed.'

X

'How do you know it's not Dillon?'

'Well, it's …' I picked up the laptop again, 'obvious, isn't it?'

'Is it?'

'Bloody *hell*, Jenny.' I'd raised my voice, startling the only other two patrons who were seated inside. 'Sorry, sorry.'

'How can you tell it's Troy,' Jenny continued in a whisper, 'when we can only see his face? It could be Dillon!'

She was right, of course. But it was the expression of the young man on the screen that convinced me it was Troy. Then I remembered the OCD traits he had displayed that day at Monroe's house, putting my chair back in its place. 'It all makes sense. The profile was spot on.'

Bradley nodded in support.

'We knew *X* had OCD. We were looking for a young man, a loner, possibly with a history of mental health issues. We've found him.'

'Don't get too excited yet, because there's more, a lot more.'

My coffee was cold, but I sipped it anyway.

'I'm all ears.'

'The problem is … well, one of the problems.' She looked at Bradley again for support. 'This evidence hasn't actually come to light, it's been hidden.'

'Of course. This is all Monroe's doing.'

'It certainly looks that way.'

I suddenly realised the significance of the nervous glances between the two of them. The video had been hidden, possibly deleted by someone without the knowledge that computer files are never really deleted unless the drive is completely wiped. Jenny had been digging in places that she shouldn't have been.

'I still say we take the recording to Nash, or someone who can help us,' Bradley said.

I realised they were both scared. 'No, not Nash. He's one of Monroe's mates. We need to be very careful.'

'We can't go to Ripley or Singleton,' Jenny said.

'But if we can't go to the Queensland Police Commissioner, who can we go to?' Bradley was getting flustered.

'It's alright, mate. We'll figure it out.' I was sick of the image on the screen staring back at me, so I closed the laptop. Jenny returned it to her bag.

'But they've broken the law, we have the evidence,' Bradley said.

Jenny remained quiet, nodding as if she were weighing up the options.

'It's not that easy, though,' I said.

'Of course it is. The law will deal with them.'

'It will, mate, it will,' I lowered my voice and leaned in once more. 'But you've got to remember who we're dealing with here – arguably some of the most powerful people in Australia. You've only got to look at what they did to Binks, and then to me. And if they've covered this up, imagine what else they're capable of.'

'If ...'

Apart from naivety, there was nothing wrong with his logic. These people had not only covered up a horrendous crime, but they'd framed a man to take the blame, and killed him. Now we had the identity of X, it was obvious that what may have begun as a cover up to save the Gold Coast from an economic disaster, while at the same time protecting the mayor's interests, had become much more than that when Monroe discovered his son was the killer. His motivation would have gone from selfish greed to the preservation of his family and his very being.

'We need to handle this carefully. Nash will be hired for the defence, and he'll pick this evidence apart in a heartbeat, then he'll focus on how we – you – obtained the video.'

'And he'll have the clout of Monroe and Singleton behind him,' Jenny added.

Bradley took off his police issue baseball cap and placed it on the table. 'So, what are we going to do? Say nothing and let Stamp take the blame?'

X

'Oh bloody hell, no. No, bloody no!' My vocabulary was lacking the vigour of my enthusiasm. 'We're certainly not going to let that happen.'

'Course we're bloody not!' Jenny threw in.

'We need more evidence. You've done a great job getting this, Jen, but it's still not enough.'

'Yes. Easier said, but ...'

'We didn't have *anything* before, but now we know exactly where we've got to direct our inquiries.'

'Wait a minute,' Bradley interjected, 'you're suspended, remember?'

'Don't you worry about that, mate. This'll be on my own time. But I will need your assistance, both of you.' I glanced at them.

Jenny nodded right away, while Bradley joined her after a thoughtful pause.

'Where do you suggest we start?' Jenny asked.

She was as good a detective as me, if not better. I guessed she already knew exactly where we'd need to begin, in fact I wouldn't have been surprised if she'd already started.

'We need to tread very carefully, but we need to focus on Troy Monroe. Check his whereabouts at the times of each of the murders and see if there have been any recorded incidents in the past.'

Jenny had retrieved her laptop and was fervently typing as she transcribed my words. Bradley jotted them down in his notebook.

'Obviously, it's going to be down to me to do all the leg work,' I continued, 'to speak with anyone who knows Troy, etc. But if you guys can discreetly take care of the technical stuff, like checking his mobile phone records, then we can report back to each other. What do you think?'

'Sounds good,' Jenny said, standing.

'I'm not sure what I can do,' Bradley said, supressing a yawn, 'they've got me on permanent night shifts.'

'You'll be an integral part of the team. Wait and see.' I squeezed his arm reassuringly.

'Okay, I better get back. I'll call you tonight, Scotty.' Jenny leaned over, kissed me on the cheek, then rushed away.

It took me by surprise. The last person to kiss me that way had been my mum.

Bradley's raised eyebrows showed he was surprised too. 'Ohh ... Jenny loves Scotty.'

'Shut up and get yourself home to bed.'

He giggled and padded off in the same direction as Jenny.

I sat for a moment looking out over the marina. A row of million-dollar yachts bobbed gently on the shifting tide while an Australian flag, aloft one of the tall masts, flapped wildly in the breeze.

My mobile phone rang. Seeing the name of the caller I sprang to attention and checked my watch. *Shit!* I answered the call.

'You bastard!'

'Todd? Hey mate, what's up?' Of course, I knew exactly what was up as I began to half walk/half run in the direction of the carpark. I was late for visiting my dad.

'You're what's up, you selfish lazy prick!'

'Tell him I'm on my way. Just got held up, that's all.'

'No need to bother coming.'

'I'm ten minutes away, tops.'

'HE FUCKING DIED, SCOTT!'

I stopped dead in my tracks. 'No ...'

'Yes. 'Waiting for you to come and see him. But what do you care?'

That familiar feeling of being hit in the chest with a frozen sledgehammer returned. 'Mate, I'm so sorry. I got held up, I was just on my way.'

'And the very last thing I said to him was a lie.'

'I'm on my way now,' I continued towards my car.

X

'It's okay, Dad,' Todd said, ignoring me, 'Scotty won't let you down. He'll be here.'

'Todd. I'm so sorry.' Those burning tears were stinging my eyes once more.

'Save it. I thought you'd changed, but you're exactly the same. Stay away from here, you won't be welcome. And don't even think about coming to the funeral.'

'Mate, I'm—'

The phone went dead.

55

He looked so much smaller than when he was alive. I held his hand; he was warmer than I expected. The room was pleasantly decorated, like a typical parents' bedroom. On the bedside cabinet was a family photo I'd never seen before, although I remembered the moment it was captured. We were at St Kilda, standing under the entrance to Luna Park, Todd and I held ice creams. I'd have been about eight years old and had ice cream around my mouth. We were all laughing. Todd had his arm around me. Mum's beautiful smile and her eyes full of happiness and joy seemed to stand out of the picture as if they'd been captured in 3D. Even Dad was laughing. This image seemed so alien to me that I hardly recognised him at first. I didn't remember ever seeing him like that – so young, so happy.

'That's because everything was about you,' Dad said.

'Was I really so selfish?'

'Yes. Still are. You even found something more important than being at your father's death bed.'

I couldn't argue with him. I could have seen Dad first, made him the priority and arranged to meet Jenny and Bradley later, but I didn't.

'Everything else is more important than your family, Scott. Always has been.'

I searched his inanimate face. The cheekbones seemed higher and more prominent. His eyes were closed, but not tightly, more as if he were having a gentle nap.

'But I don't blame you, son. You're more like me than you know.'

X

I'd never really looked at him closely before. I could only recall glances of his features. But looking down on him in the hospice bed, I realised how closely I resembled him. Unlike mine though, the hand I held was large and rough, a working man's hand, the hand of a man who had grafted all his life to provide for his family.

Todd had already left when I arrived, probably busy making funeral arrangements. Although I needed to speak to him to apologise, I was glad he wasn't there. The fact that I was having a conversation with my *dead* father didn't seem to register as unusual – it was having a conversation with him at all. I couldn't remember a time when we'd ever been alone before.

'I was a terrible son. Until now, I didn't realise how selfish I've been.'

'Don't blame yourself. It's all my fault. I didn't try with you. Our clash of personalities made it difficult for me. Todd was easier.'

The door opened and in walked a middle-aged woman. Her eyes puffy and red, she held a balled-up handkerchief tightly in one hand. 'Oh, you must be Scott. You came.' She smiled through her tears and stood on the other side of the bed. 'He went very peacefully.'

My silent stare prompted her to continue.

'I'm sorry, I'm Pam.' She dabbed her nose with the handkerchief.

My eyes must have said, 'Who the hell are you?'

'I'm your dad's wife.'

'What?' This came out as more of a croak.

'We've been married for fifteen years.'

How the hell didn't I know this? Why hadn't I been told?

'I'm sorry we finally get to meet now.' She held the handkerchief to her trembling mouth. 'Such a sad, sad day.'

'You're my ... dad's wife?'

She nodded and looked down at her husband. 'He was a wonderful man – strong, caring. I loved him very much.'

'How come ... how come nobody told me he was married?'

'You had an invite to the wedding. We tried to see you before then too, but you didn't want to see us.'

'Really?' I was squinting heavily, as if trying to wring out more of those lost memories.

'Your dad was upset. Not just by that, but for not being there for you. He regretted how he'd spoken to you when your mother died. He wanted to tell you that, to apologise.' She dabbed her eyes some more, suppressing a sob. 'He won't get the chance now. But ... but I can tell you he loved you, Scott, more than you could ever know. The biggest regret of his life was not being a better father to you.'

I squeezed Dad's hand and closed my eyes. The hot tears, seemingly triggered only by my family, were back.

'I want to tell you on his behalf, Scott, that he's sorry, and he doesn't want you to blame yourself for anything that happened.' She gently blew her nose. 'I know this because he spoke of you a lot, all of the time in fact.'

I let go of my dad's hand. It was time for me to go, not because I had somewhere else to be, but because I needed to get away and think. *Had I really blocked out so much of my life?* 'Thank you, Pam. It was nice to meet you. I'm sorry too, sorry I didn't get here in time this morning, sorry for ...'

Pam had moved around the bed. She put a hand on my shoulder, pulled me close and hugged me. 'Don't be. It's time to stop saying sorry. I'll let you know when the funeral is and if you want to come and see him again before then, just let me know and I'll arrange it.'

'Thank you.'

She was a kind lady, not unlike my mum. Dad seemed to have had a habit for attracting happy, generous women. Good on him.

X

I didn't remember leaving the hospice, didn't really regain consciousness until I was driving the Dub out of the carpark. I was trying to remember the day at Luna Park, but all I could see was me riding the dodgems, me on the rollercoaster, me playing the machines in the arcade, me eating ice cream. Mum was there of course, but it was as if my memory had forced Dad and Todd to the peripheral recesses of my mind. I began to wonder if those memories were locked away in that cupboard. And if so and I found the key, would I really want to open it?

56

I had the rest of the afternoon to myself. Jenny would be coming down to Kirra after work. Dad was obviously on my mind, but so too was the case.

A conflict raged within me. Should we keep the evidence to ourselves, safe from the knowledge of Monroe and his mates, or should we throw the dice and take it to the authorities? If we could get it to the right person, the spotlight would be returned to the investigation, but who could we take it to? My main concern was that it wouldn't just be me who ended up in jail if everything went pear-shaped. Jenny and Bradley could face the same fate for helping me, or worse, all three of us could fall victim to Monroe's dark side. Who knew what he could be capable of if cornered?

These were the thoughts going through my mind as I drove over the bridge to Sovereign Island. Because Jenny and Bradley were having to sneak around, possibly breaking the law, their fate was foremost on my mind. Would the way Jenny obtained the CCTV recording make it inadmissible evidence? Without it, we had nothing. I needed to keep digging, find something stronger, but for the first time at least we had some direction. The only choice I had was to hope that Jenny and Bradley could unearth more evidence against Troy Monroe, while I went back to the basics. The good old stake out.

I parked the Dub just down the street a bit from Monroe's house, tucked inconspicuously behind a plumber's van on the

X

other side of the road. From there I had a good view of the front entrance and the triple garage doors off to the left-hand side. I could also see the second storey windows, but most were covered with plantation shutters that made it impossible to see inside. The large atrium window framing the main staircase though was a huge sheet of unobstructed clear glass, so I'd be able to see if anyone went up and down the stairs at least.

I'd only been there a few minutes when bugger me, the front gate opened and out stepped Troy himself. A Labrador circled him, twisting and turning, its tail wagging madly. Troy pulled gently on the leash, then knelt on the ground and vigorously stroked the dog's neck. This only made the animal more excited, jumping all over his master, almost knocking him off his feet. Troy was clearly enjoying the dog's company. I'd never even seen him smile before. Now he was giggling like a little child.

With his arms almost yanked out of their sockets, he set off down the street. The leash was tight and the only thing stopping the dog from bolting into the road. I watched him pass and continue for a few metres before I climbed out of the Dub and followed.

Once again, I hoped the trusted baseball cap and sunnies would be enough of a disguise. He was moving quickly, struggling to control the dog. About a hundred metres down the road was a large vacant lot. A rectangle block covered in well-maintained turf, it led to the water's edge. The dog knew exactly where he was going, steering onto the grass as soon as they reached the block. Troy unclipped the leash then threw a tennis ball. The dog tore after the bouncing ball and scooped it up just before it reached the water's edge.

By the time I stepped onto the block, the dog was wigging out with the ball in his mouth, and Troy was running after him. He dropped the ball. Troy picked it up but this time he kicked it AFL style. It was an impressive technique. The dog followed the ball and plunged off the bank with a splash. The young man, who could easily have been mistaken for a teenager, laughed and hooted as he watched his dog swim out, collect the ball, then head back to the bank. His laugh stopped abruptly though when he noticed me approaching.

'Hi Troy, how's it going?'

His gaze dropped to the ground.

'Good to see you again, mate.'

The dog waded out of the water, dropped the ball by Troy's foot, and shook, sending a spiralling fan of droplets into the air.

Troy didn't move, it was like he'd retreated to somewhere safe.

I picked up the ball and the dog switched his attention to me. 'G'day maaaate,' I said, massaging the wet fur around his neck. He whined and nudged the ball in my hand with his nose.

'He wants you to throw it,' Troy said.

I threw it into the water as Troy had. The dog took off immediately and *splash!*

'What's his name?'

'Derek.'

'Derek the dog, cool name.'

'He's mine, nobody else's.' Troy spoke quick-fire and with purpose.

'Yeah, it's good to have a pet, eh? Wish I had a dog.'

Derek returned, but Troy ignored him, choosing instead to remain staring at the ground. I threw the ball again.

'He likes you.'

'I've always had a way with dogs.'

'You should get one.'

'You're right, I should. I've got a roommate who would probably protest though.'

'Get one anyway. Elvis is dead.'

'What did you say?'

Derek returned, only this time he didn't shake until he dropped the ball at my feet. I jumped and turned to avoid the spray. When I turned back, Troy still hadn't moved.

X

'You're a live wire you are, mate,' I said, kneeling to the dog and playfully pushing him to the ground. 'I'm taking you home with me. I'm taking you home with me,' I said playfully, tickling his wet fur.

Troy suddenly launched forwards, and with a surprising show of strength pushed me onto my backside. '*He's my dog! You get away from him!*' he yelled down at me. His fists were clenched, and his face was a shade of scarlet.

'Steady on, mate. I was only playing around,' I said, rising to my feet.

He barged right into me. His whole demeanour seemed to have changed from that of a shy young man to a bar room brawler. 'You get your own fucking dog!' He pushed me again, and this time I really got to feel his strength.

He was about to come at me again when there was a screech of tyres. Troy immediately stepped backwards and sank back into his usual self. My head turned automatically in the direction of the sound. A white Range Rover had braked in the middle of the street. I heard the driver door slam shut. Someone rounded the car and rushed towards us – it was Haley Monroe.

'What the hell are you doing?' she growled at me as she approached.

'Excuse me?'

She marched straight toward me and didn't stop until we were toe-to-toe. 'I said, what the hell are you doing?'

'I'm not doing anything, why?'

'Is he harassing you, Troy?'

Troy had fixed his focus on a single spot in the grass.

The dog jumped up and circled us. Haley turned and tried to kick him, but Derek was too quick. With his tail between his legs, he retreated and dropped to the ground for a rest.

Haley turned back to me. 'You get out of here, *now!*'

'I'm just out having a walk.'

She slapped both of her palms on my chest and pushed me backwards. 'You're a liar. I know what you're trying to do.'

'Yeah? What's that then?'

She swung around to her brother, 'Get the dog, Troy, we're going.'

Troy padded over towards the dog, clipped on his leash and headed back towards the street.

Haley watched him, her back towards me. When he'd reached the pavement, she turned back to face me and lowered her voice. 'Wait until my dad hears about this.' Her features morphed into a spiteful grin. 'You'll be back in the lock-up before nightfall.'

'Is that so? I've got nothing to lose then, have I?'

Her laugh was thick with sarcasm. 'You've already lost everything.'

'I don't mean that. What I mean is, I may as well go full bore ahead. You see, I know who *X* really is!'

The smirk dropped from her face like sand from a shovel.

'And I'm going to expose your dad for the lying, thieving fraud he is. Might just look into your history too.'

'You're nobody and you've got nothing.' She marched away.

'We'll see about that.'

57

'I've had a shit of a day.'

'Why, what's happened?' Jenny asked, settling in at the kitchen counter. It was 8.00 pm by the time she'd finished work.

I filled the jug from the tap. Elvis and Tetley were in the shed, so we stayed in the kitchen. She'd been excited when she arrived, but I'd cut her off with my gloom, telling her about the hospice.

'Oh, I'm so sorry, Scott.' She slid off her stool and comforted me with a hug.

'There's more …'

Craning her neck backwards, she looked up at me.

'Our investigation may be over before it's even started.' I told her what had happened with Troy and Haley.

'You're kidding me, aren't you?'

'No. The intention was to just stake out the place, you know, make a note of who came and went, and when. But then Troy came out with his dog, so I followed him.'

'You did more than follow him.'

'Yeah. I engaged with him. But I had no way of knowing Haley would show up.'

'Duh! Her parents live on that street. What if Monroe himself had driven by?'

'I know, I know,' I placed tea bags in two mugs, 'I wasn't thinking.'

'So, Monroe will have wind of us now.' She moved back to the stool.

'Not of you guys, only me.'

'Yes, but he's going to be on his guard. Shit Scotty, it was hard enough before.'

'I'm sorry. I stuffed up.' I stirred the teas, poured in the milk, and slid one of the mugs across the counter. 'Look, you guys stop what you're doing. Forget I asked for your help. It was selfish of me.'

'It's too late for that.' She attempted to sip her tea, but it was too hot. 'If the shit's going to hit the fan anyway, we may as well just carry on, perhaps even move up a gear.' I sensed she had more information she was yet to share with me. 'What did you find out from Troy?' she asked.

'That he's not what he seems.' I padded around the counter and sat down on the other stool. 'Didn't really get much of a chance before Haley showed up, but his behaviour definitely matches the profile. One hell of a temper.'

'Hmm, interesting.'

'So, tell me what you've got. You seemed a bit excited when you came in.'

'It's probably not the news you want to hear.' She managed a sip of her drink. 'Both the twins have solid alibis for September 9th.'

'Witnesses?'

'Yep, a whole bunch. For Dillon, the Gold Coast Suns as well as the coaching staff and God knows who else. He was at footy training.'

'Okay, so that rules out Dillon. That's no surprise to me.'

'Troy was at, wait for it—one of his anger management classes.'

'Really?'

'Apparently. You'll need to follow up, of course.' She reached into her bag, pulled out a thin Manila folder and slid it over to me. 'Here's the details of his classes. He goes twice a week. Tuesday nights, six until seven is a one-on-one session with his

X

therapist, Mia Davis. Thursday nights, seven until nine, are group sessions.'

'And four of the killings, including September 9th, took place on Thursday around nine,' I added. 'You've already checked if he was present on those evenings?'

She placed her mug down on the countertop and cupped her fingers around it. 'Yep, and he was. So, I checked his mobile phone records and they confirmed it.' She was one step ahead of me.

The coldness in my chest returned. 'I'll need to speak with the therapist to make doubly sure.'

'Yes, but I think you'll also find that most of those sessions are recorded. There'd be security cameras in the building too if nothing else.'

A rock solid alibi? My theory suddenly looked exactly like what it was – weak and without substance. My attention switched back to Dillion.

As if anticipating my thoughts, Jenny pointed at the folder. 'Dillon's phone records are in there too.'

I flicked through the documents. It was a mindless exercise. I already knew everything was in order. If the twins *were* at those locations at the times of the murders, my theory was not only weak, it was downright dead. 'But we've got Troy's image on CCTV at the scene of the murder.'

'Or Dillon.'

'There's something we're missing.'

The buzzing from my muted mobile phone as it vibrated across the countertop was almost as loud as the normal ring tone. 'Hey Bradley, how's it going?'

'Good. Listen, Adrian Stamp has just confessed to all nine of the *X* murders.'

'What?'

'The media have been informed. That's how I just found out.'

'Shit! Are you working tonight?' I gestured for Jenny to turn on the TV.

'Yes, the night shift again. Thank you, Mr Ripley.'

'Alright, take it easy out there, eh?'

Jenny grabbed the remote and turned on the TV. The news channels were indeed all over it.

This should have been looked on as reassuring news in the sense that X had finally been caught. Sure, we'd have been wrong, and our theories way off, but at least there'd be no more killings. But the news was far more than that. It was disastrous. For a start, I didn't believe for a minute that Stamp was X, so apart from the killer still being out there, it also meant the spotlight would likely return to me regarding Binks's death.

'They've either paid him off or forced a confession from him.'

'Absolutely.' I turned off the TV and took Jenny by the hand. 'Come on,' I led her to my bedroom.

'Seriously?'

Ignoring her, I plonked her down on the end of the bed and placed the folder under the incident room whiteboard. Taking centre stage now on the board was the blown-up CCTV image of Troy Monroe. I turned to face Jenny, 'You know what I'm going to do?'

'I think I've got a good idea,' she raised her eyebrows suggestively.

My mind should have been filled with the sadness of losing my father and not being there when he passed away, or of the madness and strain that had become my life in the past few days, but neither of those things occupied my thoughts at that moment. It was Derek the Labrador, jumping and running, diving carelessly into the water, retrieving the ball, returning it to his master, and bringing pure delight to the usually inanimate face of Troy Monroe.

'I'm gonna get a dog!'

'What?'

58

17 September
It was 6.00 am. I noticed the plastic venetian blinds were dusty as I cautiously opened a gap with my fingers. Crouched beside me, Jenny peered out too. I knew the press was back before I even looked. Inevitably, because of Stamp's confession, my fears were realised – questions were again being asked about the Binks's killing. The focus was back on me for all the wrong reasons, so I was sure a visit from the police was pending.

Luckily, my premonition had started the day before, so I'd moved the Dub to the street behind the house that night and asked Jenny to do the same with her car.

If the half a dozen or so reporters out front saw Jenny, the shit would really hit the fan.

My mobile phone rang. It was Ripley. I held it up for Jenny to see the caller ID.

'Hello.'

'Scott, it's Superintendent Andrew Ripley. Are you home?'

I was reluctant to answer his question but knew it would be easy for him to track my phone, if he hadn't already. 'Uhh, yes, sir, I am.'

'So, I'm guessing the press are already there?'

'Yes, they are.'

'Whatever you do, don't speak to them. But if they corner you, you tell them "no comment" due to the impending inquiry. Do you understand?'

'Yes, sir.'

'They'll soon move on, but more importantly, as long as you keep your head low, this will all go away. The inquiry could be years away.' There was a pause on the other end of the line. I imagined him shuffling uncomfortably, the way he always did when he was about to deliver something sensitive. 'You were at Monroe's house yesterday?'

'Was I?'

'You know you were,' his tone lowered to a sinister whisper, 'and this is your last warning. Back off, or we'll throw everything at you. You'll be arrested and put behind bars for a very long time. The inquiry will be brought forward, and you'll be charged with the unlawful killing of Binks, planting false evidence at the crime scene, as well as conspiracy to pervert the course of justice. And the place of incarceration won't be the kind of place where an ex-cop will be too popular, we'll also make sure of that.'

'But you know I'm innocent.'

'None of us are innocent, you know that. I need you to understand what I'm saying.'

'You want me to take the blame for all the false allegations you've laid against me, but as long as I lay low and don't say anything, it will all go away.'

'That's it.'

'Okay. I hear you.'

'Good man. Do the right thing, Scotty, and everything will be okay.'

'Thank you, sir. I will.'

The phone went dead. I often wondered how a nervous little man like Ripley could have risen to the rank of superintendent. I couldn't imagine him back in the day out on the streets as a constable or working the tough hours as a detective. He never came across as particularly intelligent, and *courage* certainly wasn't a word that came to mind. Once again, I pictured him rising from his desk, anxious, but happy for accomplishing his task. I was

X

confident he'd made the decision to call me himself, because it was a stupid mistake.

Jenny held up her mobile phone, grinning. 'Got it!'

I looked up at the ceiling, exhaled loudly and scraped my fingers through my hair.

Jenny jumped into my arms, 'We've got them!'

Our detective brains had worked as one, without the need of language. When Ripley's name displayed on the screen, I'd held up the phone and put it on speaker.

Jenny instantly took the prompt, pulled out her phone, pressed record and held it close to my phone, recording the full conversation. 'Silly, silly, Ripley.' She hugged me tight. 'Put some things in a bag.'

'What for?'

'You can't stay here. Come back to my place.'

It made sense. I needed to keep low more than ever now, at least until we got the evidence to the right people.

We showered quickly, together. Returning to the kitchen, I noticed something was different – it was quiet. I was so used to Elvis's omnipresent snoring in the mornings that my brain no longer registered it, only noticing it when it wasn't there. Since returning from the shower, it had stopped.

'Hey guys,' Elvis padded into the kitchen in his underwear. 'Jeez you two were going at it last night.'

Neither Jenny nor I took the bait.

'Listen mate, the press is back.' I flicked a thumb over my shoulder in the direction of the front door.

'Ah, great.' He held out his arms, 'Do you want me to go and have a word with them?'

'No, just "no comment," remember?'

'No worries.' He reached into one of the overhead cabinets, pulled out a bowl, then began to rummage through the under-bench cupboards. 'You haven't eaten my Rice Bubbles, have you?'

'No. Listen, things are likely to get a lot worse so ...' I glanced at Jenny, who nodded in support, 'I'm going to be moving out for a bit.'

Elvis popped up from beneath the counter like a jack-in-the-box. 'You're what?'

'Just temporarily, just while things calm down.'

'You can't move out, mate.' He obviously wasn't registering the word *temporarily*.

'It's for the best, and I'll be back here before you know it.'

'But where will you—?' Our expressions must have given him the answer before he'd finished asking the question. 'Oh, I see. You're moving in with a chick.'

'Mate, I've got to get away from what's outside that front door. And that's only the beginning, believe me. It's going to get a whole lot worse after today.'

'Why? What's happening today?' His selfish tone had turned to one of concern.

'I can't say too much, but we've got evidence to show that not only am I innocent, but that the whole thing has been a cover up.'

59

Although in many circles nowadays, the Dub would be voted the cooler of the two vehicles, Jenny's four-year-old MINI was more comfortable, more practical, and a lot quicker. I'd like to say I relaxed in the passenger seat, but relaxation was a thing my brain seemed to have rejected lately, just like certain memories from my childhood. There'd been no complaints from Jenny when I suggested we climb over the back fence to avoid the press. She was a competitive, anything-you-can-do-I-can-do-better type of girl.

We got onto the M1 at Tugun.

Jenny remained quiet, her attention on the road ahead. We were on our way to Brisbane to meet with Shana McCreary – the Bris-Vegas answer to Craig Nash, but the opposite, in that she was a prosecutor. She'd once been married to Red Jackson, the famous country singer from Tamworth. He'd been her second husband. She was currently on number four. Like Nash, she worked the high-profile cases, prosecuting everyone from football stars who ran afoul of the law, to Collin Porter, the mining magnate who was charged and convicted with statutory rape a couple of years ago. She too was often in the news, and Botox was her best friend.

Jenny had been able to make an appointment with McCreary due to family ties. She spoke of McCreary fondly as Aunty Shay. With the appointment came free parking, which was a godsend in Queensland's capital city, not just because of the expense but because it meant we were able to park in the basement beneath the building.

Jenny had said very little during the drive. I'd been studying her out the corner of my eye for the latter part of the trip. She was an intense thinker and I imagined her visualising the meeting ahead. I touched her hand as she pulled into the allocated parking spot.

'You okay?'

'Yep. We've got this.'

I leaned over and kissed her.

X

Shana McCreary's office suite incorporated the entire south-east side on the top floor of the blue glass building. As we were ushered into her office by a middle-aged receptionist, it was hard not to gasp. The views from the expansive windows took in the winding Brisbane River, including Southbank, the Storey Bridge to the east, Moreton Bay to the west, and as far south as the Gold Coast.

'Wow!' we said in unison.

'Ms McCreary will be with you shortly,' the receptionist said, showing us to seats in front of an expansive desk. 'Can I get you anything to drink? Tea? Coffee?'

'No, thank you,' Jenny replied.

'Yeah, I'll have a coffee please.'

Jenny shot me a look that said, 'Really?'

I lowered my voice, 'And is there a toilet I can use?'

The receptionist smiled awkwardly, 'Sure, if you'd like to follow me.'

By the time I returned, McCreary was at her desk, chatting with Jenny.

'Ah, Detective Inspector Stephens, it's great to meet you.' She stood and offered her hand over the desk.

I leaned over and we shook hands. Mine was still wet.

'Take a seat, please.' She rolled up her fist and clenched it as if she were wringing it out, but her eyes, a little sunken, were fixed

X

on mine. 'I've been following the *X* case very carefully,' she said. 'You've really been put through the wringer, haven't you?'

'You're not wrong.' The coffee I'd ordered was already on the desk. I picked it up and took a sip.

'Jenny tells me you have some …' she glanced towards her niece, 'new evidence?'

'Yes, we do, and it's extremely sensitive.' Now it was my turn to glance at Jenny. 'It's huge. That's why we've come to you.'

The night before, we'd decided there was only one way to handle this. We couldn't carry on with the investigation in secret. Everything needed to be out in the open, and we needed to do it now before Monroe and his entourage made their inevitable next move. The potential consequences of this were enormous, of course, but no more so than the alternative – letting Monroe rule the game, and me going to jail. That wasn't going to happen.

While Jenny spoke of the evidence we'd unearthed, Shana had sat back in her chair with intertwined fingers, gazing past us as if viewing the options on an invisible screen. Then with a little added melodrama, she looked first at Jenny and then at me, paused in contemplation, then said, 'Okay, I'm in. Show me the footage.'

60

Although Jenny's involvement so far had been behind the scenes, Shana had pointed out that it wouldn't be difficult for anyone to work out how the CCTV footage came into my possession. For that reason, she'd strongly recommended we both go into hiding.

I drove back while Jenny made some calls. The MINI was a far different ride from the old Dub – smooth, and easy to steer.

By the time we'd passed through Springwood, Jenny had booked us a holiday apartment under the name of Mr and Mrs Smith in the tallest building on the Gold Coast. Forty minutes later, we pulled up outside the iconic Q1 building.

'Okay, you wait here. I'll go get the key,' Jenny said.

After she'd disappeared through the glass doors of the foyer, my mobile rang. It was Elvis.

'What the fuck, Scotty. Where are you?'

'Hey, mate. Surfers. Why? What's up?'

'I've just had a call from Babs.'

'So?' We had complaints from the old girl next door on a weekly basis. She'd always call Elvis at work.

'You know how there were half a dozen journalists at our place this morning?'

'Yeah.'

'Apparently they've multiplied into an army and the street's chockers with news trucks.'

X

'Shit! That was quick.'

'What's going on?'

After showing Shana the CCTV footage and explaining who the person was on the close-up image, then playing back the recorded phone call with Ripley, she'd grown as excited as a greedy politician. She assured us it would only take a couple of phone calls to the right people and the investigation would be reopened. Then she pretty much ushered us out of her office, declaring action would be swift.

It was inevitable that the media would get hold of the story, but I hadn't anticipated it happening so quickly. This was obviously Shana's doing, and I began to question her motivation. Surely it would have been better to keep this from the press for as long as possible.

Jenny returned with two key cards. 'Drive down the ramp, towards the gate,' she said, handing me one of the cards and pointing towards the right of the building. 'You'll need to swipe this.'

I parked the car in an allocated spot two floors down. Within minutes, we were in the elevator, whizzing up to the fifty-third floor.

'Just had a call from Elvis.'

'Yeah?'

'Looks like Aunty Shay's gone straight to the media.'

'They're in Kirra?'

I nodded. 'Every news truck in the southern hemisphere, according to Elvis.'

'Hmm ...'

'Can we trust her?'

'Of course. She knows what she's doing.'

'But why would she go to the media first?'

'I doubt she has. She would have spoken to whoever she needed to first, then gone to the press. We can trust her.'

'I hope you're right.' That feeling of not being in control had returned. Once again, my fate was being plotted by others.

The apartment was nice with its curved outer walls, but nothing flash. The view overlooking the sparkling ocean, with hinterland glimpses to the left and right, was the reason millions of tourists visited the Gold Coast each year.

'Okay, I need to duck home and get our things,' Jenny said.

Luckily, I'd packed an overnight bag with my essentials, but it was at Jenny's.

'I'll call into the supermarket too. Do you need anything?'

'Uhh, not really.'

She kissed me on the cheek. 'Okay. Stay here, don't go out. I'll be back as quickly as I can.'

'Okay.'

It would have been great to have sat out on a balcony, but I guess the architect's vision and the design of the building hadn't allowed for them. So instead, I parked myself on the L-shaped sofa and turned on the TV.

'Here we go again.' I said out loud. Channel 7 showed the same young female reporter, this time standing on Ruby Street. 'DI Stephens is believed to be inside the property,' she announced, as the screen changed to the image of the Dub. 'His car is still parked on the street behind his house.'

'Have there been any signs of him at all?' Alex Wade asked from the studio.

'No. The only person leaving the building this morning was his housemate, a Mr Nicholadas Papageorgiou. His only comment was, and I quote, "Elvis is King!"'

With a smirk, I switched to Channel 9. A clone of the girl from Channel 7 was standing outside Surfers Paradise Police Headquarters. 'Allegations have been made that Superintendent Andrew Ripley, Gold Coast Mayor, Julian Monroe, and the Queensland Police Commissioner, Edward Singleton, framed Lawrence Binks for the X murders. It has also been implied that they purposely covered up evidence as to the identity of the real killer. Our sources tell us that Superintendent Ripley is currently undergoing questioning.'

Channel 10's reporter, standing outside the mayor's offices in

X

Southport, was a young man wearing a cheap suit and the kind of shirt that didn't accommodate a tie. The image changed to earlier footage of Monroe being escorted from the building by police through a waiting mob of media. The reporter spoke while the footage played, 'Gold Coast Mayor, the honourable Julian Monroe, was in a meeting for the proposed easing of building restrictions on The Spit.'

Audio returned to the footage.

'Is it true you plotted against Lawrence Binks, Mr Monroe?' an unseen reporter asked as Monroe was escorted through the crowd.

'What do you say to the claims that you covered up the true identity of *X*, sir?'

Monroe was ushered into the back of a waiting police car. Beside him sat Detective Dale Mason.

For the next hour, I flicked through the news channels and decided Shana McCreary had been the right person to take this to after all. Not only had she approached the media with what could be the biggest story of the decade, but she'd also gone straight to the top – as high as the governor-general.

61

We spent the rest of the day lazing around the apartment, watching movies. There was no fresh news because Monroe, Singleton and Ripley were being questioned. Jenny was on a rostered two days off, which had worked out really well. Although she'd been to the supermarket and bought some supplies, at around 6.00 pm we ordered takeaway.

While waiting for the delivery, my mobile rang. It was Pam, my dad's wife, telling me the funeral would be at Allambe Memorial Park in Nerang, 3.00 pm next Thursday. I thanked her and she hung up.

'Will you go?' Jenny asked.

'Of course. Will you come with me?'

'Sure.' Jenny put an arm around my shoulder, and we kissed. Then, responding to a text message, she headed down to the lobby to meet the Uber Eats driver.

My mobile rang again. It was Bradley.

'Hey, mate. How's it going?' I asked.

'Good. Where are you?' His tone was all business.

I told him where we were staying. He said he'd be there in about an hour and hung up.

Bugger me, before Jenny returned, my phone rang again. It was Elvis.

'Where are you, mate?'

I loved the guy, but there was no way I was about to tell him

X

where I was. He'd insist on coming around, a carton of beer over his shoulder, Tetley and Johnno in tow.

'I'm at Jenny's.'

'Oh yeah, that's right. So how are you holding up? Looks like Monroe and his mates are finally gonna get theirs.'

'It does, mate. I'm good. Just laying low for a bit.'

'So, when do you start back? Tomorrow?'

'What do you mean?'

'They just said on the news that you'll probably be reinstated as soon as possible.'

'Really?'

'You've got the media on your side again, mate.'

'We'll see.'

As always, the Thai takeaway was a scrumptious belly filler. Peering out over the ocean made me feel like I was on holiday. A text came through from Bradley. He was in the lobby. Jenny went down to get him, and a few minutes later he was breezing into the apartment wearing his suit and an enormous grin. He marched over and pulled me into a hug. 'I could have come straight over, but I wanted to go home first and change. You won't be seeing me in that ghastly uniform again.'

'Why? What's happened?' I asked, gently pulling away.

'We're back in business!'

'What do you mean?' Jenny asked.

'Well, I am, but it's only a matter of time before they call you, Scott. I'm sure of it.'

'What are you on about?'

'Ripley crumbled.'

Our open-mouthed, wide-eyed expressions prompted him to continue.

'The news hasn't been released to the media yet, but Ripley has confessed.'

'You're kidding me.'

'No, and it looks like he'll be taking Monroe and Singleton with him.'

None of this was much of a surprise. If anyone was going to break under pressure, it was Ripley. Although I didn't know him that well, I did get the sense that, deep down, he had a conscience.

'Oh Scott, that's brilliant news!' Jenny flung herself into my arms.

'I'm surprised they haven't contacted you yet.'

Just as Bradley said that, my phone rang. I didn't recognise the number.

'DI Stephens?' It was a man's voice, deep, authoritarian.

'Speaking.' I switched to speaker so Jenny and Bradley could listen in.

'Scott, this is Acting Superintendent, Jim Giles. I'd like to meet with you as soon as possible please.'

'Sure.'

'Good, but don't come here. I'm sure you know how crazy it is in Surfers at present. How about we meet at Broadbeach Police Station in an hour?'

'Sounds good.'

'Okay, I'll see you there.' He hung up.

'Told you,' Bradley said, his face beaming. 'Okay, I should have time to get to Kirra and pick up one of your suits.' He swanned out the front door.

'Wow, Scotty. Finally,' Jenny said, hugging me again.

'We don't know anything for certain yet.'

'Oh, we do. They're going to reinstate you.'

'Who says I want to go back?'

She held me back at arm's length. 'You're seriously not thinking of turning them down, are you?'

'I don't know what I think yet. Who says they're not just doing this to save face?'

'So what if they are? Don't you see? This is our chance. No more

X

sneaking around. We'll have the full resources of the law behind us again, and for the first time, we have a likely suspect.'

'I know what you're saying Jen, but—' I broke away and turned to peer out the window, 'I'm just sick of being controlled.'

Jenny wrapped her arms around my chest from behind. 'Then don't let them. Take control yourself. This is your time, Scott.'

X

Broadbeach was only a few minutes' drive. It would probably take us longer to get out of the Q1 building than it would to reach the neighbouring suburb. Bradley had returned carrying one of my suits, with only minutes to spare. As I changed into it, he insisted on standing on the other side of the bedroom door, chattering like an excited parrot. 'Ruby Street was deadly quiet, no media out the front of your house. Looks like they've all returned to Surfers. Elvis and the English chap wanted to come back with me, but I said no.'

'Good,' I said through the door.

'I chose the brown. Hope that's okay?'

'That's fine.'

We arrived at Broadbeach Police Station dead on time.

62

18 September
At 7.30 the next morning, I was standing in incident room number 3 of Surfers Paradise Police Headquarters, looking on as Jenny and Bradley reconstructed the whiteboard. Photographs of the victims mainly, but this time where the image of Lawrence Binks once took centre stage, now hung the insensible face of Troy Monroe.

Our meeting with Acting Superintendent, Jim Giles the night before had gone well. Thanks to Ripley's confession, all charges against me had been dropped and I'd been reinstated to the investigation. After the treatment I'd been forced to endure, a little part of me wanted to say, "Fuck you!" But Jenny was right–the bigger part of me was excited to finally be able to take control. Giles seemed like a good bloke, very apologetic towards my situation.

Monroe, Singleton and Ripley were charged with the same charges that had been thrown against me previously. Dion Gardner was arrested for the unlawful killing of Lawrence Binks, and held in custody without bail. What this meant for me was that I could finally get on with the job without anybody in the way, or anyone else calling the shots. Of course, this also brought with it the inevitable self-doubt. *Was I really up to it?* Time would tell. If I failed now, I'd only have myself to blame.

The first task was to put together a new team. Because I believed we were close to a conviction, I couldn't see the need for

X

a big crew like the one Ripley had formed previously. I decided all we'd need were Jenny, Bradley, myself, and the uniforms, Dee Forester and Wayne McDonald. While Jenny and Bradley tweaked the incident room, Forester and McDonald were on their way back from Monroe's house with Troy in custody. I'd instructed them to take him straight to interview room 1. Unfortunately, bringing him here meant they'd have to run the gauntlet of the press out front, but that couldn't be helped.

When the whiteboard was finished, I was surprised to see not one, but two pictures of Troy. On closer inspection, the other one was obviously Dillon – slightly longer hair with an accent of red. 'Good work, guys.'

There was a low knock on the door and Dee Forester entered. 'He's here, sir. In room 1, as you instructed.'

'Great, thanks Dee.'

'Just be aware though, his sister is with him and she's going *off*.'

'Great, the lovely Haley.'

Jenny went with me, while Bradley entered the room next door to observe through the one-way mirror.

Haley Monroe sprang to her feet when we entered. 'What the hell are you doing?' She was in my face, 'First my father, now my little brother?'

Close up, it was hard not to notice the amount of make-up she wore. I wasn't sure if it made her look younger or older. 'If you'd like to calm down please, Miss Monroe.'

'So, this is a revenge thing, is it? You're blaming our family for all of *your shit*.'

'I'm going to have to ask you to leave the room please, miss,' Jenny said.

'I'm not going anywhere.'

Troy was seated at the table, his head low.

Haley backed away from me and put her arm on his shoulder. 'I'm not leaving him alone with you bastards.'

Jenny stepped towards her. 'I'm afraid I'm going to have to insist.'

'Get away from me, you bitch!' Haley growled, her eyes blazing like hot coals.

Troy belched a nervous giggle at the word, "bitch."

'If you don't leave the room quietly miss, you'll be removed.' Jenny moved in closer, ready for a brawl.

Before Haley could reply, the door flew open and in breezed defence lawyer, Craig Nash.

'What's going on here?' he demanded, glaring at Jenny.

'Mr Nash, of course,' I said. Even this prick wasn't going to take control. That was my job now.

'Thank God you're here, Craig,' Haley rushed towards the lawyer and threw her arms around him. 'I'm so scared for Troy.' Gone was the angry, confrontational voice, replaced instead by that of a sweet, innocent girl.

'What the hell are you doing, detective?' Nash demanded, his frown directed at me.

'Absolutely nothing. We were just trying to explain to Miss Monroe that she'd need to wait outside while we asked Troy a few questions.'

'He threatened us, Craig. Said he was going to get his revenge for what Daddy did to him.'

'Oh, is that right?'

I could sense in Nash's eyes his relish for the fight ahead. I wasn't having any of it. 'No, that's not right. Now if you'd like to take a seat in the hallway please, Miss Monroe. The sooner we get this interview over with, the sooner you can go home.'

Nash gave her a reassuring nod. 'It's okay, I'll look after Troy.'

There was melodrama in her movements as she glided over to her brother and kissed him on the top of his head. 'It's going to be okay, Sprite. I'll be just outside the door.'

Troy nodded nonchalantly, as if unaware of what all the fuss was about.

X

'Good boy. Be strong.' She spoke to her brother as if he were a child. Before she left the room, and out of Nash's view, she shot Jenny a sideways glance that said, 'You hurt him and I'll kill you!'

The interview that followed could have been considered a waste of time. Nash instructed his client not to answer any questions he wasn't comfortable with. This was easily put into perspective when considering that Troy was uncomfortable with just about everything in life, so he said very little. Problem was the only evidence we had was the CCTV footage. Troy's phone records backed up his alibis, as did credible witnesses. On the nights of at least two of the killings, he was at his weekly anger management meetings.

'So, you've got nothing,' Nash said. 'Why are we here, detective?'

I handed him the CCTV photograph. 'We have a picture of your client leaving one of the murder scenes.'

Nash laughed out loud. 'Is this it? Is this really all you have?'

I didn't have an answer.

'My god, you really are out of your depth.'

'It would be helpful for the inquiry if your client would answer our questions,' Jenny said.

'He doesn't have to. The facts have done that for him. I can prove emphatically that my client was elsewhere when each of the killings took place. All you have is this.' He skimmed the photograph across the table and stood up. 'Now, if there's nothing else, we'll be—'

'I'm afraid we'll be holding your client for further questioning.' I also stood up.

'What the hell are you playing at, Scott?'

'Just exhibiting our rights.'

Nash knew we could hold Troy for twenty-four hours. 'You really do have an axe to grind. What's next on your agenda of revenge?'

I nodded towards the two-way mirror.

Bradley entered the room moments later and escorted Troy away. Nash, Jenny and I followed. Entering the hallway, we were greeted by the angry, snarling face of Haley.

'What are you doing to him?' she growled.

As Bradley led Troy towards the holding cells, everyone else's eyes had been averted towards the commotion in the opposite direction.

Dillon Monroe, red in the face, handcuffed and thrashing around like a shark out of water, was being bundled along the corridor by Dee Forester and Wayne McDonald. 'Do you know who I am, you idiots? How dare you treat me like this?'

Nash, noticeably shaken, ducked to one side. Jenny shielded him. Haley was momentarily torn. When she looked towards Dillon, her expression was pure anger. But when she looked towards Troy being led away, it instantly changed to concern. She glanced at me, and it morphed once more – this time to hate. Turning on her heels she followed Troy.

'This one didn't want to come quietly, sir,' Dee said, straining as she and Wayne guided Dillon into the interview room.

'*Do something, Nash!*' Dillon yelled from inside the room.

63

The interview with Dillon Monroe was vastly different from the one we'd just conducted with Troy. Unlike his brother, Dillon was loud and brash. Ignoring Nash's constant instructions to remain calm and not say a word, he let rip instead.

'Do you realise my father will bury you for this?' His contempt was directed solely at me.

'Just calm down, buddy,' Jenny said, 'we just want to ask you a few questions.'

'Oh, yeah, so you drag me down here against my will, handcuffed?'

'We were forced to arrest you, mate,' I said. 'It could have been a whole lot easier. Now you're facing an assault charge against an officer of the law and one charge of resisting arrest.'

'You can't hold me here.' He jumped to his feet.

The uniformed officers pounced from their positions at either side of the door and instantly forced him back into his seat.

'Do something, Craig. Jesus.' A quaver of uncertainty appeared beneath the anger.

'You don't have to say anything if you don't want to. Just remain calm,' Nash said.

Dillon folded his arms and slunk down into his seat, scowling.

'Once again, detectives, we have solid alibis and witnesses who will collaborate the whereabouts of my client,' Nash said.

'Can you tell me where you were on the night of September 9th around 9.00 pm?' I directed the question at Dillion.

'At footy training.' He sat up straight in his chair, the scowl smoothing into a cocky grin. 'I've got nothing to hide.' His eyes locked onto mine. 'What do you wanna know, dickhead?'

'Did you kill Tracey Porter on the evening of September 9?'

'What? Are you serious? Is that what this is all about?'

'And Denise Shaw on September 4?'

'You know exactly where my client was at those times. Why are you continuing with this ridiculous line of questioning?' Nash was hastily taking notes as he spoke.

'And Lisa Wei on September 3?'

'No, I did not!'

I slid the CCTV photograph across the desk.

When Dillon saw it, there was a definite change to his expression. The smirk widened to a nervous smile. 'What's that supposed to be?'

'Well, it's clearly you.'

He picked it up and studied it. 'Nah. Not pretty enough.'

'Your brother then, you reckon?' I spoke as if this realisation hadn't occurred to me.

The smirk returned. 'No ...'

'Like to hurt girls, do you, mate?' Jenny asked.

Nash rose to his feet. 'End of interview.'

'No worries. Take him away constables,' I ordered.

'You what? You can't keep me here!' Dillon pressed the palms of his hands onto the top of the table as if they would anchor him there.

'Put him in the cell next to his brother.'

Dillon jumped up. 'No way. Do something Nash!'

The uniforms grabbed an arm each.

'Just stay calm and don't say anything else,' Nash instructed.

'But they're going to lock me up for something I haven't done!'

'You'll be okay. This will all blow over tomorrow.'

Dillon tried to pull away, but the constables were stronger.

X

After a brief struggle he must have realised this, falling limp as he was led through the door.

Haley was waiting in the hallway. 'No, no, no. You can't be serious?'

Dillon's face was now a shade of ashen white, and even with the slightly longer hair and flashier clothes, he looked more like his brother at that moment than any since I'd first met him.

I was surprised Haley didn't follow him the way she had Troy. Instead, she continued to offload her anger on me. 'You really are the idiot my father picked you for.'

'Haley, that's enough,' Nash said.

She stepped closer until our noses were almost touching. 'You cunt!'

'Nice.' I stepped back and glanced over at Jenny. 'We were just saying what a lovely girl that Haley Monroe is, weren't we Jen?'

'Yeah, guess we were wrong,' Jenny offered.

I looked back at Haley. 'Must run in the family.'

Nash put a hand on Haley's shoulder. 'Come on. We're wasting time here.'

X

Bradley came breezing into the incident room, his arms filled with McDonald's takeaway bags and cartons of soft drink.

Jenny and I had been standing in front of the whiteboard for the last twenty minutes, silently contemplating the situation. Bradley's return was a welcome distraction.

'Don't get used to this,' he said, unloading the food onto a table, 'because this is against all my principles.' He detested the idea of eating fast food.

'It won't kill you just this once,' Jenny laughed, ripping open the bags and spreading them out like a throwaway tablecloth.

'Who said I wanted a Big Mac?' I said when Bradley handed me a burger.

'Sorry, what did you want?' Bradley blushed.

'Well, a Big Mac, but—'

'So, I assumed correctly.' He thrust a Coke into my other hand.

'I might have wanted a veggie burger like you blokes.' My mumble fell on deaf ears.

We sat around the table eating silently until, with a mouthful of burger, I said, 'We have a dilemma.'

'We do indeed,' Jenny said.

'Why don't you spell it out for us, Scott?' Bradley said, nibbling like a polite squirrel. 'Where exactly are we now?'

I took a loud sip of Coke through the straw, burped, and continued, 'Although for a brief period, we currently have the two prime suspects in our custody.'

'Why for a brief period? We have the CCTV footage, and we know Troy suffers from OCD. Surely that's enough to lay charges?'

Right on time, Dee Forester knocked on the door and entered, carrying a laptop.

'How'd ya go?' I asked as she placed the computer down on the adjacent table.

'Good, and not so good.' The laptop was already on. She pressed the mouse pad and skittered out of the way. Earlier, I'd instructed her to try and get some close-up images of the twins from the video footage of their interviews. A perfectly clear, freeze-framed image of Troy's face appeared on the screen.

'Perfect. And …?'

'I created a high resolution jpeg from this and ran it through the recognition software as you instructed.'

I'm sure the pause was more of a nervous response than a deliberate attempt at drama, but it was just as annoying. 'And?'

'It's a 99.97 per cent positive match to the CCTV image.'

Bradley whooped.

X

Jenny leaned over and grasped my arm. 'Congratulations, Scotty, we've got him.'

My attention, however, remained fixed on Dee. There was no sign of celebration in her face. I knew exactly what was coming next.

She brought up a similar image of Dillon.

'You can clearly see the difference,' Bradley said leaning in, 'it's the hair.'

'The original CCTV image was just of the face.' Leaning over sideways, Dee opened the image in Photoshop. Around the face was an oval outline that she had already created. 'Because of the hood, this was the only part of the head that was captured, basically the face. This is what I ran through the recognition software.'

'And?' My question was a token gesture.

'Also a 99.97 per cent positive match.'

64

As much as I would have liked to, we couldn't interview either of the twins without Nash's presence. But that didn't mean I couldn't check on them. Normally, detainees would be transferred to Southport Watchhouse, but with all the activity outside, I decided to keep the boys here. 'Hey mate. You okay?' I asked through the letterbox hatch of holding room 1.

Troy sat on the bare bench, looking straight ahead. 'I'm not who you think I am.' He spoke in that robotic tone.

'Who do I think you are?'

'X.'

'And why do I think that?'

'Because you have CCTV footage of Dillon at one of the murder scenes.'

Although I knew from his medical history that he was highly intelligent, I couldn't help speaking to him like a child. 'Is Dillon X?'

'No.'

'Who is then?'

'X equals XX.'

'What does that mean?'

He ignored me, but I detected a slight grin.

'Did you kill those girls?'

'No.'

'Then who did?'

'X.'

X

'Who is *X*?'
'*X* equals *XX*.'
'Do you know *X*?'
'Yes.'
'Why did *X* kill those girls?'
'Because *X* is angry.'
'Why?'
'Because ... *X* hates girls.'

If I'd been recording this, none of it would have been allowed as admissible evidence. What I was doing was illegal. 'Did *X* tell you that?'
'Yes.'
'When?'
He shrugged.
'Is he going to kill again?'
'Of course.'

It was no good asking the obvious questions: where were you on the night of ... etc. Speaking to Troy like this in a friendly manner was allowing me to harvest as much information about him as I was going to get.

'Did *X* tell you that too?'
He shrugged again and shook his head.
'Then how do you know? Is *X* here now?'
'Shut up, Troy. Don't say another word.' Dillon yelled from the neighbouring cell.

I strolled the few feet along the corridor until I was outside holding room 2. 'You alright in there, buddy?'
'Fuck off.' Dillon was up, leaning against the hatch with an arm on either side of the door.
'Can I get you anything?'
'Just let me out of here.'
'No worries. We can do that.'
'Really?'
'Yeah.' I lowered my voice. 'Is Troy *X*?'

Dillon put his face closer to the hatch. 'No, of course he isn't. Just leave him alone, eh?'

'Are you *X*?'

'Look at me.' He stepped back so I could see him fully. Even wearing just a plain shirt and close-fit trousers, he looked good. 'I can have any woman I want.'

'But you saw the CCTV footage.'

Dillon moved to the back of the cell and sat down on the bench. 'Are you really going to keep us here?'

'Have to.'

'Why?'

'Because one of you is a psychopath.'

He didn't take the bait.

'And you're covering up for each other.' I let that sit for a moment. 'It's only a matter of time before you slip up.'

Avoiding my gaze, he looked up at the ceiling.

'I can understand if you're trying to protect your brother, mate.'

X

Although there was no history of schizophrenia in either twin's medical records, after speaking with them, especially Troy, I began to suspect the possibility of a multi-personality scenario, which meant *X* could be a dissociative identity hiding within one of them.

'As much as I agree, Scott, we still can't hold them longer than twenty-four hours,' Acting Superintendent Giles said.

'But we can't let them go, knowing one of them is possibly a serial killer.'

'And we can't keep them both in custody knowing that one of them is innocent.'

'Surely, sir, there's got to be something we can do.'

'There is. Get more evidence. Because without proof, we have no choice but to let them go.'

X

Of course, none of this was news. I'd done my research. There was a case in the US where identical twins were held because one of them was identified as the perpetrator of a killing. But after no evidence was found to prove which twin was guilty, the case was acquitted. There was another case in Paris where an identical twin had been identified as a rapist. Justice was achieved when one of them confessed after the pair had been held in custody for almost a year. Although in Australia the law states that regardless of the circumstances, a person cannot be held without charge, we were dealing with a vicious serial killer who would undoubtedly kill again if released.

I wasn't about to let *X* back out on the street, so I charged them both with nine counts of murder.

'Jeez, the shit's going to hit the fan now,' Jenny said as we peered through the one-way mirror at the twins in interview room 1. I'd purposely sat them together in the hope that one might say something incriminating. So far, they hadn't said a word.

'Are you seriously, seriously out of your mind?' Nash said as we met him in the corridor.

'Maybe.' I showed him into the interview room.

Dillon's face lit up as we entered. Troy's remained the same. He didn't even look up.

'The trial hearing's set for 9.00 am tomorrow,' I said.

Nash nodded hastily. 'Leave me alone with my clients, please.'

'No worries.'

65

From the road, you could've been forgiven for mistaking the nondescript building for a large concrete bunker. The only two randomly placed windows visible from the side street were covered with timber slatted screens. A flush, double garage door made from Corten, rusted steel, and a matching front door, created the abandoned industrial look. The wall backing onto Hedges Avenue was windowless, rough-poured concrete. The beach side was hidden from the street.

I'd parked the Dub at Mermaid Beach Surf Club, then walked along Millionaires' Row to Haley Monroe's house.

When I rang the doorbell, a female voice immediately answered via an intercom. 'Is that really you, Detective Stephens?'

I looked up to see a security camera over the door. 'Yes, it is. Is that you, Haley?'

There was no reply. I waited patiently for a minute or so until I heard a series of locks slide, and the door slowly opened. Standing inside, smiling back at me was the unmistakable face of Haley's wife, Natalie Hinderman.

'Hi Scott. Come in, come in.' She opened the door wider and stepped back.

For some reason I hadn't imagined Natalie to be there, never mind opening the front door like a normal person. Wearing denim shorts and a singlet, she looked vastly different from the glamourous Hollywood starlet we all knew and loved.

X

I stepped through the door, feeling a little starstruck. It was well-known that Natalie was a Gold Coast girl; she'd grown up in the Mermaid Beach area.

We shook hands. 'Hi,' was all I could offer.

She closed the door behind me, and the sunlight disappeared. The small lobby was as bare as the outside. To my left, an open door led to the garage, giving me a glimpse of a black Porsche parked inside. Natalie led the way to a staircase to the right. 'Come up. If you're looking for Haley, I'm afraid she's not here right now.' Her accent was a mid-Pacific blend of Aussie and American. 'She's due back at any moment though,' she continued, without looking back.

I followed her up the stairs to a small landing. As soon as she opened the door at the top, sunlight flooded in. We stepped through into a huge open-ended room to be met by the gentle *swish* of the ocean. The air was warm and breezy. 'Wow.' I'd yet to venture further than one syllable since arriving, but it was all that was required.

'Can I get you a drink?'

I nodded.

Natalie grinned, and I got the impression she was used to people acting this way around her.

The room was open plan, made up of an enormous contemporary kitchen, dining room and living space. There were no windows on two sides, but the wall looking out onto the beach was a floor to ceiling row of glass concertina doors that were fully open. Outside, a resort-style infinity pool seemed to spill over to the beach beyond as if the coast had been cleverly incorporated into the building.

'Wow,' I said again.

Natalie giggled while she swung open the fridge door and retrieved a jug of iced tea. I must have been standing with my mouth open.

'Hope you don't mind tea. This is a dry house, I'm afraid.'

'No, that's fine.' Thank goodness, I'd found more syllables.

I followed her outside to a Bali-style gazebo. The shade it offered was welcome as we took seats on either side of a stone table.

'Cheers,' Natalie said.

'Cheers.' We touched glasses.

'So, what did you want to see Haley about?' she asked after taking a sip of tea.

'Oh, nothing much really. Just wanted to have a chat. I think we got off on the wrong foot.'

'Well, you did just arrest her brothers.'

I should have sipped my drink, but whether it was because I was nervous at sitting one-on-one with the most successful Australian actress of all time, I gulped down half of it in one go.

'Are you okay?' Natalie asked, my pained expression alerting her.

'Yeah, I'm fine, sorry.'

'Brain freeze?'

'Yep.' I massaged my forehead with my fingers.

She giggled again.

I was beginning to feel a little more relaxed. She was beautiful close-up, but she still had that carefree Aussie way about her. 'How well do you know the twins?' I ventured.

'Troy mostly,' she replied.

'Do you think he'd be capable of killing anyone?'

'No! That's ridiculous.'

'Why do you say that?'

'Troy's a little boy. He wouldn't harm a fly.'

'And Dillon?'

'He wouldn't have the time or the brains.'

'You said you know Troy mostly?'

'He comes for a sleepover sometimes. He has a few issues, autism, you know. He has a temper, but he's having therapy for it.'

'Would you say he suffers from OCD?'

'Oh gosh, yes.' She laughed. 'He can't stand anything to be out of

X

place, but no more so than the rest of the family. I think you'll find it's actually a Monroe trait.' I couldn't tell if she was joking or not.

There was a clunk and a muffled groaning – the sound of the garage door opening.

'Uh, oh. Look out, the master's home,' Natalie grinned, 'I hope you brought your armour.'

From our seats, we had a clear view of the door leading up from the garage. It swung open and in walked Haley. She went straight to the kitchen, threw down her car key on the centre island, went to the fridge and poured herself an iced tea. Then looking around as if searching for Natalie, her eyes met mine.

I braced myself as Natalie had suggested, but I needn't have worried. Haley padded through the house, kicking off her shoes as she went. She reached the table, leaned down and kissed her wife. Then she put down her drink, slid out a chair and took a seat. 'Thought you might show up.' There was no sign of animosity.

'Yeah?'

'Yep, either that or drag *me* in for questioning.'

'Why would I do that?'

'Because you know I'm the only person who really knows my brothers.'

She was spot on. I had considered bringing her in, and after realising that trying to speak to her parents would have been a waste of time, I'd come to the conclusion Haley was the only person I'd get some sense from. Hauling her down to the station wouldn't have gotten her on side though, so I'd decided to approach her from a different angle, non-threatening and in her familiar surroundings. 'Look, I know we don't see eye to eye,' I glanced at Natalie, and she nodded in support, 'but I want to apologise for what's happened.'

She shrugged and sipped her tea. This was a completely different Haley Monroe than I'd been in battle with only a couple of hours before.

'I'm truly sorry, and I realise how upsetting it must be, having your brothers held in custody.' I noticed a slight flinch. Was she struggling to hold her composure? And was I subconsciously baiting her?

'It's okay. I'm fine because … now the initial shock has worn off, I realise you have nothing, so it's just a matter of time before they come home.'

'Is there anything you can tell me about your brothers that could be helpful?'

'Like what?'

'Well, I've heard Troy has quite a temper.' I purposely avoided looking at Natalie.

'That doesn't make him a killer.'

'Has he ever had a girlfriend or …?'

Haley's laugh was a strained one. 'I don't think so.'

'Is he capable of killing those young girls?' This wasn't the plan. I was supposed to be winning her over, not goading her.

'Of course he's not!' She didn't yell, but there was a cat-like spit in her reply.

'What about Dillon?'

'Dillon's only interested in football, swimsuit models and tequila.'

I had to admit, she was retaining her composure.

'More likely to be Troy then?'

She jolted slightly and her fists clenched very briefly, like she'd just received a zap of static.

'Why are you doing this, detective?' Natalie asked.

I wasn't buying the calm routine from Haley. This wasn't who she really was. Perhaps not quite in the same league as her partner, but she was a bloody good actress all the same. 'Look, everything's going to come out in court. If there's anything we need to know, it's better you tell us now, rather than we find out later.'

'They're innocent! That's all you need to know.'

X

X

'It's a good result,' Jenny stated as we shared a bottle of wine back at the Q1.

We'd booked the apartment for a week, so had decided to enjoy it.

'What now though? We'll still need more evidence if we're going to get a conviction.'

'I know, but if my faith in Nash is correct, the twins will be remanded on bail. That'll give us more time. They'll be under twenty-four-hour surveillance, which means if one of them *is* X, he won't even be able to leave the house.'

'So, what do we do now?'

'Something will come up. It always does.' When I spoke those words, I had no idea of what that *something* could have been. But come it did – the very next day.

66

19 September
The hearing was set for 9.00 am and would be the first of the day at Southport Magistrates Court. Jenny and I arrived at work for seven and were met at the top of the stairway by Dee Forester.

'Morning, sir, ma'am.'

'Morning, Dee. What's up?' I got the feeling she'd been looking out for us to arrive.

'There's someone to see you, sir.'

'Someone?' We turned into the corridor.

'Mayor Monroe.'

'Ahh, awesome. In holding cell number 3, I hope.'

'No, sir. In your office.'

'Great. Can you bring us three coffees please, Dee?'

She nodded and ducked away in the direction of the kitchen.

Seated with his back to the door, Monroe jumped up as we entered my office. 'Scott.' He held out his hand. 'Thank you for agreeing to see me.'

There was no actual agreement, but I shook his hand warmly. The person standing before me was far different from the confident billionaire we loved to hate. His face was gaunt, and the fake tan was sallow on his dry skin. His cheekbones were more prominent and there was less of a shine to his eyes, while the plain, grey suit was a deflating contrast to the bedazzlers he usually wore.

'Mr Monroe, what can we do for you?'

'I was hoping I might have a word in private.' He glanced at Jenny.

X

Circling my desk, I took off my jacket and placed it over the back of my chair. 'That alright with you, Jen?'

'Sure.' Jenny left the room and closed the door behind her.

'Take a seat, sir,' I gestured with my hand as I began to roll up the cuffs of my shirt.

We both sat.

Monroe, fidgety, looked back at the door as if to make sure it was closed. 'You're not recording this, or filming us or anything, are you?'

'No.'

There was a knock and Dee Forester entered, carrying two coffees in paper cups. She placed them down on the desk.

'Thanks, Dee.'

When we were alone again, Monroe shuffled in his seat. 'Firstly,' he picked up the coffee but didn't drink from it, 'I wanted to apologise for my behaviour over the last couple of weeks.'

'Hmm … you *have* been a bit of a dick, Julian.'

The back-straightening flinch was another sign that he wasn't used to being spoken to this way, but the momentary 'how-dare-you' glare instantly dissolved, a clear signal I was the one in charge now. He averted his eyes down towards the coffee cup. 'Yes, I suppose I have.'

'So, what is it you want to tell me?'

'It was never supposed to go this far.'

I lifted my coffee and took a sip while keeping my eyes locked onto his, prompting him to continue.

'I only had the coast's best interest at heart. Binks wasn't supposed to have died. Gardner took that upon himself.' He took a mouthful of coffee, which surprised me because it was bloody hot. He didn't seem to notice and carried on speaking, 'He was supposed to have been brought in and charged. The court case would drag out over the next year or so, but in the meantime, the coast would return to normal.'

'The developments, you mean?'

'Yes, well, no. Not just that, but the tourism and the overall welfare of the people.'

'How many billions is the cruise terminal costing? And the new casino?'

'That's irrelevant.'

'Not when you realise that you had the most to lose if the investors pulled out.'

'But don't you see how disastrous that would have been for the coast?'

'But bringing Binks in wouldn't have changed the fact that the killer was still out there, unless ...' I paused, not purposely adding my own little sense of drama, but because it felt damn good to be the one asking the questions, 'Unless you knew who the killer was. Your son, perhaps?'

'No, no, that's ridiculous! Troy isn't a killer, we both know that.'

'Do we? What about Dillon?'

'That's just silly.'

'But if you knew Binks wasn't *X*, what was to stop the killer striking again?'

'Binks *was X*. Don't you see that? We just didn't have enough evidence, so we—'

'Fabricated it. Planted the knife at the scene, even went as far as procuring blood from the last victim and placing it on Binks's clothing.'

'Yes, but our intentions were merely to get the result that every single person on the coast wanted.'

'You set up an innocent man!'

'No, we got the right man, but we went about it the wrong way.'

'And DI Williams? What about poor old Des?'

'He would never have gone along with it, so we needed someone else in charge of the case. Someone who—'

'Someone without the brains to see what was really going on.'

'Yes.' He took another mouthful of coffee.

X

I leaned forward. 'Well, you got that wrong, didn't you?'

'Yes, well, Ripley did.'

I wanted to gloat, make him squirm, but remained professional instead. 'Which one of them did it?'

'Excuse me?'

'The twins. Which one of them killed those beautiful young women?'

'Neither of them, of course,' he snapped back. 'Are you not listening to me?'

'Of course I am.'

He placed the half empty cup on the desk and straightened his jacket. 'My apologies. I'm just–I'm under an awful lot of stress at the moment.'

'I understand. It's not a very nice feeling, is it, when the media's attention is suddenly thrust upon you for the wrong reasons?'

'No, no it's not.' He glanced at the door again then back at me. 'I was hoping we might ... come to some kind of arrangement.'

'Okay.' I lowered my voice to match his sinister tone, 'What kind of an arrangement?'

'I want to take my boys home today. They're innocent.'

'How do you know they're innocent?'

'They're my boys, of course I know.'

'But how?'

'Let's just say ...' he glanced towards the door again, 'I know.'

'So, you know who X really is?'

'Oh, for crying out loud!' He jumped to his feet. 'Binks is dead, for God's sake. The last killing was a copycat. We both know that.'

I remained quiet to see where this was heading.

'Tell me what you want.' Now it was his turn to lower his voice as he leaned over the desk. 'I'll give you anything, anything at all. Just let my boys go.'

'I'm afraid that's not going to happen, mate.' Ignoring his offer of bribery, I checked my watch. 'In just over an hour's time, they'll be up before the magistrates court, facing nine counts of murder.'

'But you can't charge them both.'

'Already have.'

'This is all about revenge, isn't it?'

'I don't know what you mean.'

'Yes, you do.' The words came out like a spit in the face. 'I know all about what happened with you and Gladys that night.'

'Who?'

'Don't try and play smart with me, it doesn't work for you.'

'I don't see your logic, mate. I have it off with your missus and I'm the one looking for revenge?'

'Because you blame her for your mother's death.'

'That's ridiculous.'

'Is it? And do you remember how good you felt when you assaulted me? How cocky you were when you strutted out of those toilets, leaving me reeling in agony. You put me out for the rest of that season and caused lasting damage.'

My shrug was purposely nonchalant. 'I seem to remember it was self-defence, three against one. Sounds like you're the one most likely to be seeking revenge.'

He laughed and looked me straight in the eye. 'At the very moment you were flaunting your victory, your mother was crushed to death, and all because of you.'

I didn't take the bait.

67

The trial hearing went exactly as I expected. Nash was no match for Shana McCreary. The twins were granted bail of $1.5 million each, placed under house arrest and ordered to wear security ankle bracelets, with a trial date set for three months' time. Dillon was suspended from the Gold Coast Suns indefinitely. Both boys would be confined to Monroe's mansion. Although the killer still wasn't behind bars, at least it meant whichever one of the brothers was the culprit, he'd be monitored 24/7, with no freedom at all.

The bumbling unknown detective who'd been plucked from obscurity and plonked in front of the media only a couple of weeks ago, was no longer present. The man who approached the podium outside Southport Magistrates Court was upright and confident. I read from a statement Bradley had prepared earlier, basically just sharing the facts we had so far. I wasn't holding back any information from the press. I knew I needed them onside. It was me who released the CCTV footage, along with the tantalising logline: Monroe twins charged with *X* murders.

Nash had warned me against doing that, and while he fought to get a restraining order to prevent it from happening, I released it anyway.

When I finished reading the statement, questions came at me from the large crowd of reporters.

'Do you have any idea which of the twins is the killer?'

'No, not at this time.'

'But you've charged them both?'

'Yes. This is an unprecedented case. We're sure one of them is the killer, but that also means one of them could be innocent.'

'Could be?'

'There is a chance it could be both of them, but we have no evidence to back that up at this time.'

'But aren't you worried now they've been released?'

'No. They're not free. They'll be under twenty-four-hour surveillance until the trial.'

'Who put up the bail?'

Normally questions like this would have a *no comment* reply, but I was having none of that. 'Mayor Monroe.'

'Are you confident of a conviction?'

'Yes.'

'But you're going to need more evidence, surely?'

'Yes, and we have time to find it now, but at least the streets of the coast will be safe while we do so.'

I would have been happy to have stood there all day answering their questions, but I had somewhere important to be. I ended the press conference, thanked everyone present, then returned inside the courthouse.

Bradley was waiting in the carpark with the Range Rover. 'We've got plenty of time,' he said, while I joined Jenny in the back seat.

'Well done.' Jenny squeezed my knee. 'You were great!'

'Thanks.'

'Probably a bit too forthcoming, but very confident.'

'Nah. It's better coming from my mouth rather than them concocting their own stories.'

'Nash isn't going to be happy, or Monroe.'

'I know. Good, eh?' I grinned.

X

X

The aroma of mown grass and freshly cut flowers on a gentle breeze greeted us as we stepped from the car into bright sunshine. A white hearse was parked under a wide portico. A small crowd wearing their Sunday best congregated around the entrance to the chapel. From inside, I could hear gentle organ music playing The Beatles' 'Let it Be.'

My dad's wife, Pam, broke away from the pack and came to greet me. 'There you are,' she said, putting her arms around me.

'Pam.'

She gently pulled away. 'And who is this?' she asked, looking first at Jenny, then Bradley.

I introduced them. I think she thought they were a couple, until Bradley spoke.

'Come on.' She took my hand. 'The family's already inside.'

There was a small gauntlet to pass through at the doorway, handshakes and hugs from people who seemed to know me, but of whom I had no recollection. Inside was dark until I took off my sunglasses. The first thing I saw was the coffin, resting on what appeared to be a small stage at the front of the chapel. To the left I saw Todd, sitting next to a woman who must have been his wife. Two children – a boy of about ten, and a girl of perhaps five or six – sat next to their mother. Apart from a vacant space for Pam, there was no more room on the front pew, but the one behind it was empty. While Jenny and Bradley took their seats, I stepped forward and placed a hand on my brother's shoulder. He looked up, offered a forced smile, and nodded. His wife's smile was more genuine. The children looked up at me inquisitively. It was the first time I'd seen them, which somehow added an extra layer of sadness to an already sad occasion. We didn't speak. I took my seat next to Jenny.

During the service, the celebrant spoke of a man I'd never known, and when she listed me as one of the family members, it felt very alien. When the curtains finally closed in front of the coffin, my eyes remained fixed on the spot.

Jenny took my hand. Todd stood, walked past me, and received condolences from those seated behind us.

His wife didn't pass me by though. 'Hi, I'm Liz.'

I stood and went to shake her hand.

She smiled and pulled me in for a hug. 'It's good to meet you at last.'

The little girl was standing shyly behind her mother, tugging at her dress.

Liz turned, 'And this is Juliette. Juliette, this is your Uncle Scott.'

'Daddy's brother?'

Her munchkin voice stabbed me in the heart like a blade cast from guilt. Why was I only now meeting this precious little girl?

My nephew was introduced to me as Tom. 'G'day mate,' I said, shaking his hand.

'Hi.'

'How's it going?'

'Good.' He was shy, uncertain perhaps, about the strange uncle he'd never met before.

Pam gave me another hug too. 'Thank you for coming.'

'No worries.' I had no idea of what to say or how to act in a family situation.

'Are you coming back to the wake?'

I looked at Jenny. She nodded quickly and looked away.

'Yes, of course.' When I introduced the kids to Jenny and Bradley as my niece and nephew, the blade twisted a little deeper.

X

The wake was held at Southport Surf Club. I got to meet members of the family who I'd never met before, although most of them assured me I had. Todd was purposely avoiding me, moving around the room in the opposite direction. When people started to leave, I approached him and gently shoved him out onto the balcony.

'Thanks for coming,' he said. There was no gratitude in his eyes.

'Listen, mate. I'm really sorry for not being there when Dad passed.'

He shrugged. 'Can't be helped. Too late now.'

'No, I mean it. And not just for that.' I was shaking. 'I'm sorry for being such a dick all these years.' My eyes were heating up again with those bloody hot tears. 'I looked at your wife, Liz, and your beautiful kids today, and I thought, why don't I know these people? Why aren't they in my life?'

Todd was looking out to sea.

The tears began to run down my cheeks. 'I'm sorry, mate. Sorry for everything. I'm going to change.'

Todd's hands shot to his face, and I noticed he was crying too.

I grabbed him and pulled him close. We hugged and sobbed.

'I'm sorry too,' he said through the tears. 'I was never a good brother to you. It was always me and Dad.'

'That's because I wasn't interested in anyone except myself.'

A little voice came from nowhere. 'Why are you crying, Daddy?'

We looked down to see Juliette staring back up at us with innocent concern.

'Nothing, peanut. Daddy and Uncle Scott are just upset about Poppy.'

The little girl held out her hands, wanting to be picked up. Todd obliged. She threw one arm around her father's neck, one around mine, and she pulled us close. 'Don't be sad. Poppy is in heaven with Nanna now!'

Goodness me, the floodgates really opened. We group hugged tightly and stood together for what seemed like forever. When the sobs finally subsided, Juliette asked, 'Can we have cake now?'

68

It was early evening by the time Bradley dropped Jenny and I back at the Q1. Bradley had somewhere else to be, so we changed into our civvies and headed into Surfers for a bit of dinner. We ate roast lamb with veggies and Yorkshire pudding at Kitty O'Shea's. In remembrance of my old boss, Des Williams, I had a pint of Guinness. Jenny did too.

'Poor old Des, he was a victim of all this just as much as anyone.'

'Yep, and Monroe is responsible,' Jenny said.

It had been a long day, so we didn't stay out late.

'Where do we go from here?' Jenny asked as we strolled arm-in-arm along the esplanade. 'What if we never find out which one is guilty?'

'The twins being under house arrest will prevent any more attacks, which could go some way to proving one of them is *X*.'

'Yes, but which one?'

We'd walked north along the esplanade in the opposite direction to the Q1. The sea breeze was cool and made us shiver in a welcomed way. We turned around at the Indy chicane on Main Beach and headed back. When we were in line with Orchid Avenue, my phone rang. It was the number of the surveillance team outside Monroe's house.

'DI Stephens.'

'Sir, it's Constable Miller. Dillon Monroe's ankle bracelet has malfunctioned. It could be damaged, or it could have been removed.'

X

'Is he still at the house?'

'As far as we know, sir, yes. We haven't seen him leave.'

'Get in there now. Find out where he is.'

'Yes, sir.'

'Then get back to me.'

The phone went dead.

'What is it?' Jenny asked.

'Dillon Monroe. Looks like he might have gone walkabout.'

We headed briskly to the station on Ferny Avenue, and just as we reached the entrance my phone rang again. A different number I didn't know.

'Scott, it's Haley Monroe.' It was the first time she'd addressed me by my first name, but her tone was rushed and urgent.

'Yes Haley, what can I do for you?' I turned to face Jenny.

'I need to speak to you. It's … it's about Dillon.'

'Where is he?'

'He's gone. I don't know where he is.'

'Did he remove the bracelet?'

'Yes, and he left in a rage.'

'Okay, where are you?'

Jenny didn't need to hear the other side of the conversation to know what was being said. She got straight on her phone to the surveillance team.

'I'm not far away,' Haley continued. I could tell by the background noise that she was driving. 'I think he might be coming for you.'

'Are you saying Dillon is *X*?'

Apart from the distorted traffic noise, there was silence for a moment. 'I need to speak to you in private.'

'Okay, come to the police headquarters.'

'No. The press could still be hanging around and I can't be seen. Be at the Helm Bar construction site in ten minutes.' The line went dead before I could protest.

Jenny's phone conversation ended at the same time. 'He's

definitely gone. The bracelet was on the jetty. Looks like he may have taken one of the jet skis.'

'Haley's on her way to meet me.' For some reason I didn't tell her where the meeting was. 'You go in. Let Giles know what's happening. Get some coppers out on the streets, and the water police on the lookout for a jet ski. We need to find him, and fast.'

X

The site of the old Helm Bar, overlooking Nerang River, backed onto Ferny Avenue and was only a hundred yards or so from the police station. The building had been demolished some months ago, and there was a temporary construction fence around the small parcel of land. Next to a flimsy gate was an architect's rendering of an eight-storey apartment building.

There was a good view of the street, but no sign of Haley and nowhere for her to park, so I decided to check the river side to see if she was waiting there.

The alley between the site and Vibe Hotel was dark. I was about to increase my pace when I suddenly sensed someone behind me. Swinging around, I was confronted by a hooded figure. And he was close. In a split second, an arm rose into the air and came down like a guillotine. The blow was aimed across my neck from the top left to the bottom right, but I managed to jerk my head backwards. Something sharp nicked me just below the ear.

'Dillon!' I yelled, raising my arms in defence.

But he was quick, and he was strong. With the hood string of his tracksuit pulled tight, it was clearly Dillon Monroe. He struck again from the opposite side. I turned and lowered my head. This time the blade sliced above my right ear. There was little pain, the combination of the razor-sharp blade and the adrenalin pumping through my veins made sure of that.

X

He came at me again and I realised he had another knife in his other hand.

Hitting out blindly, I caught him in the mouth. He staggered backwards, but recovered and lurched forwards again. In his right hand was a small, hooked knife. I managed to grab his wrist but was only able to raise my other arm against the inevitable blow from the other knife. The longer straight blade skewered the palm of my hand. The adrenalin didn't do much to spare the pain this time.

I pulled my hand back and felt it slide free from the blade.

Without the luxury of conscious thought, I drove my hand forward again, narrowly missing the blade but driving the heel into Dillon's chin. Once again, he staggered backwards, but came at me again.

This time I kicked out – that same kick I'd delivered to his father all those years ago, the kick of a full forward worthy of a fifty-metre goal – and it hit him square in the nuts.

Only it didn't. And it didn't stop him in the same way it had Julian. He kept coming.

I'd managed to step back and gain a little ground between us. My stance was stronger now, boxer-like. Dillon's was more martial arts style. He lunged forward again, slashing from left to right with both hands. I dodged the blows. 'It's over Dillon, give it up.'

He didn't speak, just continued to attack, but he was tiring. I saw my chance and lunged forward. This time I blocked his left hand with my right forearm, then drove my right elbow into his face. There was a yelp and I felt him shudder, but I'd taken my eye off his other hand, and he drove the longer knife deep into my shoulder. I reeled backwards while still holding onto his other arm. He let go of the knife, leaving it embedded in me. The searing pain from my wounds throbbed like unearthed electricity. I was losing a lot of blood.

He punched me in the mouth with his free hand. I blindly stepped to one side so my right leg was at the side of him. With both arms now, I yanked his arm, causing him to twist and fall over my leg, schoolyard style. He went down, but I went with him.

The strength was seeping from me with each drop of blood. The throbbing was so intense that my vision was beginning to fail. We wrestled, but he pulled his arm free and raised the little knife into the air.

Wide open and with what could easily have been my last action on this earth, I reached to my shoulder with my right hand and pulled out the longer knife that was still embedded there. Feeling the weight shift in Dillon's body as he recoiled, ready to launch his attack downwards with as much force as possible, I thrust the longer knife upwards. The momentum of his downward thrust meant that little force was needed on my part. The blade impaled him just below the chest, travelling upwards at a right angle and into his heart. Suddenly his whole weight was on my arm. I couldn't hold him, and he slumped down on top of me.

For a moment I lay still, panting. Although the pain from the vicious attack was unbearable, I managed to push Dillon's body to one side.

I checked his pulse.

He was dead.

Then I called Jenny.

'Good news,' Jenny said, before I could speak, 'we've got him.'

'What?'

'Dillon, we've just picked him up. Where are you?'

I could barely speak, but I managed to tell her my location and that I was badly hurt. The phone fell from my hand. Within minutes, the area would be swarming with police. I needed an ambulance.

I somehow managed to turn the body over and remove the hood. The gasp that left my lips had nothing to do with the intense pain. It was one of shock and surprise.

69

I sat on the ground, leaning up against the construction fence. The only sound was the traffic from Ferny Avenue. The features of the face that looked back at me were distinctly Monroe. Smooth, unblemished skin, blue eyes and blonde hair that differed only from the rest of the family by subtle salon curls. Without the usual make-up, the eyes looked smaller, the cheekbones less pronounced and strangely masculine – attributes from both parents.

The first sound of approaching sirens carried in the night air, but instead of getting louder, they drifted into my subconscious, along with the staring eyes of Haley Monroe.

19 September

'He's lost a lot of blood, but his signs are stable.' The female voice was almost childlike in one sense, but compassionate beyond its years in another. 'He just needs to rest and build up his strength.'

I didn't know where I was or when I'd become aware of the conversation, or who was even speaking. I was just there. My eyes were closed, but there was light beyond the lids, and movement. Gradually opening my eyes, I made out two blurred figures, one standing either side of me.

'Scotty.' It was Jenny's distinctive voice. She took my hand and squeezed it gently.

'Mr Stephens, can you hear me?' The face of a young girl appeared in my vision as she leaned over me.

I felt like I was floating. There was a delightful tingle through the whole of my body. No pain. No signs of anxiety. Only wellbeing and contentment. I tried to speak, but my mouth was too dry. Two more figures appeared on either side.

'Hey mate,' Elvis and Tetley said in unison.

A blink and a slight nod were all I could manage.

The young doctor shone a light in my eyes. 'You're going to be just fine.' She lifted my head and held up a bottle of water to my lips. 'Just a little for now.'

'How are you feeling?' Jenny asked gently, rubbing a hand across my forehead.

'I'm feeling great. What happened?'

'You stopped X.'

The vision of Haley Monroe's dead eyes flashed through my mind. 'Haley?'

'Yep.'

With more water intake, recollection of the previous night began to seep back into my memory. 'Haley Monroe was X.' I tried to sit up, but the doctor held me down.

'Steady on, buddy.'

'Just take it easy, Scott,' Jenny said, 'everything's under control.'

Then the doctor made an adjustment to the drip in my arm, and I drifted back to sleep.

20 September

After twenty-four hours of sleep, I felt much better, sitting up and eating a bowl of cereal. I was in a private room with a TV. Annie, the nurse looking after me, showed me how to work the remote. Flicking through the news channels brought back the memories and reality of the case.

Jenny and Bradley came in at 10.00 am. Bradley was a bustle of smiles and admiration, while Jenny was all business.

'Although Haley's home address was the house she shared with

X

her wife on Hedges Avenue, she also had an apartment in Surfers that not even her father knew about.'

'Searched it?'

'Of course. There wasn't much of any interest except for two identical tracksuits hidden at the back of her wardrobe. Not real evidence, but we don't need it.'

'What about Dillon? Where was he?'

'He was picked up by the Gold Coast Water Police, not far from the Helm Bar site,' Bradley said. 'He was sitting on his jet ski, intoxicated, waiting for his sister to collect him.'

My quizzical frown prompted him to continue.

'Haley had taunted Dillon, telling him he'd probably be set up to take the fall, just like Lawrence Binks. She plied him with alcohol, then cleverly changed her point of view by faking sympathy and convincing him the only way out was to make a run for it. Then she offered to help him get away.'

I nodded at the realisation that Haley's actions all made sense.

Jenny took up the thread and continued, 'In his alcohol-fuelled anger, Dillon took the bait. Haley came up with the plan for Dillon to escape by jet ski via the Broadwater. She arranged for him to meet her on Chevron Island.'

'So, the plan was to kill me,' I said, 'then go and meet her brother?'

'We found a suicide note in her car. It was also a written confession for your death and the *X* murders. It was signed *Dillon Monroe*.'

'Right, so after taking care of me, she was going to kill her brother and leave a counterfeit suicide-slash-confession note with his body.'

22 September

Because none of my vital organs were affected, my recovery was surprisingly quick. On my release, Jenny and Elvis were there to take me home.

'We've got to go out through the basement,' Jenny said, 'the press is out front.'

I already knew this from the news coverage. Seems the media got wind of my release.

'You're the Golden Boy again.'

When she said basement, what she really meant was the morgue. There was a loading bay down there with its own private entrance. Waiting for us was an unmarked police van with Dee Forester in the driver's seat.

'So, where's home?' I asked as the van whizzed past the Griffith University campus.

Elvis and Jenny glanced at each other awkwardly.

70

In less than three weeks, I'd been the unwilling student of a great many lessons. For a person to go through the things I had, you'd expect two possible scenarios as the outcome. Either come out the other side a stronger, more grounded individual, or be a complete basket case. I wasn't sure yet which category I subscribed to. In what felt like only a few days, I'd been plucked from my happy, carefree life and thrown into the lion's den. I'd been manipulated and controlled like a puppet, lifted to the greatest heights of adulation and fame, then dropped to the lowest depths of public loathing. During that time, I'd also learned that my childhood wasn't how I'd remembered it. And to top it all, when I'd had the opportunity to make things right with my dad, he'd died before I had the chance to say goodbye.

But now I was the hero again. I had a new life ahead of me, and the security of a higher paid job. I should have been happy.

I couldn't really say I'd grown from the experience, but I certainly hadn't crumbled either. Perhaps this was a product of the old Imposter Syndrome. Feeling somewhere between stronger and crazy, there was a growing need for getting back to normal.

I was relieved at Jenny's reaction when I said I'd be going back to Kirra. Although the last few days being with her were great, staying at her apartment in Burleigh, then enjoying the luxury of Q1 together, we were both detectives with the same uncanny ability of reading people. I guess because we were so alike, living together would be impossible. A tension I'd noticed in her over the last couple of days seemed to disappear when I made my decision. She squeezed my hand in the back of the police van and nodded knowingly.

At the other end of the spectrum, there was no hiding Elvis' feelings. 'You bloody ripper!' he yelled, turning to face me from the passenger seat. *'El tres Wankas del regreso!'*

I didn't have the heart to tell him at that moment that things were going to be different. I'd let things calm down a bit and tell him later.

We arrived in Kirra about thirty minutes later. Secretly ducking out of the hospital basement to avoid the press had been good, but there would be no hiding from them now. Still very sore from my wounds, going in the back way and climbing over the fence was out of the question. I would have to face the masses.

'DI Stephens, how does it feel to be exonerated?'

'DI Stephens, how does it feel to have captured *X*?'

'DI Stephens, is it true you unlawfully killed Haley Monroe?'

'DI Stephens, will the Monroe family be suing you?'

'DI Stephens, what are you going to do now?'

When we finally got through the front door and into the house, Tetley was there waiting with two bottles of beer in hand. 'Here you go, lad,' he passed one to me, the other to Elvis. Skittling into the kitchen, he got two more from the fridge and handed them to Jenny and Bradley. Retrieving a half-empty stubby from the waistband of his underpants, he held it in the air. 'A toast – to the luckiest sod in town.'

We repeated the toast in unison and swigged our beers.

Jenny and Bradley left soon after. One beer was enough. I shouldn't have even had that with the medication I was on, but as ever, peer pressure won through. Suddenly feeling tired, I needed to recuperate. The doctor had warned me of this and urged me to rest as much as possible over the next few days. When I told the boys I was going for a lie down, something in their expressions told me they understood.

'Oh, okay mate,' Elvis said quietly.

X

Even Tetley didn't fire back with the usual banter. 'Is there anything we can get you?' he asked, sounding just like his mother.

'No, I'm good.' I carefully made my way to my bedroom.

X

The next two weeks were probably the longest of my life. Due to my injuries, surfing was out of the question, which was a real bummer. I'd finished the course of medication, so I was able to drink again, but I chose not to, not like before anyway.

When I returned to work, I turned down the use of Des Williams's old office. For now, I wanted to be just plain old Detective Constable Scott Stephens again. Acting Superintendent Giles seemed to understand. The media had shifted focus and were leaving me alone, but people were still recognising me in the street; strangers shook me by the hand and took selfies. It was getting a bit annoying, but I remained polite. When the nominations for the Australian Police Medal and the Order of Australia came up, I turned them down.

X

Trial dates for Monroe, Singleton and Ripley were set for the following January, but Gardner's date hadn't yet been fixed. Monroe had been hanging low since his arrest. Gladys had left him but retained the family home. Monroe had moved into a sprawling penthouse in one of Surfers' newest residential towers.

I wasn't enjoying the job anymore. Life at home was different. No, that's wrong – life at home was exactly the same. I said the experience of the case hadn't really changed me, but it had taken these last couple of weeks to realise it actually had. Instead of hitting the booze with Elvis and Tetley every night, I was purposely working late, then turning in as soon as I got home, or finding somewhere else to be. Jenny and I were still firm friends and I'd quite often go around to her place. We'd listen to music and talk. Real talk. The kind of conversations I could never share with the boys. She told me she'd be leaving for far North Queensland in a week's time. Her brother, the local copper in a small seaside town, was getting married. She'd be going to attend the wedding and asked if I'd like to go along. I said I'd think about it.

One afternoon I finished work early and didn't fancy going home just yet, so I just drove the Dub around the coast. Without much thought or planning, I found myself parked outside Monroe's mansion on Sovereign Island. I'm not sure why I was there. After a few minutes, the front gate opened, and Troy appeared with his dog. They set out along the street towards the block of vacant land, which I guessed was their usual daily destination. I got out of the car and followed.

By the time I reached the block, the dog was already off the lead and chasing the ball. When he saw me approaching, Troy's gaze lowered to the ground as it had before.

'Hey, Troy. How's it going?'

'Good.' He didn't look up. Derek the dog returned, dropped the ball at his feet and began to circle him.

I picked up the ball and threw it.

'Do you remember me?'

'Of course. You're Detective Inspector Scott Stephens. You killed my sister.' His response was delivered in that same quick-fire way.

'It was self-defence if you remember.'

'Yes. She was going to drain you, like those girls.'

'Then she was going to kill Dillon.'

'Yes.' A smirk flickered briefly.

The dog returned and dropped the ball. I knelt and began to stroke him. He rolled over onto his back. 'Listen, I'm sorry about what happened. To you, I mean, dragging you down to the police station.'

'Don't be sorry. It was bingin.'

'Bingin?'

'Yeah. Good fun.'

X

'Okay.'
Derek was growing more excited.
'Gee, I wish I had a dog.'
'You're a good person. Derek only likes good people.'
'Thanks.'
'Haley was a bad person.'
'Yes.'
'So is Dillon.'
'Is he?'
'Yes, and my dad.'
'What makes you say that?'
'Derek hates them.'
'Right ... and Derek knows.'

X

I wasn't intending for it to be a party, but I knew from experience that a gathering on Ruby Street would inevitably end up being one. I'd made a decision and I wanted to share it with my family and friends.

Tetley and Johnno were already drinking in the man shed when my first guests arrived, but this was nothing out of the ordinary for 5.00 pm. Todd, his wife Liz, and their kids, Tom and Juliette, arrived with Dad's widow, Pam.

Although the tension between Todd and myself had eased, our relationship was still not what it should have been between two brothers. I was hoping time would fix this. The kids, however, were a different matter – no inhibitions, just a sense of pure, innocent fun. I think they looked upon me as the famous uncle, which only made things more exciting for them.

Dale Mason and the team arrived at the same time as Chilly the barber and the drifters from Kirra Hotel. Bradley showed up with a friend called Terrance. Jenny was the last to arrive. Strangely, she came in the back way with Elvis in tow. My spider senses were tingling.

When I was sure everyone was present, and before the Kirra crew got too wasted, I turned off the music and stood on the couch. 'Can I have your attention please?' It took a few minutes for the chattering to stop. 'Firstly, I'd like to thank you all for coming.' *Shit the wedding speech again.*

Tetley sniggered. Jenny gave him the death stare.

'I uhm ... I've asked you all here tonight mostly to say thank you for your support over the last few weeks. I'm a lucky bloke to have such great mates. And now,' I looked over at Todd and Liz, the kids and Pam, all huddled together in one corner, 'I've got a family to look out for too.'

Todd smiled and nodded.

'But there's another reason I asked you all here today.'

Jenny's eyes narrowed. Had her detective mind already worked out what was coming?

'I've come to a decision, and it's not one I've made overnight.'

The room was deadly quiet, except for a strange whining sound coming from the back yard. I ignored it and continued, 'This is something I've given a lot of thought to recently—'

'Get on wi' it, lad,' Tetley said, 'you're killing us!'

'I've decided I'm going to ... leave the police force.'

'What?' The question was a collective one, riding the wave of a communal gasp.

It was only Jenny who didn't show any emotion. Although we'd talked about this during an early morning walk around Burleigh Headland, I hadn't actually said I was going to do it, but I got the impression she wasn't surprised.

'What the hell are you going to do?' Elvis yelled.

'Haven't decided yet.' It was a white lie. I knew exactly what I was going to do.

There were no congratulations or well wishes, which was to be expected. I think most of them were worried I'd finally lost my mind. I noticed Jenny and Elvis duck out the back door. The kids

X

were nowhere to be seen either. I followed to find them all in the garden, shielding something from my view.

'Close your eyes, Uncle Scott,' Juliette said.

I frowned at Jenny. 'What's going on?'

'Do as you're told, Uncle Scott.'

I closed my eyes and heard some rustling, and what sounded like something being slid across the grass.

The kids were whispering and giggling, then Jenny said, 'Ready ... okay ... open your eyes.'

I did as I was told.

A cardboard box sat at my feet.

Juliette could hardly contain her excitement, dancing on the spot as if she needed a wee.

The box moved.

I knelt, opened it, and out sprang a tiny puppy! Ejecting itself from the box, it landed in my arms and covered me in puppy breath kisses, yelping with excitement.

'A Staffy! Is this for me?' It was a silver-coloured Staffordshire Bull Terrier.

The kids couldn't contain themselves any longer and joined in with the petting.

'Thought you might need a new partner,' Jenny said. Her knowing smirk told me she'd figured out my plans. 'Every private detective needs one.'

'Private detective?' Elvis repeated, wide-eyed.

My casual nothing-certain-yet shrug was ignored, while the puppy bounced around in my arms.

'Brilliant. You can have the office upstairs from mine.' He was already thinking ahead.

I passed the dog to the kids.

'What will you call him?' Jenny asked.

I looked over to see the little bloke nestled under Juliet's chin, gazing up at her.

The name came to me just like that. 'Romeo!'

ACKNOWLEDGEMENTS

As a proud Queenslander, I'd like to begin by acknowledging the traditional custodians of this land which we inhabit, and pay my respects to the Elders past and present.

I will always be indebted to Queensland and in particular, the Gold Coast. The beaches, the hinterland, the people, the weather—a lifestyle I could only ever have dreamt of when growing up in the UK.

Although the theme of X touches on the world of corruption, this is by no means a reflection of the current Gold Coast mayor, or Queensland Police and the great work they do. I'd like to acknowledge the frontline workers of Queensland Police for protecting us and keeping our streets safe. Thank you!

As always, a big thank you to my long-suffering wife, Jane. We have shared many adventures over the forty plus years we've been together—riding pillion on a vespa, while researching fictional murder scenes around the Gold Coast, is a recent pastime she's endured.

Thank you also to my editors, Karen Collyer and Julie Guthrie, for your patience and knowledge, and your positive feedback and encouragement. I'm proud of what we've achieved.

ABOUT THE AUTHOR

ANDY M^{C}D (aka Andrew M^{C}Dermott) lives on the glorious Gold Coast of Australia and is the CEO of Publicious Book Publishing. His first novel (*The Tiger Chase* - 1st edition) was published in the US in 2002, which was followed up with the launch in San Diego and a book tour of the US, including LA and Las Vegas. More titles followed.

2022 sees the unveiling of the new brand ANDY M^{C}D, and the launch of Andy's exciting new novel set entirely on the Gold Coast called *X*. This will be followed by the launch of three more titles throughout the year, with more to come in 2023 and beyond.

Andy was born in Nottingham, England. A naturalised Aussie he has lived on the Gold Coast for the last 32 years with his wife, Jane. He is a patron of the Gold Coast Writers Association, and currently resides at Kirra Beach.